Praise for The Third Mrs. Durst

"_The Third Mrs. Durst_ is a slow, dark burn that leads to a fantastic explosion of an ending."

—Victoria Helen Stone, bestselling author of _Jane Doe_

Also by Ann Aguirre

THE
THIRD
MRS.
DURST

ANN AGUIRRE

THE

THIRD

MRS.

DURST

MIDNIGHT INK
WOODBURY, MINNESOTA

FIRST EDITION
First Printing, 2019
Hardcover with dust jacket

Book format by Samantha Penn
Cover design by Kevin R. Brown

Midnight Ink, an imprint of Llewellyn Worldwide Ltd.

Library of Congress Cataloging-in-Publication Data
Names: Aguirre, Ann, author.
Title: The third Mrs. Durst / Ann Aguirre.
Description: First edition. | Woodbury, Minnesota : Midnight Ink, [2019]
Identifiers: LCCN 2019012024 (print) | LCCN 2019013526 (ebook) | ISBN
   9780738761732 () | ISBN 9780738761312 (alk. paper)
Subjects: | GSAFD: Suspense fiction.
Classification: LCC PR9200.9.A39 (ebook) | LCC PR9200.9.A39 T48 2019 (print)
   | DDC 811/.6—dc23
LC record available at https://lccn.loc.gov/2019012024

Midnight Ink
Llewellyn Worldwide Ltd.
2143 Wooddale Drive
Woodbury, MN 55125-2989
www.midnightinkbooks.com

Printed in the United States of America

To the survivors:
This story is for you.

now

Some people just need killing. And maybe I'm one of them.

My husband certainly thinks so, but then, he feels that way about most women. I may not survive his style of love.

His first wife didn't. Neither did his second.

The flames are everywhere now. It's getting hard to breathe.

We'll see who dies today.

PART ONE
THE BEGINNING

1

I got on a bus when I was sixteen. Everything I owned fit in a backpack I stole from my cousin, and I left behind a shotgun shack with five younger brothers and sisters. Maybe they cried when I left, just like I did when Dee struck out on her own, but I had no mind for their tears. We didn't have electricity and none of us ever had shoes at the same time. I'd like to say my mother tried, but she fell into the hillbilly heroin that was the only attraction our two-bit town offered and never stood up again.

I was lean and leggy back then, fierce cheekbones and big eyes. Not because I saw that look in fashion magazines and coveted it but because I often went days between meals. My jeans had holes in them, and my T-shirt was so thin that it was transparent. In winter that might've been a problem, but it was sweltering, heat shimmering off the pavement like some evil wizard had cast a spell. Men swiveled their heads at me as I trudged down the street, but I was used to that.

Even then I was old enough to understand the danger, but I'd also known that if I stayed in Barrettville, I'd end up like my mom—pregnant at sixteen, having babies I couldn't afford, no way out except drugs or death—so I stole enough pennies over a long year to afford a one-way bus ticket, and when the time was right, I made my getaway. I'd rather die on the streets of Nashville than become an old woman by twenty-nine.

I'd been living rough, watching this Burger Boy for two weeks. I'd heard that a man I needed to meet sometimes stopped here. Del Morton was known among the city street kids; if he took a shine to you, your life changed. Period. I was determined to snatch that golden ticket, one way or another.

Washing dishes for a few dollars under the table kept my belly full, but I still didn't have a safe place to sleep. Things would change, soon. I had nothing but determination back then, and if sheer willpower could push me to succeed, then my plans were already etched in the atmosphere, skywriting that promised *MARLENA ALTIZER WILL MAKE HER DREAMS COME TRUE*.

I spent a couple of dollars on a value meal, waiting to see if Del Morton would show.

The fries were greasy, salty, and I savored each bite of the burger, too. Eating like that, I made the food last almost an hour, hiding the fact that I had nowhere else to go. My lingering didn't seem to bother the employees. One boy cleared the tables near me, wiping them longer than necessary as he tried to make eye contact.

He couldn't help me in the slightest, so I didn't pay him any mind. Jenny Song came in then. She was a girl who had helped me find my current squat, younger than me but more experienced at living on the street.

"Any luck?" she asked.

I shook my head. "Nothing yet."

She was incredibly beautiful, even at fourteen, with long black hair, delicate features, and light brown eyes that shone like topaz. "The supermarket just tossed out the expired stuff. I got some food for us."

"I saved you half my burger and fries." I slid the tray toward her, and she gave me a smile that never failed to sparkle through me like fancy fizzy water.

After Jenny ate, we couldn't loiter anymore. She headed for the bathroom while I strolled toward the door. I nearly ran into a man in a crumpled business suit. He had high color in his cheeks, more than two days of stubble on his jaw, and wore a straw Panama hat. *Del Morton. Finally.* I'd promised Jenny that if I got him to sign me, I'd get her in too. Somehow.

All part of the plan.

His gaze swept over me in a way I was used to, more than I should be, except his pale eyes lacked that usual spark; this was more of a sweeping assessment. The look lingered on my bulging backpack.

"You ran away from home," he said, instead of "pardon me."

"No running involved. Not that it's your business." I nodded at him as I passed by, feigning indifference. His reputation didn't give me the impression that Morton was a groper, but I'd been grabbed enough to half expect a hand on my ass anyway.

He stopped me with his words instead. "Let me buy you a Coke. We might have something to talk about."

Smiling, I followed him to a table, where I sat down to wait while he went to the counter. He got my Coke, and for himself, only coffee, a big one, that he gulped black and hot despite the sweltering weather. Normal girls wouldn't chat with an older man like this, but their mothers had probably spoken words of warning, whereas mine had been telling me to take the hand of anyone with money to spend for as long as I could remember. I sipped at my Coke, relishing the infusion of sugar.

"Sorry," he said. "I've been driving for eight hours."

He did look like he'd come a far piece on a hard road. "What do you want?"

"I should introduce myself. I'm Del Morton." He pulled a business card from his wallet, slid it across the table.

It read *UMAX*, his company name, and below that *Del Morton, Talent Agent*. Finally, the card stated his contact information, including a cellular number. I'd heard of mobile phones, of course, but I didn't know anyone who had one. He must bring in good money.

"What does a 'talent agent' do?"

I already knew, but men liked it when they believed they were teaching you something, Wide eyes and a curious expression had gotten me all the way here. Just then, Jenny came out of the bathroom and stopped where the tiled hallway met the side doors. She raised her brows, her wordless question evident.

With an imperceptible nod, I confirmed it. *Yes, he's the one.*

"An excellent question. The simplest answer is that I scout photogenic young men and women and find them modeling work."

"Bullshit." That was expected. If I hadn't already done my homework, I'd be skeptical of this offer. Since I'd been angling for this—and starving for it—I could hardly control my euphoria.

"If you don't believe me, walk away. I'm almost done with my coffee, and I have a meeting in forty minutes." But a hungry light sparked in his eyes. The fact that I was reluctant must have made me seem like a better catch.

"Maybe I'll ask a few more questions," I said.

"Such as?"

"What kind of jobs do you find?"

In reply, he produced a folded page from his inner jacket pocket. "This flyer features two of our models."

It was an advertisement like you might notice posted at a bus stop or on a telephone pole, promoting a sale at a sporting goods store. The models were all geared up like they were about to go play tennis or golf.

"What else?"

"We've placed people in department store shows and local catalogues, a few regional TV commercials. I can't promise to make you famous, but with that face, you could make some money, enough to pay for college, maybe."

College would've been impossible in Barrettville; I didn't tell him I'd stopped school after junior high. People in the hills where I'd lived were born in bathtubs, not under lucky stars. But maybe I could change my fate. I beckoned Jenny over then.

"If you sign me, you take Jenny, too. She's even prettier than I am."

He gave her a once-over, same as he had me, and he tilted his head, thoughtful. "It's rare that I do this, but all right. You've got a deal. Does that mean you're willing?"

I nodded, and Jenny bounced beside me. We were on our way. "So what's the first step?"

"First off, I'll get your teeth fixed. Then we take some pictures and send out your headshots, add you to our company portfolio."

"Just tell me where I go," I said.

The business card he'd given me didn't have an address printed on it, so he took it again and wrote it on the back. "What's your name? Miss...?"

"Altizer," I answered. "You can call me Marlena. And this is Jenny Song."

"Nice to meet you both. We can probably launch you under your first name. It has a classic ring."

"My mama thought so anyway." I wasn't about to list all the things she'd been wrong about; maybe my name wasn't one of them.

Del Morton seemed to be thinking, then asked Jenny, "Do you have a Chinese name in addition to an American one, Miss Song?"

"Song Li-hua. Why?"

"It's pretty. I just thought I might be able to market you better in the East if you did."

"I don't mind working under either name," she said.

He nodded. "I'll be in touch. If you need a place to stay, I've written down my office manager's name. She's often willing to let aspirants sleep in her spare room until they sign officially, and we assign them a bed in one of the apartments we rent for our models."

"You supply room and board?" I hadn't heard that.

Morton shook his head, his foot tapping with a touch of impatience. "I don't pay the bills, but my name is on the lease. You may end up sleeping in a closet, but you already know I'm not promising glamour. Modeling is tough and competitive. You should know that from the start."

Smiling, I nodded as he drained his coffee and stood. This promise of a bright future—of pretty, straight teeth that would let me smile without sealing my lips like I knew a secret—those changes would open so many doors. Somehow Jenny and I stayed calm until he left, and then we were jumping and screaming right there in the Burger Boy.

"I can't believe this worked." Her arms went around me, tight and close, and I hugged her back.

"We should call that office manager. There's no reason to go back to the squat if we have a better choice." Tugging her toward the pay phone, I realized I didn't have enough to call, but Jenny added a dime.

The phone rang twice, then a woman said, "Hello, this is Pamela."

10

"Hi there. This might seem strange, but Del Morton just gave us his card and your number. He said you might be willing to let us stay for a few nights. He asked us a sign a contract with UMAX—"

"Mr. Morton just called me. He does like picking up strays," she said. "But you must be beautiful because he doesn't waste his time on less."

"Thank you," seemed like the appropriate response.

"This must seem overwhelming and a bit risky, but my house is likely safer than wherever you're staying now."

Since Jenny and I slept in turns, this woman had it right. "I'm ready. What's the address?" I got a pen and a scrap of paper out of my backpack, jotted down the information, then repeated it back to her.

"Thank you. We'll be there soon."

"It's a couple of miles," Jenny said once I hung up. "Are we really doing this?"

With a firm nod, I took her hand. "This is all we've talked about since we met, practically. You heard about what happened to Dee ... and we can't turn aside now. Are you in for the long haul?"

In answer, Jenny pulled me toward the door.

2

We stayed that night at Pamela Morgan's house. She was a motherly, middle-aged woman with auburn hair and a warm smile. Her guest room had a full-sized bed in it, so Jenny and I slept together. Neither of us minded, and it was heavenly to take a shower instead of washing up in a gas station sink.

Just as Pamela promised, her two-bedroom bungalow was clean and safe. If she'd ever been married, she didn't have a man now. In the morning, she drove us to UMAX to sign the contracts.

Del Morton hadn't lied.

After we signed, he took me to the orthodontist and I got braces that I paid for in installments, small deductions from each modeling job. The work wasn't glamorous, and while Jenny and I didn't end up in somebody's closet, we did live lean, six girls in a two-bedroom apartment. We had bunk beds, just like at some summer camp, but it wasn't bad. The more of us who lived there, the smaller our portion of rent and utilities was, and a couple of us were often traveling to a shoot.

Plus, the older girls showed Jenny and me the ropes, explaining which photographers were professional and what jobs I should pass on because the company liked to pay in trade. Which meant getting clothes instead of cash. Most of us had a second job to cover bills while we hustled to get our faces out there. I wasn't old enough for the cocktail waitressing that Dana and Stephanie did; Wendy and Alexis both had part-time receptionist jobs, and I didn't have the skill for that, either, so I got a job at the car wash with Jenny. We didn't do much except stand around in shorts and a crop top holding *SALE* and *HOT WAX* signs, but it paid our monthly bills. It would get significantly tougher as fall rolled into winter.

After I turned eighteen, I started working on my GED. I also opened my first bank account, as things were rough when I was underage and forced to use cash for everything. I breathed a sigh of relief as I blew out my birthday candles with Jenny, because there was no way anybody could send me back to Kentucky.

Everything was a struggle, but it felt like I was gaining ground, especially when my braces came off. I had the straight teeth Mr. Morton had promised, and after a good cleaning, it felt like shaking the clay off my feet. Since I didn't eat right growing up, they had to take out some teeth, do some bridge work, but that didn't show in my smile.

And then I got my big break.

A rockabilly band saw my face on a flyer, one I did for a furniture store, and they wanted me for a music video. Some of the models at the agency had dance training; others were taking acting classes. When Mr. Morton offered me the job, I was worried. There was nothing like that in my background.

He just laughed. "There's no trick to it, Marlena. You pose, toss your hair, you pout. Haven't you ever watched MTV?"

"Not really."

"Then stay here and do some market research." He clicked on the television and tuned it to the music video channel. "I figure you'll get the gist pretty quick."

He was right about that.

After a bit, I saw the pattern Mr. Morton mentioned and noticed that the girls in these videos never talked. I could do it, I figured. On the way out of the office, I nearly ran into a tall man in a tailored suit, not handsome but lean, with brown hair and pale blue eyes. That was my first encounter with Michael Durst.

That, too, was part of the plan. His interest was probably piqued by the fact that I *didn't* fawn over him. Even then, he'd been in society pages, covered in business magazines for his successful property developments.

He steadied me, hands on my shoulders. "Are you all right?"

"Fine, thanks. Mr. Morton's not in, though."

Frowning, he checked the time on what looked like an expensive watch. "He's expecting me. The receptionist told me to go in."

"He'll probably be along soon. Have a good night, sir."

"That's quite an accent," he said, smiling.

He didn't keep me longer, and I hurried out, down the hall, through the small waiting area where Pamela sat reading a true crime book. "All done?" She gave me a friendly smile.

Sometimes she mothered us with questions like "Are you taking regular birth control?" or "Did you eat something besides celery today?" This afternoon, however, she only sent a worried look down the hall. "Mr. Durst is early. I'll try calling Del again."

Durst was a VIP, the sort of man you didn't keep waiting. Maybe he was trying to book a bunch of models, which meant Mr. Morton couldn't afford to piss him off. Either way, it wasn't my worry; timing was everything, and I had to do a facial and get plenty of sleep before filming tomorrow.

————————

For the shoot, they'd rented out a farmer's fallow field and contracted with some midway company to set up a private carnival. That seemed like an incredible waste of money, and they'd even bussed extras out to wander around looking like they were having the best time ever, carefully *not* paying too much attention to the band, who was too famous for a venue like this.

A harried bald man grabbed me the minute I arrived. "Did your agent explain the concept to you?"

"Vaguely." That probably wasn't the answer he wanted, proven when he shoved some papers into my hands.

"Read this. Fast."

"This" was a basic summary of the "story" they were trying to tell: simple country girl goes to county fair, falls in love with aspiring musician, and then they part ways after one amazing night. Someone else would be playing the older version of my character later in the video: a woman in her thirties with a teenage daughter who looked like the aspiring musician—who was now a wildly famous guitarist. I didn't know much about music videos, but the idea seemed pretty good, if a little mushy, especially when I read the lyrics.

I mightn't have had much schooling, but I knew exactly how that older woman would feel because I'd seen that look in my mama's eyes more than once. And this story about the passing regret of a famous man? It brought bile to my throat, since it was nothing compared to the struggle of the woman who'd chosen to raise a child alone and couldn't afford that decision. It didn't touch on how the daughter felt, either.

Sighing, I crumpled the page and got herded to makeup, set up in a tent. I couldn't get too excited about playing a yokel who was about to get boned and abandoned, but Mr. Morton would've had my ass if I'd quit for such a personal reason. They did my face and braided my hair into two loose plaits; they must have been going for a sexy farmer's daughter vibe because I had to put on cutoff shorts and a red plaid shirt, tied up under my boobs.

The weather was good, typical of late summer in the South, and we had enough sunlight to do the carnival scenes in one day. Staff ran around like crazy, and I didn't know what to do except wait. It wasn't like I had a trailer, unlike Bobby Ray Hudgens, the lead singer in the band. In my opinion, he was too old to be playing someone messing with a girl at a carnival, but I kept quiet as the director gave me all his notes.

I wouldn't say I was an amazing actress or anything, but it was surprisingly easy to get swept up, to *become* that starry-eyed girl who locked eyes with a handsome bastard playing a guitar. When I rose onto my tiptoes to see over the other girls, it wasn't in the notes, but they just kept rolling. The director didn't stop us when Bobby Ray pulled me out of the crowd, either. I stumbled onto the stage, all shy excitement, and I didn't dance; I held on to him and hid my face, a move that would later become part of my trademark. Lots of pictures that showed off my hair, the slope of my neck, or the angles of my back.

Scene change.

After the show scene was over, they filmed us running wild through the carnival, hand in hand. I went on rides that made me queasy, had to pretend it was the most fun ever. Bobby Ray's hand was sweaty, and his eyes shone like he was on the good stuff. Oddly, that made me feel right at home because of all the time I'd spent with my mama when she wasn't truly there.

The director didn't say anything about a kiss scene, but Bobby Ray pushed me up against the side wall of the ring toss and gave me a wet one, plenty of tongue. Fighting him would've ruined the take since I was supposed to be in love with this asshole, so I twined my arms around his neck and didn't kick him when he slid a hand up my thigh. High. Higher. He kissed my neck, and I arched it, closing my eyes because that would make me seem like I was enjoying this.

"Cut!" the director called.

Bobby Ray had both hands full of my ass and was pulling me against his crotch, so he wasn't listening to instruction. It took a couple of grips to haul him away. He flashed me a grin as he swaggered off and winked like that was something we both wanted. His mouth tasted like beer and cigarettes, and I spat as soon as I could.

They hadn't offered me anything to eat or drink all day, but there were coolers and what they called a craft services table with sandwiches, chips, fruit, and various snacks. When I headed over that way, the people nearby stopped talking.

"Hey," I said.

The two extras gave me a look and then the taller one asked, "Are you screwing Bobby Ray?"

"What?"

"I wanted your part," the other one complained, "but they wouldn't let me audition, and our agency is way better than yours."

They both sounded the right kind of Southern, the kind that made people think of delicate belles and cotillions instead of backwoods hillbillies. Conscious of that, I'd always tried to talk more like the reporters who gave the news out of Atlanta. My success was limited, though, and when I got mad, my accent only got thicker.

"How is that my problem?"

The girls laughed. This was why I'd stopped going to school, and I hated when people looked down on me. Instead of getting food,

I stomped off and hid in the makeup tent, where one of the artists was nice enough to bring me a bottle of water. I stayed there until nightfall, when they needed to film the farewell scene against a dreamy field and a starry sky, with the brightly whirling rides behind us.

Until then I'd had no idea how much trouble it is to film at night, how much work and running around it requires. Since I was tired from the long day and sad from dealing with those girls, it didn't take much for me to cry when Bobby Ray let go of my hand and climbed into his battered van and drove away, leaving me standing on a dirt road, alone in the dark. Closeup on Marlena's weeping face. I did it silently, like I had at home, where if I made a lot of noise I'd get a whipping.

The director loved it.

"One take, Marlena! I think you've got a future. Bobby Ray's waiting for you in his trailer. He wants to thank you personally for your hard work."

3

Inside the trailer, it smelled of stale cigarette smoke, booze, and sweat, with the ripe scent of pot from the joint in Bobby Ray's hand. He took a deep drag and shooed out the two ladies who were already showing him a good time. The women gave me shitty looks as they pushed past. I hovered near the door, not wanting to step in farther, but he caught my wrist and pulled me. A stumble put me on his lap, and his lazy smile said he thought I should be glad to be there.

Thinking he was clever, he sang the first few lines of "Three Marlenas," a song that I'd loved when I first heard it on the radio. I would never feel the same about it again.

Rape wasn't always brutal. Sometimes it was a man with all the power and a girl who hesitated to say no. While I was thinking, he decided for both of us. My face scraped over a couch cushion as he bent me over, yanked down my shorts, and took me from behind. He was fast and sweaty; it had hurt a lot more the first time, one of my mother's boyfriends and I was only eleven. I set my jaw and stared at the bobblehead dog that nodded with each thrust. *"One, Two, Three Marlenas."* The damn song wouldn't stop playing in my head. I counted sixty-two head bobs before Bobby Ray groaned and got off me. He slapped my ass as a signal we were done and I pulled up my clothes, with his semen making me feel filthy.

Outside the trailer, I knelt in the dust and gravel and puked up the water that nice makeup artist had brought me. I curled my hands into fists, focusing on the bite of my nails on skin. For a moment I considered filing a report, but since I hadn't said no verbally, since I hadn't fought, since there were no bruises, I decided it would only hurt me more.

One day, I'll be powerful enough to get back at Bobby Ray.

Shakily, I got to my feet and stumbled to the bus that was chartered to take all the extras back to town. They had room for me and I dropped down on the front seat next to some middle-aged woman. I leaned forward and put my face in my hands.

"You had a long day," the extra said. "But you did excellent work. If I'm any judge, you'll get plenty of casting calls after this, more modeling jobs too, probably."

I sat up slowly. "Do you know me?"

"Not as such, but you did your best today. Under some trying circumstances."

She had no idea, but her words did make me feel better. I swallowed a second wave of nausea and emptied my mind until I got back to the apartment. My roommates were out or asleep, which meant I had a clear path to the bathroom. Normally we took fast showers because of the bill, but I sat in there until the water went cold, scrubbing and crying. Only stopped because I didn't want to mess up my skin. I still had to work the next day.

That night, I didn't sleep much, stretched between bad memories and dreams of vengeance. Jenny crawled into my bunk bed when she heard me whimper and I wrapped myself around her, breathing in the smell of her strawberry shampoo. She didn't ask, and I didn't tell her. We both had demons to wrestle in the dark.

On the way to the agency, I stopped at Planned Parenthood. People had been talking about this new morning-after pill, and I'd be damned if I ended up like my mother, having some asshole's baby.

They got me in fast; it was a quiet morning, and the doctor didn't ask that many questions. I guessed I didn't look traumatized and should maybe get into acting after all. An hour later, it was all done, and I went on my way, outwardly unchanged. But I'd learned an important lesson. In this business, I needed to protect myself because nobody would do it for me.

Things took a turn for the worse when Mr. Morton praised me for doing such fine work on the music video. Apparently I'd been so fantastic that Bobby Ray Hudgens himself sent along his good wishes and a nice bonus for my pay packet. Did that mean he knew I didn't want him and he figured five hundred dollars was the price of my silence? Bile rose in my throat as I took the check from Mr. Morton.

"You all right, Marlena?"

The worst part of this was, nobody cared. Even if I'd told Mr. Morton what happened, I couldn't be sure he'd take my side. He'd probably wonder if I'd encouraged Bobby Ray, and or maybe he would even ask me to keep quiet. This job was all I had, and I couldn't bring myself to test him. He'd been honest so far, but my trust didn't reach far enough to open my mouth. In my experience, men stuck together.

There'd been a time back in Barrettville when my mama didn't want Ernest Ford coming around, and he didn't listen to "no" either.

I remembered the way she'd screamed and cried, and how us kids huddled together because we didn't know exactly what was happening. Later she tried to get him locked up, but the sheriff swore Ernest Ford was out fishing with him that night, and was my mama sure, wasn't it likely that the drugs had just given her some bad dreams?

Not likely. She had my youngest brother nine months later. But Ernest Ford never saw consequences, because you didn't get lower than the Altizer brood in Lee County. That was a lesson I absorbed early on, and looking at Mr. Morton, I just couldn't speak. So I swallowed hard and nodded.

"Fine, sir."

But when Pamela asked that same question five minutes later, I broke down. She came around the reception desk in a hurry and her words stopped. Her hug was like a mother's, only Pamela smelled fresh and clean, with just a touch of lavender. Mama always reeked of sweat and whatever she'd been eating.

"I won't ask you to talk if you're not ready," she said. "But I'm always here for you girls, and I'll do whatever you need me to."

Somehow, I couldn't stop crying. Nobody had ever said anything like that to me, and maybe she didn't even mean it. I held on like the world might tip me off if I didn't.

Afterward, she made tea and got a cold pack for my eyes. By the time I had to leave for the catalogue shoot, you couldn't tell that I'd been an unraveled ball of yarn before.

That extra was right, too. She'd predicted I'd get more jobs, and the offers came in numbers high enough that I got to pick and choose. A few of them paid for me to fly to their location, which was beyond exciting. Hard not to look on this success as blood money, though. I'd certainly paid a high toll in Bobby Ray's trailer to reach the next level.

The next month, I got my first cover, a regional magazine similar to *YM* called *Carolina Girl*. Nobody cared that I wasn't from either of the Carolinas, and I had a full-day fashion shoot, different outfits, new hairstyles, and they even gave me some input on which pictures I liked best. Until that moment, I'd mostly been treated like a prop that smiled and posed. Let me say, that fresh regard—or maybe respect—was heady.

By then, I was earning enough for Mr. Morton that he started coming with me to shoots, and he deterred the assholes; they didn't even try. I wished I'd had that buffer sooner, but it also sent me a message. Money made you more important and more untouchable. At that age, I didn't have career goals as such, but I decided it then: I needed to get rich, or pair up with someone who was. Even then I understood that my face wouldn't be popular forever.

That fall, I did a lot of traveling around the South and my bank account got healthy. The better I did, the less my roommates liked me. Pretty soon I quit my job at the car wash, and Dana stopped speaking to me altogether because she was only twenty-six and already hearing that she was "too old" for some jobs.

The more I worked, the less I saw Jenny. She wasn't booked as much as me, though she'd just done a shampoo commercial. Since we'd met on the street, Jenny hadn't said too much about her past, but I knew she had a white mother and a Chinese father who had passed away. We were both working the same shoot, a print ad for a beauty salon, and I steered her away from the photographer.

"You don't want to be alone with him, trust me."

Guarding Jenny became a habit for me. There was no way I'd let her pay the same price I had for success. I was there when I could be, whispering tips and blocking those who would hurt her.

On our next job, I made full use of our first break. "Another thing, steer clear of Bobby Ray Hudgens. And don't take offers that let you bypass the normal audition process. There *will* be a hidden cost."

Jenny linked her arm with mine. "Thanks. I don't know what I'd do without you."

"You'll never need to find out," I said softly.

4

Just before Christmas, I went to an audition for a bit role in some indie movie. I didn't get it, somebody else played that part, but for some reason, Mr. Morton was waiting for me with champagne. The cork popped in a grand sound and white froth poured out. We both knew I was underage, but that was the last issue on my mind.

"What's all this about?"

"Congratulations, Marlena. I didn't know you met Michael Durst, but evidently you made an impression, and he's been following your career."

"He has? Why?" I suspected I already knew.

"I could give you a long answer, but you'll prefer the abridged version. He's wealthy ... and important." Mr. Morton tapped on his computer and brought up a page that slowly loaded a photo. "This is Michael Durst."

"Oh, right. I met him coming out of your office one time."

"Well, he's recommended you for a spot in a German trade show."

"What kind?" I didn't know much about the world of high-couture, but even I got that this wouldn't be Fashion Week.

"Lingerie. It'll be in February, so you need to apply for a passport and put a rush on it. Do that at the post office, except the pictures. Handle those at a drugstore for quick service."

Mr. Morton hustled me out of his office, and in a daze I went off to do as he'd instructed. It wasn't until later, after I'd gotten my photo taken and paid all the fees and filled out the forms, that it struck me as odd. I'd only spoken with the man for a minute, so why did he want me posing in German underwear? There was something off about it, but Mr. Morton was so excited that I figured this must be a fantastic opportunity. And it played to my plans as well.

Maybe I'd end up doing real runway shows and get my face in *Vogue*. If anyone in Barrettville saw, they'd be so surprised. In retrospect, I can see how that was the turning point. If I'd said no, if I hadn't gone to Germany, my life would've been so different.

I chose the road that looked prettiest from a distance, but I didn't know, then—sometimes the horizon is bright because it's on fire.

———

Getting ready for my first overseas trip, I didn't pay a lot of attention to my roommates, not even Jenny, who sometimes slept with me when one of us had bad dreams.

She perched on the edge of my bed as I packed my suitcase. "You aren't coming back here, are you?"

"Not likely, no. You know it has to be that way."

"I'm aware. I just didn't think it would hurt this much. We've been together for so long, and I don't know if I can live without you."

"You have to," I said firmly. "So do I. We'll get through this. I'll write. And call."

"Knowing something is necessary doesn't make it easy. I ran away from my stepfather because I knew one day he'd do something I couldn't walk away from. I'm scared for you, Marlena. I have a bad feeling."

I sat down on the bed next to her. I'd never pried into her past, but it sounded like she had badness behind her as well, badness she could see coming. In Barrettville, there'd been a woman everyone called Granny June, who did Tarot readings and always seemed to know when somebody was about to be born, die, or suffer some catastrophic luck. People went to her on the sly for hexes and charms, and for backwoods birth control, too. I'd known folks to cross the road to avoid her supposed evil eye, and I'd seen some strange stuff in Kentucky. So I wasn't about to tell Jenny she had no gifts, especially when her instincts had kept her alive.

When I put my hand on hers, she glanced up in surprise. "Let's say it's true, and that there's a good reason for you to worry," I said. "I'm tough. I can handle myself. And I won't forget you, I promise. We'll finish this together, just as we started it."

She laced her fingers through mine. "You promise? Dana said—"

"She's just mad that she looks older than twenty-six. We're together forever, and that's the truest thing I've ever said."

Jenny hugged me then, and she didn't feel like any of the sisters I'd left behind. I loved the silkiness of her hair, and the sweet honey scent of her skin. We used the same lotion after our showers, but it smelled better on her somehow. I stroked her back and let her nestle close. Sometimes Jenny seemed like she might have a crush on me, but I couldn't be sure. That night, we curled up in my bed together, and I crept away before dawn feeling like I was leaving a lover, but I had a plane to catch.

Mr. Morton was waiting for me downstairs, car parked at the curb. He leaned on it, heedless of the dew still misted on the metal. "You ready to take on the world?"

"More or less," I said.

He laughed, like I was trying to be funny, and chucked my suitcase in the trunk. "You may already know this, but Mr. Durst will be in Germany on business. Make sure to thank him properly if your paths cross."

I studied Mr. Morton as he started the car, but he showed no sign he'd meant anything by that other than its surface meaning, so I relaxed a little. "I'll do that. But ... can you really travel with me like this?" I didn't want to say that the other girls were shunning me over special treatment, but it was true.

"It's not just for you. I have connections to make, wheels to grease, so don't worry about it. When you start making more money, I'll see about hiring you a road manager."

In all honesty, I only had half an idea what that meant, but I'd seen pictures of celebrities going around with an entourage. I didn't think I'd ever get to that level, and I put the offer out of my mind as we parked at Nashville International Airport. I'd never left the country before, and I probably would've been scared if Mr. Morton had sent me on my own. He herded me through the process like a good cattle dog, nipping at my heels when I paused too long.

Finally we were waiting at the gate, with about half an hour till our first flight, when a boy came over to me, timid as a chipmunk. With those freckles and front teeth, it was a solid comparison. "You starred with Bobby Ray Hudgens in that Mad Misfits music video, right? I can't believe I'm meeting a famous person."

Goose bumps prickled my skin and my smile froze. For about ten seconds it felt good to be recognized, until he reminded me that no matter how bright the flames, they always threw a shadow. "That was me," I said softly.

Mr. Morton stood a few feet off, talking on his cell phone. No help there.

The boy didn't seem to realize I wished he would walk away. "If it's not too much trouble, do you mind signing this?"

"This" was his boarding pass. I wrote my name neatly, but the cursive looked childish. He didn't seem to mind.

"Thank you. I'll be your biggest fan from now on!"

Mr. Morton's return drove off my admirer, who hurried toward a gate nearby. "Was he bothering you?"

Yes.

"No," I said.

"You'll get used to people coming up to you. There's an art to making them feel acknowledged without spending too much time on it."

———

Berlin was nothing like I expected. After the bustle of the airports in Nashville and Chicago, the airport was small and relatively quiet. In just a few steps, we went from immigration to the exit, where a Mercedes town car was waiting. The driver got my door, earning a nod from Mr. Morton. Shivering, I slid into the backseat and wished my coat was a little thicker.

"Straight to the hotel to drop Marlena off, then take me on to my first meeting."

"Yes, sir."

I hadn't had much idea what to expect from Germany, but Berlin was a practical city, square and industrial, not much to admire as we drove. The sky was heavy with pink-shot clouds, cool and bright with wintry sunrise. We'd taken an eight a.m. flight, traveled for fourteen hours, and now it was five in the morning, my first time losing a day like that.

The early hour meant light traffic, so we arrived quickly at a small hotel in the heart of the city. Rectangular and blocky, it looked like it had been built in the fifties, and the lobby was orange and cream, polished floors and smooth countertops. Mr. Morton got me checked in and once I had the room key, a card I had to swipe, he said, "Get some rest. The driver will collect you at noon."

If I hadn't been so tired, I might've been nervous about the lingerie show, but ten hours on a plane had me ready for a shower and bed. After setting the alarm, I crashed for six hours. The buzzer was raucous but it did the job. I made myself presentable for my first meeting with the show producer, then hurried down to the lobby to wait for the driver.

He arrived five minutes early and didn't say much in performing escort duty. More alert now, I had butterflies dancing in my stomach as we pulled up at the exhibition hall. It was domed on top with lots of windows, what I guessed would be considered modern architecture. Other than that, I didn't have words to describe it.

"We're here, Miss Altizer."

"Thank you."

Compared to what I was used to, it was still bitterly cold, and I hurried into the building, following the signs to where Mr. Morton was waiting, all smiles and hearty booming voice. He was chatting with a woman in her fifties, bright blond hair and vivid blue eyes, decked out so well in a slim black suit that she must have been a designer or a stylist.

"Marlena, come meet Clotilde Weber, the CEO of Celestial. She agreed to give you a chance as a favor to Mr. Durst." The subtle emphasis was clear.

"Thank you, ma'am."

"Please, call me Clotilde. Turn for me, child."

That was abrupt, but I obeyed, moving as I'd been taught. The designer nodded in approval. "She'll do," she said to Mr. Morton. To me, she added, "Run along and meet everyone else. We'll start work in earnest tomorrow."

The butterflies from earlier hadn't settled; they were more like bats, but I did as I was told. Before I got to the lounge, I heard cheerful chatter in a variety of languages, and already I felt at a disadvantage. I'd probably find it hard to talk to these people; peering through the doorway only confirmed that impression. All the models in the room seemed to be taller than me, more beautiful, and better dressed. Even the staff were impossibly chic, surpassing standards I couldn't have envisioned in Barrettville—wall-to-wall luxury brands, shoes that cost thousands of dollars, and handbags so precious I couldn't believe they were dangling off anyone's arm.

"Are you nervous?" a male voice asked.

Startled, I almost dropped my own purse and he caught it neatly. As he glanced back up, I recognized Michael Durst. Quickly I shook my head, reaching for my bag. He didn't relinquish it.

"No," I mumbled. Then I remembered to add, "Thank you. For recommending me for this show."

He laughed. "My pleasure. Let me tell you a secret, miss. The secret to success is believing you're at least as good as anyone in the room. Confidence can carry you farther than you'd ever imagine."

5

Jenny was right.

I never did go back to the apartment in Nashville. That lingerie show went so well that I signed an extended contract with Celestial and there were catalogue shoots and more shows. Mr. Morton sorted out my work visa with help from Clotilde, and I ended up in a little flat with three other models: two European, one African. They were all better educated and more sophisticated, so we didn't bond.

They had stylish boyfriends who picked them up in shiny sports cars and they came home giggling drunk, with more presents than they could carry. Part of me wanted in on that world, but I feared it too, because every man might be Bobby Ray Hudgens beneath the skin. Money just lacquered over the awful, hiding the base violence of a place like Barrettville, and even there, the haves did what they wanted to the have-nots.

Sometimes I missed my brothers and sisters, but any money I sent, Mama would confiscate and pour into her habit. If there was a way out for any of them, they'd have to find it on their own, just like I did. Maybe that made me heartless, but if any of them managed to track me down, I would help then.

When I wasn't working, I took language classes, learning German, French, and Italian. I picked up German faster than the Romance languages, but overall I had a knack for it. From time to time I felt guilty about how I'd left Jenny, so I sent money to her, kept in touch via email. Her words on screen kept me from feeling too lonely, most days.

Everything's okay here. Still working at the car wash. I don't like the new girl, and I miss you. But I heard you suggested me for a European shampoo commercial. Thank you for that! I didn't get it, they went with someone "less ethnic." I did some catalogue work for that sportswear company in Galveston recently and I guess I'll be doing a department store show next month. I'm working on my GED, just like you told me, because I don't want you nagging me. Write soon, OK?

Jenny and I texted a lot, too, just quick updates more than actual conversations because of the time difference. Still, it was nice waking up to a heart or a smiley face from her, especially since I didn't have friends here. Ostensibly I was still repped by Del Morton, but he'd opened his hands to let me sink or swim with Celestial.

I swam.

By the end of the first year, I'd accepted a couple of television commercials, and I was the face for an expensive Italian rejuvenating cream, too. As my initial contracts expired, the offers were still coming, and the money was seductive, but I watched girls around me succumb to eating disorders and drug addiction to stay competitive and decided to leave under my own steam.

Once I settled into my new life, I figured, maybe I could send Jenny tickets for a visit. She'd been hinting that she wanted to come for a while; she'd never been to Europe, and it would be fun having her here. I had to get sorted out first, separate myself from the world of wine for breakfast and ecstasy in my bathroom and white powder spilled on my damn coffee table when I woke up.

The next day, I went to inform Clotilde that I wouldn't be signing on for another year. Her office always intimidated me, all cream and gilt, with feminine touches that defiantly asserted her power as chief executive officer of a profitable lingerie company. Mannequins had been brought with the next season's designs and she was still considering them when the assistant ushered me in.

"What do you think of this one?"

It was a matched bra and panty set in cerulean, satin, and lace. Cocking my head, I considered. "Pretty, but it's something you wear for a lover."

"As I thought. Did you come to sign the contract, or will you be bringing Del to badger me for better terms?"

I shook my head. "No, it's an excellent offer with generous conditions, and you've been good to me … so this is hard. But it's time for me to pursue other opportunities."

A few photographers had suggested that I could make the transition to couture, but I was an inch too short to stand out as a supermodel, and I didn't want to fail upward. I'd never coveted fame. I had a rep for being a buzzkill, and some men who'd tried me said I was a frigid bitch behind my back. There was a reason I lived so chastely, however. People always talked, and I needed a certain reputation to get back to anyone who might inquire about me. Men tended to want what they couldn't have, so it wouldn't do at all if I appeared to be an easy acquisition.

Hence my resignation from Celestial. I had to be driven and determined, committed to self-improvement. Everything that happened from this point forward had to seem like Michael Durst's plan, not mine.

Clotilde didn't take it well. "Why, Marlena? Are you going to Luxe-wear? Because you should know—"

"No." Interrupting was rude, but I needed to set the record straight. "I want to go to school here. I've heard that there are opportunities for international students."

That revelation appeased Clotilde, once she realized I was resolute. "It's not bad for you to take a long view. Most girls only think about being famous." Briskly, she went on to confirm what I'd heard about German universities and offered to have her assistant compile a list of schools that might be a good fit. "There's one here, in fact."

"Again, thanks for everything."

"Juliet will email you with the information. Take care, Marlena."

As I stepped out of Clotilde's office, I met Michael Durst again. It wasn't a coincidence; I'd chosen to give notice at that time because I knew he had an appointment. From what Del had told me, Durst had been watching over me from a distance. It was reasonable to take that as tacit interest, which would increase or decrease depending on my moves.

I suspected he'd respond, now that I'd resigned as a model.

Durst owned shares in Celestial and in UMAX entertainment, along with several other businesses. Those were minor aspects of his portfolio, according to what other models had said. In the last year I'd seen women try to hook up with him, but it rarely worked, possibly because they knew to a decimal point how much he was worth and what real estate deals he was currently closing. He seemed like a shark, far too canny to be suckered by a gold-digger.

This man didn't age. Four years earlier, he'd looked to be in his late thirties, and *still* seemed to be; an immortal in his prime. Like the first time I'd seen him, he was dressed well, in a custom-tailored gray suit,

Rolex on his wrist. His gaze raked over me, coolly impersonal, and his smile told me nothing at all.

"Have you made a decision?" he asked.

"It's time for me to move on," I answered.

"An excellent choice."

"Is it?"

"Indisputably. You don't have what it takes to succeed at the highest levels. There's no sense in throwing yourself at a glass wall like a brainless bird."

That conjured a vivid, awful picture of a wren slamming into a window, dropping broken and bloody to the ground. I blinked to clear that image. "If I didn't agree with you, I might take offense."

"You're too clever for that," he said.

"How do you know?"

"I know you, Marlena. From the first moment I saw you in Del Morton's office, I knew you would belong to me. I also understood that you were too young, and that I had to let you realize it on your own."

It was equal measures heady and overwhelming, hearing that from a rich and powerful man. In truth, I'd made up my mind to have him long before we met. He was destined to be mine the first time I saw his picture in the tabloids, so from my perspective, this *was* inevitable. I admired the shine of his expensive Italian leather loafers, and the promise of a Cinderella story for my very own. I remembered the shotgun shack and being unable to sleep for my stomach chewing at my backbone.

The devil had a run at me, whispering, *With him, you can have anything you want. He'll make the world kneel at your feet.*

That's the dream, right?

Because a girl who used to scrub chimneys was pretty, the prince wanted her, and when she ran, he kept her shoe as a souvenir and hunted her down, relentless in his desire. Little girls were raised wishing for that fate, but it always seemed strange to me that she could be *claimed*. On a prince's whim, she left her old life and became a princess in a fancy room. Did anyone ever ask what came next? Whether she missed her pet mice, or whether she was happy in her ivory tower, even though the prince wouldn't let her do her own shopping and she couldn't choose her friends, because the prince *wanted* her, and he got her, and he *owned* her, forever after.

Tilting my head, I smiled up at him. "Shouldn't you ask me to dinner first? Seems like you're getting ahead of yourself."

His mouth curved. "I don't mind dancing with you, as long as you know where we'll be when the music stops."

6

Michael Durst's courtship, if you could call it that, started the next night.

He picked me up at my Berlin flat in a luxurious town car. The driver opened my door with a flourish and I climbed in beside the wealthiest man I'd ever met. We drove past quaint bistros and cafes with patio seating, portable heaters burning away because it was chilly at night, even in May.

I expected we'd go somewhere posh, but I couldn't contain my surprise when we headed west to Kurfürstendamm. When I'd stepped out of the flat, I'd felt beautiful in my black sheath dress; it was Anne Klein, simple and elegant, one of the nicest I'd ever owned. Now he wanted to *Pretty Woman* me because I wasn't fine enough for wherever we were going?

"Wait here," he instructed the driver. "We won't be long."

He led me into a boutique with an array of beautiful clothes and accessories, shoes embellished with real diamonds. "You look pretty, Marlena, but you should always wear the finest quality, and I will ensure that you do."

I let him sweep me into the glamour and I relished the fact that he was dressing me in an ivory Dior gown, especially when he added a collar of diamonds, a matching tennis bracelet, and the prettiest Louboutin shoes I'd ever seen, all sheer silver and sparkles. The salesgirls whispered in German as they rang up the purchases, a mixture of awe and envy, and I *liked* being the girl they wanted to be.

"Should we wrap up her dress?" the tall one asked.

"No need. Donate it." He handed over a platinum card with casual assurance while I twinged over having my best cocktail dress discarded like it was garbage.

That feeling soon rushed away when we arrived at our destination, a restaurant so exclusive that it took months to get a reservation, and even then, it helped if you knew someone. We strolled past the people trying to bribe their way in, ushered in by an unctuous host in a suit. The place was all amber lighting and polished onyx tabletops, ultramodern decor with a stunning view of the Berlin skyline.

"Getting in here means something," he said, once we'd taken our seats.

"That you're rich and powerful?" Probably, I shouldn't have said that.

My candor made him smile. "Among other things."

When the waiter came, Mr. Durst ordered for both of us, high-end steak and potatoes, as if I didn't know how to read. After the food arrived, I watched him to see what silverware he used; a pause he noted, to my chagrin.

"You have a lot to learn," he said. "If you're willing, I'd like to teach you. In my hands, you can shine as you've never imagined."

He saw himself as Pygmalion, creating his perfect woman from unshaped clay. The artist didn't ask his medium how it felt about the form being forced onto it ... and why would he? Clay had no thoughts or feelings; it existed to be molded. It would seem strange if I let him do it with full awareness, so I pretended to be oblivious. Durst didn't want a *clever* woman, so I had to hide any hints of that.

"Can't we just date?" I asked, eyes wide.

He laughed quietly. "If you give when you should, yes. I find you delightful, Marlena. Your eyes ... your eyes are extraordinary."

Given his intensity, he must have believed they were. I'd been counting on that, based on pictures of women who'd clung to him for a night or two. I'd get much, much more before I was through.

I said demurely, "Thank you, Michael."

I took my first bite of the steak. In my whole life, I'd never had anything so good—tender and meaty, but somehow buttery as well. Likewise, the potatoes were the fluffiest, airy and delicate, and I almost cried over how exquisite everything was. He taught me about wine that night, an informative lecture about what types came from which regions, and I drank more than I should have, so I leaned on him when we left the restaurant hours later.

Through dizzy eyes, I caught Durst smiling, eyes bright with some emotion I couldn't identify. His arm tightened on me as we slid into the town car. "Tonight, I'll take you home. That won't always be the case, but ... I'll ensure that the timing is perfect."

As we drove, I figured out that he meant sex. Maybe it was because he was older, but he talked around things that made him seem ... if not repressed, then old-fashioned. I wasn't drowning in the desire to fuck him anyway, but if I did, I'd be richly rewarded. The diamond tennis bracelet weighed heavy on my wrist.

He saw me safely to my front door like a gentleman. "I have a question for you … and it's important, as it will dictate what happens between us from this point on."

"That sounds serious."

He nodded. "Tell me the truth, Marlena. Have you ever had a boyfriend?"

My stomach lurched. I knew what he was really asking. I could've told him about Bobby Ray Hudgens and that asshole boyfriend of my mom's who made sure I was never innocent like a child should be. Instead I told the technical truth, knowing what he'd make of it. "No. You're the first."

"I thought so," he said, lucent with satisfaction. "I'll call you soon, princess."

I'd heard that before, but he meant it. He'd staked a claim on me, one he wouldn't relinquish readily. I could have shouted in triumph, but I'd been planning this for so long that I could never break character. Not once. Not ever. The way most girls dream of the future in a general sense, I had been making notes about Michael Durst.

One of my roommates, Imani, was home when I stumbled in. Her dark eyes locked onto my new wardrobe and she gave an approving nod. "You finally saw the light. Who is it?"

"Michael Durst."

Perfect brows shot up. "Be careful. I've heard some things, and you're too green to start swimming in the deep end."

"What things?"

"I know a girl who dated him, and he's a real control freak. You wear what he buys, go where he wants to, and God help you if he catches you looking at another man."

"Is he into kinky sex stuff, too?"

Imani sighed. "You just can't be told, can you? Fine, have it your way, but don't come running to me for help later."

"I won't," I said.

She meant well, but she didn't *know*. Not about Dee leaving, or the Kentucky hills I'd run from, determined I wouldn't end up like my mother. No matter what, my story would have a different ending.

One date turned into ten, and then twenty, each more extravagant than the last. Michael convinced me to study European art history. My last night in Berlin, only Imani was around. The other two girls had dates or jobs; I didn't really keep up.

"Are you sure this is wise?" she asked.

I'd already toured the apartment in Heidelberg, and it was bright, modern, with hardwood floors, stainless steel appliances, and clean white walls. Not large, but it didn't need to be, and it was close enough for me to bike to campus. I had my admission letter in hand, ready to begin the next phase of my life.

"What, moving? Or college?"

"Relying on Michael Durst."

I'd planned to attend a public university in Germany, because international students qualified for low-tuition costs, but Michael had argued in favor of the more prestigious Heidelberg University. At first I objected, but when he held my hands, gazed into my eyes, and said, "Marlena, I want to do this for you. Let me," I yielded.

He was just *so happy* when I put myself in his hands, you see, trusting in his judgment. I'd have to be an idiot to reject a free, first-rate college education, so I ignored Imani's cautionary words. "I know what I'm doing. Take care of yourself."

The movers came the next day and hauled my stuff to the new flat. This was the first time I'd ever lived alone, and it was past time for me to invite Jenny. She'd be so impressed that I was enrolled at such a good school. I wished I was studying languages, but I did like the prospect of earning my bachelor's degree in six semesters.

In the moving van, I wrote a quick message to Jenny. *Here are some pics of my new place. Let me know when you have time off. I want you to visit if you can. Miss you!* Before I could finish the message, the phone rang, so I quickly hit send.

"Hi, Michael."

"Are you on the way?"

"Everything's wrapped up in Berlin," I confirmed.

"Good girl."

That was the first time Michael steered my life the way he wanted, but it wouldn't be the last. I set a pattern of giving in, and then he'd reward me with some glorious gift; sapphire earrings or a Chanel bag. When I wasn't stuffing my mind with interesting facts about dead artists, we were jetting to Monaco or St. Tropez, and I let him shape me to his desired form.

Already I'd noticed the change in the way men looked at me. Before, there had been greed and desire, but now it was tempered by caution, like I'd become a treasure too dear for the common man to hope for. Their eyes skated over me, lingered in admiration, and then kept going. I *loved* that part, and so I wore what Michael bought, studied as he thought I should, and never questioned his decisions.

7

As it turned out, Jenny couldn't come before I graduated. She was in school at Tennessee State University, working on a computer science degree, and she was dead gifted, too. She had her own dreams to chase, and we were always together at heart.

Soon after I got my diploma, I also received a marriage proposal. It was what I'd been angling for, but I could hardly contain my delight and triumph. *Look at me now. Look how far I've come.* For Dee's sake, I'd walk this path, even if it was difficult. I'd push this all the way to the end.

Michael saw something in me, something he wanted for life. So there I sat, gazing across a white-linen tablecloth, candles flickering between us. The black velvet ring box was open, displaying an incredibly beautiful platinum and diamond engagement ring. He'd never spoken of love, and our sex life was ... well.

Sleeping with him wasn't exactly a hardship. He liked me to lie quiet and still and not make a sound while he did it. In fact, sometimes he made me roll over so he could do me from behind, just pumping and grunting while my face slid against the pillow. He didn't want me to pretend to come, either. All I had to do was hold still and wait, and afterward, he praised me for being his good girl. That was fairly messed up, but I couldn't let go of this golden ticket. No matter where the ride carried me.

I whispered, "Yes," and he slid the ring on my finger as the waiter and waitresses cheered and popped the cork on some expensive champagne.

A week later, I was sitting in a conference room at a law office, poring over the thick packet of papers that made up the prenuptial agreement I was being asked to sign. Best I could reckon, if I cheated on Michael or left for any other reason, I got nothing.

The attorney was standing at my shoulder. "You'll receive an allowance of a thousand US dollars weekly, for the duration of the marriage. That money will be yours to keep. We've also noted your current assets, which will remain separate from Mr. Durst's interests."

My savings account didn't even have enough in it to cover one year of tuition at Heidelberg University, so I smiled at the idea that Michael might be trying to con me out of money. But then I started doing the math. Four thousand a month, forty-eight thousand a year. Considering his personal fortune, that was probably a pittance to him, but my mother had only a quarter of that annually.

"I'm fine with all of that," I said.

The pale-eyed lawyer looked surprised. "Then sign here, initial here, and a final signature on the last page."

Michael came in as I stood, done with the paperwork. "Go on out. I need to talk with Anton for a moment."

I paused outside the door, a curious imp prompting me to listen. "Did she argue?" Michael asked.

"Not at all. It seems you've chosen well this time, Mr. Durst."

Chosen well? The question circled in my head as I hurried to the bathroom to wash my hands. They shouldn't catch me eavesdropping; that would undo all the points I'd earned by not haggling like I was buying fresh catfish.

Soon, I would stop being Marlena Altizer and become Mrs. Marlena Durst. It was even spelled out in the agreement—that I had to take his name. He was firm in that regard, probably some assertion of ownership. I couldn't claim I didn't know what I was getting into. I'd studied Michael Durst, and Imani had warned me as well. His patterns were easily discernible to anyone who took sufficient time and interest.

In the mirror, I could scarcely recognize myself. I'd changed so much in a few years that I doubted anyone who'd known me in Barrettville could identify me. I'd felt the same way the first time I saw Dee's picture in the newspaper. Was she *always* that beautiful? And why didn't I know it, when we were supposed to be closer than real blood sisters? At least that was what she whispered before she went away.

Shrugging it off, I went to look for Michael.

For once he drove me home personally, though he didn't enjoy being behind the wheel. When I asked why, he changed the subject. He had a way of turning topics so I wouldn't delve, and I absorbed the message that I was an accessory, not an emotional necessity. Maybe I needed to alter that to secure him on my hook. On reflection, probably not. He didn't need to love me; desire was enough.

"It feels like I've been waiting forever to make you mine," he said. "I don't want a long engagement, and I can't take too much time away from work."

"Okay." That was what he wanted from me, continual agreement.

"Pack up your things, enough for two weeks or so, and I'll have the rest sent to the penthouse in Manhattan. You'll love it."

Will I?

He didn't ask if I wanted to go back to America, but my time in Europe was done, apparently, whether I liked it or not. At least it should be easier to see Jenny. New York to Nashville wasn't nearly so much distance.

Taking comfort in that, I asked, "Is that where we'll be living?"

"For a while. I travel a lot, and I'll want you to come with me, whenever possible."

Okay, that sounded good. I was feeling relatively cheerful when I went into the flat and began boxing up my worldly goods. If I'd had close friends there, I would have called them up for a bachelorette party, but I never managed to form close ties at university, just knew people I messaged for notes when I missed class. Thinking back, there were people who'd tried, but I always had plans with Michael or I was waiting for him to call. He didn't like it when it took me too long to get back to him, and *I* didn't like the nerve-wracking sensation of pissing off the person who was paying my tuition.

Just like in Berlin, I wrapped up my life in Heidelberg alone.

It had been a while since I'd written Jenny more than a quick note, so I typed a long email, talking about graduation and the upcoming wedding. I closed with, *Hope you're well. It's weird since we haven't seen each other in so long, but you're still my closest friend. Keep me posted, OK? And know that I* really *wish you could be my maid of honor.*

Despite the time difference—it must have been four a.m. there—she wrote back right away. *I'd love that, if only I could. But some of us aren't engaged to sugar daddies and can't hop on a plane anytime we want. I demand pics of the big day. Promise?*

Guaranteed, I sent back. We got on Skype and talked until she had to go to class; that was the closest I would come to a wild celebration ending my days as a single woman.

Two weeks later, I married Michael Durst in a small, private ceremony at a lovely chapel in Ibiza, all whitewashed simplicity, terracotta tiles, and nineteenth-century stained glass. With only a few of his closest friends attending, the ceremony was far less ostentatious than I expected. I wore a Versace gown that Michael chose, and my hair was done as he'd instructed: in an elegant twist, with baby's breath and white roses pinned around the top like a tiara of innocence. He'd even inspected the makeup artist's work before we spoke our vows, earning a teasing rebuke from the stylist.

"You can't see her now. Don't you know it's bad luck?" She spoke in Spanish first, and then repeated the warning in English.

Michael ignored her, leading me out to greet the guests in defiance of the custom that dictated my family should give me away. But none of them were there, and his expression unnerved me a little, as if he wouldn't let go of me, ever, for any reason. Out in the sunlight, I forgot that feeling as I drank excellent champagne and swayed to the romantic strains of a small orchestra.

After a few dances, Michael stepped away for a moment to talk with a man I didn't recognize. He seemed out of place for the occasion, in his dark shiny suit and blood-red dress shirt. I didn't linger long on the tattoo crawling over his collar, a snake that twined around his neck and was about to bite his ear off.

The lawyer who had overseen the prenup came over to congratulate me. Anton, I vaguely remembered, though I couldn't produce a last name. "The wedding was lovely, and you look beautiful. Would you care to dance?"

"Sure," I said.

It was an entirely proper waltz, and neither his hands nor his eyes wandered, but Michael cut in before the song finished. He smiled with his teeth, not his eyes. "Overstep again, counselor, and I'll have to kill you."

We all laughed, but I wasn't entirely sure my new husband was joking. The awkward moment melted away as someone gave a toast, and then there were presents to open, and a beautiful sunset to admire, while the photographers madly snapped pictures, committed to capturing these perfect moments.

I promised to send Jenny a picture.

In that rosy haze, I was happy for a while, because Michael went out of his way to please me. Anything I wanted, I could have. He took a couple of weeks off and we cruised the Mediterranean on a yacht he bought because I casually said it might be fun. In those early days, Michael was like a genie who existed to grant my wishes.

But wishes are never granted without a hidden price, just as the most beautiful roses have barbs the better to bleed you dry.

8

At first, Michael took me with him everywhere, and I was on his arm constantly. I understood then why he wanted me to study art history; it was a topic that made me seem smart and cultured to the people he needed to schmooze. Doubtless he wouldn't have put it that way, but old men liked it when I could talk for ten minutes on *Girl with the Pearl Earring*, describing my impressions of it from memory. We'd taken a day trip to the Hague when we were in Amsterdam, including a visit to the Mauritshuis, which let me also discuss how beautiful the museum itself was, converted from a Dutch count's private residence.

With such talk, I was charming a rich old real estate mogul who owned some land on the west coast that Michael wanted to buy. I didn't ask, and he never shared his business concerns with me. We were at Jack Denney's Malibu beach house; it was late, so the moon was up, reflecting on the water.

"You make me want to go see it myself," the gentleman said, smiling. "But where are you from, my dear? You have such an interesting accent."

I blushed. Despite my best efforts, I hadn't been able to eradicate the hills from my voice entirely, but I'd gained a patina that made me sound almost exotic due to living in Europe for the last four years. Americans never seemed to be sure if I was one of them at first glance, and talking to me didn't clarify matters either.

As I was about to reply, Michael said smoothly, "She was born in a little village in Croatia, but her father is a diplomat so she's lived all over the world. Marlena speaks four languages, isn't that right, my dear?"

Okay, this wasn't part of the plan. Not remotely.

His fingers dug into my upper arm, telling me I'd better agree with the pedigree he'd assigned. My smile tightened but didn't falter. "That's true."

It was highly unlikely that a random American businessman would speak Croatian, but still, I couldn't breathe properly until Jack Denney walked away. I wanted to scream, because this was a much bigger issue than wearing the clothes Michael picked out. Now he had me pretending to be a different person, and if his contacts discovered the deception, I had no doubt that I'd pay the price, not Michael.

"Shhh," he whispered, leaning close, pretending to kiss my cheek, but it was more of a controlling move. "We'll talk about this later."

Normally I'd just smile and let it go, but since this meant maintaining a long-term pretense, I broke the subject wide open as soon as we got in the car. "Why Croatia? I don't speak a word of Croatian, Michael. I've never even been there. If people find out—"

"Breathe," he cut in. "And shut up."

I did, because the edge in his voice chilled me. He'd never used that tone on me before, though I'd heard it aimed at staff who pissed him off. He raised the partition between the chauffeur and us, then turned on some mood music. Maybe the smooth jazz was supposed to be calming, but it exacerbated my already raw nerves.

"It's Croatia because I know people there, and there's a man willing to acknowledge you as his daughter. Your maiden name was Novak, by the way, and your parents are Henrik and Anya, an American expat. After graduating from high school early, you came to the US to work as a model."

"You can't just rewrite my past," I said softly. "People know me. Like Mr. Morton—"

"I own twenty-five percent of UMAX, Marlena. Do you really think he'll disagree with any story I care to tell?"

That didn't assuage my concerns at all. "I guess not."

And it bothered me that my whole identity had to be paved over. Barrettville was nothing to brag about, but I wasn't ashamed, either. I had no control over where I came from, only where I was going.

He sighed and glanced away as if I'd disappointed him. The air in the car chilled my skin after the warmth of the summer evening. "You're not ready to be my helpmeet. I'd hoped … but no. You need more training. Etiquette, deportment, and you need to learn Croatian. You always wanted to study languages, right?"

Not like this.

My head was reeling from these sudden demands. Now that we were married, dressing me wasn't enough for him. Neither was fucking me. Now there was another hurdle for me to jump: becoming his ideal woman even though it was a lie he was selling to enhance his own status.

"I don't understand."

"There will be a dossier waiting for you at the hotel. I want you to memorize everything in it until you can give those answers in your sleep. You must be worthy as my wife, Marlena. You need to be perfect."

I had no idea who had set this criterion, but his mood was dark, and I didn't like how icy he'd gotten, as if we were strangers. I whispered, "I'll try harder."

"Good girl. I won't be staying. I'm flying out for Munich tonight, and then I have some meetings in Moscow, so I won't be home for a few weeks. I expect you to be on board with making me proud when I get back."

"I will be. This is just … sudden. That's all." I couldn't say what was on my mind.

That was when the honeymoon ended and my husband peeled off his latex mask. I didn't like what I was glimpsing underneath. But this? This was only the tip of the iceberg.

I'd had some inkling that the transformation from prince to beast might be forthcoming, but I'd thought there would be more forewarning. I was so, so wrong. Now that he had my ownership papers in the form of the marriage license, I supposed, he thought there was no more reason for a pretense of gentleness. From this point forward, I would receive good treatment only if I earned it.

"Go upstairs. In the morning the driver will take you to the airport, and you have tickets on the nine a.m. flight back to New York."

I might've said something, but Michael was already signaling the driver to open my door, and he turned away as I climbed out of the car, making his displeasure crystal clear. For reasons I didn't entirely understand, the prospect of losing his approval felt like the end of the world. He'd made me, after all, and if he lost pleasure in his creation, wouldn't I be nothing at all?

I trudged into the five-star hotel and took the express lift to the penthouse suite. The room was huge—with an incredible view—but I could see only the file on the immense dining table. I didn't even change out of my evening clothes before I started reading.

This ... this was a complete life, created just for me, along with pictures that had been beautifully photoshopped. I almost wished that these smiling people *were* my parents, because they looked so proud at my graduation, and we seemed to be having such fun together beside a crystalline lake. It seemed that I was an only child, lavished with affection and sent to the best schools, as evidenced by my graduation at sixteen.

The depth of this charade staggered me. But really, what was the point? To Michael, it mattered so much for the world to think he'd married the perfect woman. He didn't have the flawless personal background required to actually woo and win such a perfect woman; *he has to make do with me.* I took the file to bed with me and woke to a call from the front desk.

Hurriedly, I packed my things and met the driver in the lobby. It was never the same person twice, and they never made eye contact. All my attempts at small talk failed, too.

After the first-class flight to New York, yet another stranger picked me up and I decided to test a theory. "I'd like to change my destination, please."

"Excuse me, madam?"

"I'm not going straight home. Can you take me to Bergdorf's instead?" That was a department store that Michael favored, not too far from our condo in Manhattan.

"I'm sorry, I can't do that. My instructions were very clear."

"Right. Well, take me home, then. I'll go shopping after I drop my things off." With a tight smile, I settled back in the town car, a knot in my chest.

The ride took forever because of traffic. Given my preferences, I would take public transportation, but Michael would rather die. So we sat in gridlock, though I could've walked the last five blocks much faster. Eventually we got there and the driver carried my luggage up, escorting me past the doorman all the way to the penthouse.

"You don't work for a car service, do you?"

He was a large man, burly and brown-skinned with skull-cut hair, and dressed in the black and white of the professional driver, but somehow I had the feeling he did more than drive. The man's eyes slid away from mine, giving me an answer before he spoke.

"No, madam. I work for Mr. Durst."

"Which means you won't be leaving when I go inside. Do you have orders to stop me if I try to go out?" I tried to keep the question casual, but all this affluence and protection was starting to close in on me like I was a rabbit in a snare.

"I'd need to speak with Mr. Durst, which is currently impossible."

"He wants me to sit quietly in the apartment until he gets back?"

Impassive look, though I thought I caught a flicker of sympathy. "I couldn't say, madam. Mr. Durst doesn't confide his private plans to me."

"Okay then. I won't make your life difficult." I paused, trying to decide if there was any way to gain ground. Being friendly never hurt. "What's your name, by the way?"

"Vin. I mean, Vincent Rivera."

"Then good night, Vin."

This was so damn much to process, but best I could figure, I'd pissed Michael off, and now I was a prisoner until I made him happy again. Shivering, I hurried inside the condo and shut the door behind me, leaning on it because my knees wouldn't hold and my breath was coming in gulps that might make me hyperventilate if I didn't get it under control.

My first instinct was to message Jenny, but as I glanced around the condo, I realized I didn't know if I could trust my phone—the one Michael had bought for me. Everything I owned, he'd given me. The stuff

55

I'd owned before we got married he'd made me donate to charity, as it didn't befit my new role as his wife.

When I took those vows, I hadn't realized it was a life sentence in the same vein as being locked up for murder.

9

I tried calling my husband, but like Vin had said, he didn't answer. He might have been on a plane or in a meeting. Either way, I wasn't going anywhere that night.

The chef who came in once a week had left frozen gourmet meals that I only needed to microwave, and I had over a hundred channels of premium satellite TV. In the library, there were volumes of classic literature, priceless first editions. I could get some air on the rooftop terrace, call up a private masseuse, order anything I wanted and pay extra for next-day delivery, or soak for hours in the gilt and marble tub that was big enough for two mermaids to frolic in.

I didn't do any of that.

Instead, I had some water to counteract the dehydration of a cross-country flight and settled in with the file, determined to become Michael's perfect woman. He shouldn't be tired of me yet. I'd done everything he'd asked. So, according to his pattern, I figured I should have a couple more years before the situation escalated. I was ready for that eventually, but the timing was off, and I hadn't laid any of the groundwork for my perfect exit strategy.

Maybe he's not angry. Maybe the guard is for my protection.

That comforted me a little as I memorized facts about Marlena Novak, the girl from Croatia with a homemaker mom who dabbled in watercolors and a diplomat father. None of it was glamorous but it was all deeply respectable, and maybe that was what Michael needed. I stayed up late that night and the next two.

It was so lonely and quiet in the penthouse that I thought I might lose my mind. Each time I peered out into the foyer, Vin was there, and late in the evening it was a stranger, some man whose name I didn't know.

On the fourth day of my enforced isolation, I heard movement in the hallway outside and activated the screen on the intercom to see what was up. A tidy, professorial-looking woman offered something to the guard, and he let her ring the bell. The gray hair and horn-rimmed glasses combined with a no-nonsense black suit gave her a faintly intimidating air. I answered at once, because at this point any distraction was welcome.

"Good morning, Mrs. Durst." She spoke with a faint accent, German or Austrian. "I am Frau Schmidt. I'll be tutoring you in deportment and etiquette, three hours a day. In the afternoon, your language teacher will arrive."

To help me learn Croatian, I figured. Otherwise, this complicated backstory Michael had manufactured would fall apart.

There was nothing wrong with improving myself, but I still felt sick and shaky over the way I was being hidden from the world until I met some standard that had never even been explained. It wasn't like I burped in public or licked butter off my knife at fancy parties, but Michael probably didn't approve of the way I waited to see what everyone else would do, a silent tell that I didn't belong in refined company.

"Let's get started," I said.

That set the tone for the next week and a half. I didn't despise working with Frau Schmidt, though she was harsh when I couldn't remember who took social precedence or when I couldn't tell a tea spoon from a dessert spoon. I enjoyed my lessons with Monsieur Girard, an elderly Frenchman who spoke an astonishing twelve languages. I tried to get him to teach me more than Croatian, but I was fast coming to the comprehension that people did *not* deviate from whatever Michael Durst had asked of them.

Two weeks to the day after I had gotten home, my husband finally returned, late in the evening. He hadn't called or texted in that entire time, and in a normal relationship, I could've cried or shouted at him. But I was walking a narrow line, and I didn't care to consider what would happen if I stumbled.

I pinned on a bright smile, took his coat and briefcase. "Welcome home. Should I warm something up for dinner?"

There were cleaners who came and went, but they didn't live with us. Michael was ferocious about guarding his privacy. Just then he looked tired, as if things hadn't gone according to plan overseas.

"I ate on the plane," he said, scrutinizing me. With impersonal fingers, he gripped my chin and turned my face to the side. "Your skin is a mess, look at those dark circles. Haven't you been using the products I bought?"

"I am." Not every single night, though.

"Then we need to switch brands. I want results, not a tired hag greeting me when I get home after a long trip."

That stung, because if I was exhausted, it was from trying to meet his standards. I'd been burning the midnight oil every night that week to get conversant in Croatian, and it wasn't easy without a partner to guide me as I went. I swallowed my instinctive protest.

"You haven't been eating properly, either." In a different tone, this might have registered as affection, but he was eyeing me critically. "You're too thin, and I don't think you've been working out either. You're losing muscle tone, Marlena."

I closed my eyes against the sting of furious tears and then opened them with fresh resolve. *I can do this. I can.* I'd known going in that this wouldn't be easy. I had to shrug off hurt feelings and pretend to view him as my lord and master, the only star shining in my night sky. *Pretend, pretend. Say it like you mean it.*

"I'm sorry. I was too focused on my studies. I'll take care of myself better."

He finally softened. "Good girl. Remember, everything about you is a reflection on me, and you need to be healthy so we can have a baby in two years."

Shit. Michael had apparently decided—on his own—when I would bear his young. He probably figured I would be up to the mark in other ways by then, worthy of growing his seed. Admittedly, I hadn't loved this man when I married him, but it was getting harder to feign affection for so many reasons. I'd have to find a way *not* to have his kid.

"I'll do better." I was starting to feel like I should record that.

"See that you do." At last, he drew me to him and kissed my forehead. "Remember what we talked about before I left?"

I nodded.

"And where do you stand on that?"

"I'm doing my best," I said quickly. "Gleaning as much as I can from Frau Schmidt and Monsieur Girard."

"Excellent. I knew you'd see reason. Now I just need you to sign some documents pertaining to finalizing your status."

"What? Why?"

"On paper, you'll really be adopted by Henrik and Anya. It's nothing to worry about, just a formality, but it lends credence to have documentation. Just sign here and here."

"I don't..." At his look, I decided not to argue and wrote my name where he said. "This won't affect my citizenship or anything?"

He took the forms and put them away in a manila folder. "Not at all. Be a good girl now and report on what you've learned."

This close to him, a wave of panic washed over me, but I battled it down and dutifully explained what I'd memorized about table manners, introductions, and social precedence. Before he could ask, I switched to Croatian and spoke a few simple sentences to demonstrate my growing proficiency.

"Excellent. If you manage your time a little better and care for your body while you're sharpening your mind, you really will be the perfect woman."

I was supposed to take pleasure in that, so I held on to my smile like a rock climber slipping off the rope. His hand settled in the small of my back and he guided me toward the bathroom. This was the signal that we'd be having sex; he must have been pleased with my progress. Michael liked scrubbing and inspecting every inch of my body before we did it. At first I didn't mind, but since I couldn't decline the offer or wash myself, the ritual had long since crossed my comfort line.

That didn't matter. It never had.

I suffered through the invasive cleansing and waited in bed while he showered. Afterward, he came in and scrutinized the white cotton gown I had on, then he flipped me over. As he got in bed, I whispered into the pillow, "I don't want to."

Michael didn't hear in the rustling of covers, but I didn't think it would've changed anything even if he had. He wanted me. He took me.

"You're mine, I made you. And you'll *always* be mine. Every inch of you."

I said nothing.

He pumped harder. "Say it, Marlena."

"I'm yours. You made me."

That prompted an awful sound from him and a flurry of movement. I squeezed my eyes shut and waited for it to be over. My silent disgust might have made it better for him because I suspected he didn't think women should enjoy sex.

The kindest thing I could say was that he was quick and clean; he wore condoms though I was on the pill and he didn't flood me with semen. He also didn't mind if I got up to wash because he always did the same. Then we got back in bed and he held me. Some people loved cuddling afterward, but his arms felt like another trap, preventing me from moving or even breathing. Only after he drifted off and started to snore could I squirm away and relax on the other side of the bed, not touching him anywhere.

In the morning I made breakfast, fresh food not frozen. He didn't seem to notice the difference, busy with his phone and the morning paper. I had to broach the subject while he was in a good mood or God knew how long I'd be imprisoned.

As Michael finished his meal, I said, "With your permission, I'd like to join a few charity committees. It would be good if I made some helpful connections."

I also wanted Jenny to come for a visit, preferably while he was away, but I couldn't ask for what I truly wanted straight off. He laid down his paper with a contemplative expression and then he smiled. I got a tender pat on the hand.

"That is some excellent initiative. Before my next trip, I'll give Vin a list of approved events, fundraisers, and social clubs. You can pick and choose what looks most interesting, though I'd recommend something art-related so you can truly shine."

"I'll bear that in mind. But ... it's tiring to stay home all the time. If Vin goes with me, do you think I could run in the park sometimes? And maybe go to Bergdorf's? Shopping online isn't the same. I can't evaluate the fabric or try things on."

I wanted those small freedoms so badly my hands were shaking, so I knotted my fingers together beneath the table while I waited for my husband's judgment.

10

"**O**f course," Michael said after a brief pause. "Vin is *your* body-guard, princess. You may not be aware, but I have enemies. If they can't get to me, they'll hurt you instead. And I will never allow that."

I blinked at the surprising intensity of his tone. At moments like this, I could almost believe he did care for me—that maybe I'd misunderstood those four days that I spent in total isolation. He meant for me to study and rest, not feel like a songbird battering her weary wings against the bars. But I knew too much about him to be taken in by his false tenderness.

There was a story of a village that used to chain a virgin to a rock to protect them from the violent gods of the deep, but in my case, I'd stepped into the chains of my own free will. I'd locked the manacles onto my own ankles, knowing what would be coming to claim me.

"Thank you for taking care of me," I said, because that seemed to be what he expected to hear.

Michael rewarded me with a broad smile. "I'm home for a week this time, so why don't I take you shopping? I have some conference calls to make this morning, but we can go this afternoon and have a nice lunch somewhere."

"I'd like that."

It meant that my lessons would have to be compacted, but I was so happy to leave the condo at last that I worked my ass off and got ready in record time. When I came out to the living room, Michael looked me over and then gestured me back to the bedroom.

"Something nicer, Marlena. I didn't spend all that money on your wardrobe for you to dress like you shop at Walmart."

I flinched, because in my childhood I'd only *dreamed* of getting new clothes there. Everything I owned had been passed down multiple times from cousins who had more than we did, and they bought their stuff at thrift stores. All my clothes had been worn by five or six people already. It wasn't unusual for me to patch and darn my shirts until they fell apart in my hands.

In our bedroom, where we shared a huge closet, I had *so* many clothes that most of them still had the tags on. I must've stared too long because Michael came in after me and pulled a few things out. "You'll look perfect in this."

Hate that fucking word.

The urge to scream startled me. I swallowed it and took the outfit he'd chosen, more ivory and beige. It was like he thought wearing bright colors would tarnish my innocence. I put on the clothes and the jewelry and the shoes and came out a few minutes later to receive his approval like it was a communion wafer.

"You're lovely."

Vin shadowed us in the elevator and through the foyer, where the doorman tipped his head. I again marveled at the ostentatious luxury: marble floors and gold-framed revolving doors, braided pillars outside and two magnificent potted plants to frame the entry. The street was clean and quiet, as it should be for a building where a one-bedroom condo cost close to three million dollars. I hadn't known that on my own; Michael made sure to tell me.

"Could we walk?" I asked.

"To Bergdorf's? I don't see why not." Michael took my hand and wrapped it around his arm, a statement of ownership to other passersby.

Bergdorf Goodman wasn't the sort of place I'd come to on my own. It seemed like all the assistants were staring at me and not in a good way, though they greeted Michael graciously. He was probably in their VIP gold club or whatever it was called. I didn't want to shop, but my husband had a limited sense of what constitutes an acceptable pastime. I bought a purse and a new necklace and he whipped out the platinum card.

Afterward, we had an extremely elegant lunch, but it was hard to relax with Vin dining at the next table over. Michael might have been paranoid, but if he wasn't, then I'd married a man who was constantly in danger of being murdered.

Hard *not* to be freaked out. I had my own plans, of course, but they didn't include all the people who wanted to kill Michael Durst. There was no way I could compile what must be a tremendous list. In his scramble for the top, he must have stepped on a lot of people.

On the way out, an older couple—probably late fifties—recognized Michael. By the way they were dressed, I knew they must be old money, Park Avenue for life. Michael's expression told me that they were important, and I resolved to shine. Pleasing my husband *should* mean more freedom, right? He waited for a break in the conversation and eventually introduced me to Helen and William Stone.

"Oh, I heard about the wedding," she said. "But our mutual acquaintances didn't do justice to your lovely bride. So nice to meet you, dear."

I took her hand in both of mine and gave such a warm smile that hers brightened. She'd had work done on her face by a superior surgeon, and the veneers on her teeth were excellent. On second look I gathered she might be as old as seventy, carefully preserved. Surprisingly enough, her husband stood up to closer scrutiny, and he couldn't have been more than fifty-five. Probably not her first marriage, I guessed. All this information I collected in the time it took to shake her hand.

"The pleasure is all mine. It's such an honor to meet you, after Michael's stories." Offhand, the only thing I could recall was something about her getting drunk at a yacht club, but that counted.

William laughed and touched my arm playfully. "All good, I hope?"

"Certainly."

To my surprise, Michael pulled me to his side, wrapping a tense arm about my shoulders. "I'll call you. We can get drinks sometime soon. Are you in the city long?"

"A month or so," Helen answered. Her eyes twinkled with a not-entirely-benign light as she took in the possessive clasp. It was all I could do not to squirm away. "I see you can barely keep your hands off her, darling, so we won't keep you."

Steely fingers wrapped around my wrist, hauling me out of the restaurant. I stumbled, but Michael didn't look back and it was Vin who steadied me, taking three long steps to make sure I didn't faceplant on the sidewalk. Then my husband leveled an icy gaze on my bodyguard, pointedly staring at the hand beneath my elbow.

Vin let go. The tension made it hard to breathe and I expected a rebuke, but Michael only began walking again in furious silence, towing me so fast that my shoes scraped my heels raw over the few blocks we had to cover. Vin had my bags but I couldn't take them; Michael gave me no chance.

Averting his eyes, Vin didn't speak in the elevator. Silently he took up his post in the hallway. As soon as the penthouse door closed behind us, Michael slung my arm away with such force that I tumbled over the nearby ottoman and hit the floor with a vicious bang. If Vin was really my bodyguard, not my jailer, he should break the door down when I cried out.

He didn't.

"What the *hell* did you think you were doing?"

I drew my elbows up and in, reflexively protecting my face. It had been a while since anyone had hit me, but a few of my mama's exes had been fast with their fists. I got good at dodging and running long before I left home, but here there was nowhere for me to go, no place for me to hide.

"Well?" he shouted.

"T-trying to make a good impression."

"Don't lie to me, Marlena. I know what flirting looks like. Does it make you feel good when other men look at you, when they want to have you?"

Since I'd been talking to Helen Stone when her husband responded to me, I couldn't begin to understand this mood swing. We'd had a good day, and then I was trying my best to please him, but—

I could only get out, "I'm sorry you're upset, but it wasn't like that."

"Are you calling me a liar? I know what I saw, and it wasn't only with that bastard Will Stone. You tried it on Vin too, with your big eyes and that helpless smile."

"No. It's just ... a misunderstanding. Vin just helped me when I tripped. You were walking really fast."

"It's my fault then?" In a motion so calm that the violence scared me more, Michael picked up a glass statue from the end table and lobbed it as hard as he could. The delicate figurine smashed into the floor dangerously near my arm and fragments peppered me, covering my hair in glass dust. "Understand this, Marlena. If you work Vin, if you try to undermine his loyalty and make him your person instead of mine? It won't end well for him. You grasp that?"

I was shivering so hard that I couldn't even answer for a few seconds. "Got it."

He stormed out, then, and I heard him shouting at Vin, audible even through the door. "You're supposed to be impervious. You got eyes for my wife?"

"No, sir." That was all. No excuses, no explanations.

For at least five minutes, I just sat on the floor amid the broken glass until a quiet knock sounded. I eyed the door like this was a trap, but I got up and opened it anyway. Since security in the building was tight, it had to be Vin or someone Michael had sent to punish me.

"I'm sorry," Vin said, handing me the purse and necklace I no longer wanted.

Had never wanted.

"For what?"

"Getting you in trouble. I'd heard that your husband is ..." He stopped talking, probably unable to find a word that fit this situation. "Anyway, I should have been more careful. I will be, in the future."

I closed the door in his face because there was nothing else to say, and if Michael checked surveillance footage, I didn't want to give him more reasons to flare up. To him, this ten second conversation might seem like an orchestrated seduction. It took all my energy to get a broom and clean up the mess. I couldn't leave it for the maid in the morning; there would be talk, and that would hurt Michael's reputation, and I had to make him happy.

Have to. Make him happy.

Even if it killed me.

11

When I finally checked my messages on the phone I didn't entirely trust, I had seven emails from Jenny. The last one simply read, *if you don't answer me, I'm coming to find you.* Since we'd kept in touch no matter what else was going on, I didn't doubt her.

Sorry, I've been so busy since the wedding. What's new with you?

Jenny wrote back, a long, breezy email about the assholes in her computer science program. Those problems distracted me from my own, and I replied. We even Skyped, like in the old days, and I listened with half an ear for the door to open. Nothing but silence.

I ate alone, slept alone, and I even put on workout clothes to see if he'd kept his promise about talking to Vin. The bodyguard didn't object, and we went running in the park. He stayed five feet behind me no matter what pace I set. I was tense by the time I got back to the condo and waited for some sign that I hadn't been abandoned. That evening, I was braced for a stranger to deliver divorce papers.

On the third day, Michael finally came home. When he did, he brought flowers. Warily I took the white roses, trying to contain my urge to flinch away from the hand that then dropped onto my head. I shivered, controlling my reaction with significant effort.

"You're upset," he said. "I may have overreacted, but the idea of losing you … it drives me crazy. I only reacted that way because I love you so much."

When he put a pretty pink diamond ring on my finger to conclude the apology, I let him draw me close and rested my head on his chest, vowing not to make him feel insecure again. I'd never considered myself irresistible, but Michael clearly thought other men couldn't see me without wanting me.

Stroking my back, he went on. "Men are animals, Marlena. You're too innocent to understand that, and that's why I have to fight twice as hard to keep you that way."

I swallowed hard. What would Michael say if I told him I already knew? One of my mother's boyfriends had shown me when I was eleven, and then later, Bobby Ray Hudgens reinforced the lesson. Before, I'd never thought those violations made me dirty, but I had no doubt my husband would feel that way. He'd probably think I was some little Lolita, seducing men with a sway of my hips.

"Oh." It was the only sound I could make.

My lack of response didn't matter because he was in the mood to talk. "I've never told you this … because I'm not proud of it, but I was married before. She … left me. And it took a long time for me to get over that."

Left you? Is that what you're calling it? My heart hardened into titanium, untouchable, impenetrable. But I couldn't let on how much I already knew—about his past, and I couldn't think on it too deeply or he might read that awareness in my expression. I understood far too well to be drawn in by diamond rings and repentant smiles.

71

But I kept up the pretense. "There's never been anyone else," I said softly.

"I do know. It's part of what makes you perfect. But sometimes I lose the thread, and I'm sorry for that."

It amused me to test him, though, and to see how he'd respond. "I went running in the park yesterday. Vin took me. But there was nothing personal about it."

Michael nodded. "He gave me a full report before I came in. Now that I've had some time, I know you weren't leading him on. And what happened with Will Stone, well, he's a lecher, but that's not your fault."

It was tough to get the words out, but I could only cower for so long. "Next time you're upset, if you could dial it down … I was really scared."

There, I said it.

"I'll never hurt you," Michael said. "You are my most precious possession, and it's my greatest joy to protect you."

That wasn't what I wanted to hear. I wanted an *I'm sorry, I'll do better,* like he always forced out of me. And the fact was, he *had* hurt me. I had a circular bruise around my wrist from where he'd hauled me around and another on my hip due to my tumble over the ottoman, deep and blue, fading to green. I bit in the inside of my lip against an instinctive protest. *I'm not your possession. I'm not.*

"Okay," I said.

For months, I walked on eggshells, me taking lessons and Michael traveling as much as he stayed home. I made sure not to do anything that would anger him when he was around. It got to the point that I sighed a little in relief as soon as he took his travel case and left for the airport. Nothing had been solved; I was still somewhat afraid of him and he still didn't trust me.

How little became clear when I dropped my cell in the bathroom and it bounced into pieces. I swore, kneeling to collect them, but I didn't think it be could repaired. Seconds later, Vin rushed into the room, drawing up short when he saw me in my robe, bits of broken phone in my hand. I stared, because there was no way in hell he could've heard such a small sound from outside the penthouse.

When he didn't speak, I said, "Explain yourself. Now."

"Mr. Durst texted me. He said I should check on you."

"Why?" Deep down, I knew. I must have known, but I wanted him to say it.

"Because he lost your signal."

"Which means there's a tracking device on my phone, and he knows where I am at all times."

I glanced around the bathroom, wondering how far this obsession went. Were there cameras in here so Michael could watch me piss from Germany? Sometimes I masturbated in the tub—long, luxurious orgasms—and a cold wave broke over me. That probably didn't fit with his mental perception of my supposed purity.

Vin seemed to be reading my mind. "There's no surveillance in the condo, as far as I know. It stops in the foyer."

Relief all but drowned me ... and how *pathetic* that I should be grateful for privacy in the fucking bathroom. I wasn't sure I could trust Vin, but he had no reason to lie, either. As I thought about it, I decided it made sense: because, if Michael could check on me via some illicit video feed, he wouldn't have sent Vin in, where I could tempt him with my irresistible wiles.

"Good to know," I muttered. "You can go now, unless you're staying for the show."

I slid my robe off one shoulder, more an angry gesture than a seductive one. The bodyguard's gaze never shifted from my face. "No thank you, madam. I need to report to Mr. Durst."

"How can you work for someone like him? He's basically holding me hostage and you don't seem to care."

Vin paused. He'd already stepped out of the bathroom into the hall. "I just work for the man. You're the one who married him. If you're unhappy, leave."

"Would you even let me?"

At that, he turned. "If it's your genuine desire to flee, I won't stop you. But you should go before he gets back and hide yourself thoroughly. Mr. Durst is not a man who takes rejection well."

I'd recently read an article about how women who married up were screwed by the rich men they were trying to leave. The men hired high-power lawyers and accused their soon-to-be-exes of all the sins they'd committed: abuse, infidelity, and more. When I took Michael on, it would require careful planning.

This isn't the time.

I just had to suck it up and live with what he dished out. If Durst followed his usual playbook, then I could respond in kind—with measures I'd already taken. But it was important to go step by step, or everything might fall apart. I couldn't let Durst get away, even if it meant suffering like this.

"He'd probably take it out on you, then," I said. "If you let me go. So I won't do anything that'll explode in your face. Come to think of it, I'll tell him personally that I can't stand it anymore. I have to be brave, right?"

Vin startled visibly, his brows shooting up. "Don't factor me into your calculations. I can take care of myself."

He left without looking at me again, but things were different after that. Sometimes he spoke to me when we ran in the park and he brought me coffee from my favorite cafe once a week. No longer did he call me "madam" in that icy tone, either. Occasionally I made him smile, such a delicious break from his normal severity. Since we couldn't run side by side, I talked him into getting Bluetooth earpieces so we could chat with no trail for Michael to follow. Vin didn't argue over it, a sign that he felt closer to me. I never pushed him, never touched him, but I wanted his friendship. Needed it.

There might come a day where my life depended on it.

12

The stars finally aligned for Jenny to visit.

Michael had a long trip to Russia planned. He would be too tied up to entertain me if I went with him, and things were too volatile there for me to go sightseeing, even with Vin to protect me. He agreed that it was a great idea to invite Jenny for a couple of weeks so I wouldn't be lonely.

For her part, Jenny had scheduled job interviews in New York, and I really hoped she'd get one of them and move here. Spending time with society acquaintances felt like work because I had to be on guard every moment, remembering my role as a Croatian diplomat's daughter. Michael had been right in that it did open certain doors, but I worried they would slam with a vengeance, and I'd get blamed when the shit hit the fan.

Vin drove me to the airport the night Jenny flew in. "I'll wait in the car. I may have to circle, so text me when you've got her and let me know which doors you're near."

"Gotcha."

I no longer fretted about whether Michael had cloned my phone and was reading my messages. As long as I didn't send anything he shouldn't see, it would be fine. And it would prove that he truly could trust me.

I hurried into the arrivals area and headed for the kiosk where we'd agreed to meet. Jenny was already waiting, and I greeted her with a huge hug. She held on hard and we were both jumping like teenagers before we let go. Her hair was much shorter than in the last picture she'd sent, but the pixie cut looked incredible on her.

"How cute are you?" I teased, leading her toward the exit.

Jenny didn't let go of my arm even as we walked. We dodged people with luggage who were running to join the security lines. "I hardly even recognize you," she said. "You look so ..."

She gestured, and I got it, because I was dripping designer labels, head to toe. "Michael insists. He'd self-destruct if I put on anything else."

"Your husband sounds like a nouveau-douche."

I couldn't stifle the laugh. "He's definitely not old money. He cares too much about getting into the right circles."

"Then he should've married some snotty blue blood instead of you."

Quickly I got out my phone and sent Vin the text about where we were. "This way. The driver is circling."

"*Driver*," Jenny mocked gently. "You know the girls all hate you, right?"

By "girls," I guessed she meant our former roommates. "Nobody has sent me any hate mail, but they weren't my biggest fans when I moved out."

"You're living the dream."

It was a balmy evening, no jacket required, though the air smelled heavily of exhaust. Jenny wrinkled her nose as I waved to Vin, who pulled up in the shiny black BMW 325i, not a huge car nor an especially memorable one. Her eyes widened as she took in Vin's severe haircut, sharp jaw, and broad shoulders.

As he stowed her luggage in the trunk, she whispered, "Fringe benefit?"

I shook my head quickly. "He's protection, that's all."

Her eyes widened. "Have there been kidnapping attempts or something?"

That was the sensible view. I was glad that she couldn't imagine the truth—that Michael didn't trust me and that he wasn't one hundred percent a legitimate business man. I'd overheard enough one-sided phone calls to be sure he was involved with some shady people who strong-armed deals for him. If there was land he wanted to acquire, he got it, one way or another.

Vin opened the door in time to catch her question. He settled in behind the wheel before answering, "It's my job to prevent that."

Jenny smirked at me as the car swung away from the curb. Traffic was a mess that night, so I knew it would take forever to get back to the condo. "Tell me what else you do besides look gorgeous," she said.

I filled her in on my various charity groups. "Other than that, I study languages, go to museums, work out." If I didn't, if I lost a pound or gained one, I heard about it. Michael had very particular requirements, and he wouldn't even touch me if I didn't meet them. It was a lot harder to be someone's permanent arm candy than the general public might believe. My tone drew a flicker of concern from Jenny, so I added quickly, "What about you?"

She didn't seem to realize she'd been distracted and told me about the companies she'd landed interviews with here, all entry level in IT, but she was so damn smart I had no doubt she'd be management in no time. I'd heard of some of the places but I didn't have much background in corporate.

"You've been doing freelance work, right?"

"I had a few offers in Nashville, but I don't want to stay there. It's..." She trailed off, and I could see her past creeping up on her.

"I know." Likely Tennessee had bad echoes for her, just like Kentucky did for me.

"Move to New York. I can help you find a place to stay."

Vin flicked me a look in the rearview mirror, but with the headlights shining on bright as the cars passed on the other side, I couldn't get a hint of what he was thinking. Whatever. Jenny had been with me for years, since we'd met on the streets and joined UMAX together, and she used to sleep in my bed when the nightmares hit. I needed her support, now more than ever—in so many ways.

"If I get a good job offer, I'll take you up on that."

We chatted for over an hour, when traffic finally gave enough for us to slip into the parking garage beneath the building. Michael had a spot right next to the doors, which was a big deal if you knew how those things worked. I didn't until he told me.

Vin let us off at the doors to the garage lift. "Go on, I'll bring up Ms. Song's bags after I park."

In the small but lavishly appointed elevator lobby, Jenny nudged me. "Now *that's* service. I could get used to this."

Not if you met Michael.

We took the express elevator straight up, and she gaped at the decor in the foyer. Over time I'd gotten used to all the gilt and marble, the lavish flowers and ornate moldings near the ceiling. Everything was black and gold and white, with Renaissance touches that tried to give the impression that this was some gorgeous historic building in Europe, not a structure that had gone up in 1990.

"Damn," she said.

"Wait until you see the rest."

I'd be lying if I said I didn't enjoy giving her the grand tour: the huge living space, the formal dining room, library, rooftop terrace, master bath, and enormous bedroom. Everything in the condo had been picked out by professionals who knew how to make things look expensive and exquisite. It was a showroom more than a home, but it did impress, as Michael intended.

"What does your husband do again?"

Before I could answer, Vin knocked on the door. Jenny opened it with a wide, flirtatious smile. "You're fast. I like that."

"My pleasure, madam."

I smiled a little, because I hadn't heard that in a while. She wasn't deterred by it, though. "Hey, *I'm* not married to your boss. Call me Jenny."

He smiled back, unable to help himself. She often affected people like that. "If you prefer. Here are your things. I hope you have fun while you're here. Jenny."

"That's what I'm talking about. Want to come in for a drink?"

Vin glanced at the camera behind him so quick that only I caught it, then shook his head. "Thank you anyway, but I'm on duty."

"Does he *ever* relax?" she wondered, closing the door.

"Not much. He does get days off, though. An older man fills in then."

She sighed and shook her head. "Your life is so complicated."

"I'm aware. Should we have that drink you mentioned?" Without waiting for an answer, I got a bottle of costly and delicious wine from the rack in the kitchen.

When I came back, Jenny had her phone out with a message typed as an unsent text. *Is it safe to talk?*

I loved her for having kept up the pretense in front of Vin. Though I was working on him, I hadn't brought him onto my team yet, so

Jenny was correct that in case of external surveillance, she needed to seem like a clueless friend I had to protect instead of a committed conspirator. I wouldn't have put it past Michael to bug the condo, despite what Vin thought, so I made a gesture that said I wasn't sure.

She nodded at that, keeping up the bright chatter as she typed. *There's no way I can talk you out of this? I'm worried about you, baby.*

Silently I shook my head, taking her phone to respond: *You know better than anyone why I have to do this.*

Jenny had been with me, those long nights when I cried over Dee, and when I made what might be an impossible promise to myself. She had sworn to stand by me, and that had never changed over those long years. Hell, though she didn't say so, I understood why she'd studied computer science.

If you're sure. It's probably not too late to back out.

I married him. At this point, I can only push forward. You know that.

Sighing softly, she cupped my cheek in one hand and touched her forehead to mine for a brief moment. Then she typed, *Fine, I get it. In your shoes, I might even feel the same. Then we're committed to this epic struggle between good and evil. What's next?*

I wrote it out for her.

13

Still busily feigning ignorance about Michael Durst, putting on a show for a bug that might not exist, Jenny got out her phone, talking to herself as she scrolled and skimmed. "Huh. I can tie him to various development projects but I'm still not sure what he actually *does*."

"Mostly? He buys land and then builds stuff on it."

"Boring." Jenny drew out the word in a drawl, gently mocking the country accent I'd worked so hard to eradicate. "Let's see what else we can find."

I drank while Jenny fiddled with her phone. I ignored her one-woman performance until she gave me a look that hinted she was about to get mischievous. "What?"

"Did you know he's been married before?"

With my eyes, I warned her to stop. "He told me. Apparently, she left him."

But nope, Jenny was determined to rattle Durst's cage. "It's not *she*. It's they. You're his third wife, Marlena. He was married to his first wife for only a year. She died in a car accident while they were traveling in Croatia."

How well I know.

None of that was news to me, but I took her phone and skimmed the article as if it were. If you lied enough, eventually the lines blurred and you forgot the truth. Living like that was necessary for someone else to believe it.

There wasn't much coverage about Michael's short marriages, but I got the sense the world viewed him as tragic and possibly cursed. At this point, we'd been married fifteen months. I had outlived his first wife, and his second only lasted two years. That didn't bode well for me with our second anniversary approaching. One accident, Deborah Neuman. One suicide, Leslie Talbot. Soon it would be my turn.

Michael Durst was nothing before he married Deborah Neuman. He'd had almost nothing to his name, but an insurance payout after her death changed everything. Suddenly he was a major player overseas, buying land and making investments like he'd been born with a silver spoon in his mouth.

I'd gotten one postcard in my whole life, and I still had it, sewed up inside a homemade potpourri bag. Postmarked from Croatia. *Dear Marlie, I'm so happy …* It was the last time I heard from Dee.

Silently I got up, motioning Jenny to silence. It was time for her to see what I'd found. All those days I'd spent locked up in the condo hadn't gone to waste. She agreed to wait in the living room to keep watch while I tiptoed into the study. Michael thought I was too cowed to intrude on his private space, an image I'd cultivated carefully.

He'd hidden the key to his file cabinets in an empty mint tin in his first drawer. I knew there couldn't be a camera in the office or my initial intrusions would have been noticed. If he'd planted a listening device, I could come up with some excuse for being in there. It wasn't the biggest risk I'd taken.

Quickly, I dug out the old policy agreement and carried it back to show Jenny. Maybe before now, she'd thought I was misguided or in denial over how and why Dee died. She read over the documents in silence. I already knew what they said. Before Durst married Deborah Neuman, he took out a sizable policy on her, one with an accidental death rider. If she'd died of natural causes like pneumonia or a heart attack, he would have received much less. The rider for a car accident was in the millions.

You were right, Jenny typed, quietly handing the papers back.

I'd suspected, and for years I'd wondered, but it wasn't the same as holding the insurance paperwork in my hands. This wasn't proof, of course. At least not in a way that made the courts concerned, or Durst would have already been in prison. But it was good enough for me, and knowing this, I could never quit with it half done. Jenny read that in my expression.

The second wife had been a suicide. I'd checked into that years ago, before I left Barrettville, and I recalled what I'd learned sitting in the oppressive heat of a library that didn't have air conditioning and offered only one working computer for public use. I brought up the site for Jenny so she could read the details. *Varies between companies,* the insurance information website said, *but the general rule is that there is no payout on a policy if the purchaser commits suicide within the first two years. After that, the beneficiary receives full payment, and it is up to the insurer to contest cause of death, if applicable.*

I might find a similar insurance policy for Leslie Talbot if I kept digging, but I didn't need additional motivation to push forward. Silently I replaced the files, locked the drawers, and replaced the key.

"Marlena? You look strange." Jenny touched my arm when I got back. That was more than she should say aloud, probably.

I put a finger to my lips. "Too much wine, I suspect."

"Do you think you married a Bluebeard?" she asked.

Grimly, I forced a light tone. "That's crazy, right?"

"I don't know," she said finally. Her cautionary words made sense in the context of friendship, and I savored the idea of Michael squirming if he overheard this conversation. I'd just defend him strongly enough to make him feel safe.

"There was an old lady on our block, seemed so sweet," Jenny went on. "Turned out she'd poisoned two husbands, one son-in-law, and a neighbor. It's hard to tell what people are capable of, even if you think you know them."

"That doesn't make me feel any better," I mumbled.

"It's not supposed to. We've been watching our own backs since long before we should've needed to. Here's what I can promise, though. Now that I'm here, you'll never be alone with this. If there's ever a moment where something feels off, you cut and run."

Time to play my role to the hilt.

"You've seen too many cable TV movies, Jenny. Michael would never hurt me. He treats me like a princess. I can have anything I want, anything at all. You wouldn't believe how intense he is about making sure I'm safe."

Jenny rolled her eyes at me but responded in kind, thankfully. "Fine, I get it. You're the luckiest and I should be jealous."

"Exactly. Let's get some sleep."

I had missed having her in my bed. When we were younger, we'd cuddled a lot, twined together, and tonight it was sweet and soft, just like old times. Except it wasn't, because she stroked my cheek, my hair, my shoulder, while gazing into my eyes. When she kissed me, it was beyond delicious, so good that I moaned into her mouth. I melted beneath her hands, her lips, and in just a few short moments, came harder than I ever had in my life.

Afterward, breathing hard, I whispered, "You wanted this, all those nights you crawled into my bed?"

She kissed my lower lip. "Desperately. You never took the bait."

"Because you were too young."

"We were both horny teenagers," she said.

"Not a teenager. Still hungry for you." I proved it by making her twist and gasp and moan until she nearly passed out.

The next morning, Jenny let me pretend we were lovers with nothing to worry about as we ate, shopped, and gossiped about people we'd known from UMAX.

"Mr. Morton got married? To who?" I demanded.

"Pamela, if you can believe it. I guess they had a thing for years."

I had fond memories of the woman who'd mothered all of us from the reception desk. "That's so sweet."

Vin trailed us everywhere, of course, and Jenny had a tough time ignoring him, but once she understood that it was for my safety—for more than one reason—she got with the program. By day, we were old friends, and at night, well, it was the honeymoon I'd always dreamed about. She aced her interviews, so at the end of the trip, she had to decide between three excellent job offers. We celebrated her final choice with an expensive dinner at a place Michael had taken me to when we'd first arrived in New York, and it felt pretty good waltzing Jenny past the folks waiting in line, on the strength of the Durst name.

After she took a bite of the steak, she said, "I see why you stick around. Once you've had a bite of this, it's hard to walk away."

I again appreciated her for playing the role, even in public. I had to seem awestruck, if not lovestruck, and a bit silly, for the rest of my plan to fall into place. The last thing I wanted was for anyone to learn how far I'd calculated, how deep I was playing the odds.

"It's not *only* that." I laid out my fake four-year plan, which had to do with getting as much out of Michael as I could before he tired of me and swapped me for someone younger and prettier. Since that behavior was a staple in our set, nobody would think twice if that was my actual life goal.

Since Jenny knew the truth, she snorted a laugh and covered by taking a deep drink from her wine glass. Vin's gaze sharpened, but I didn't think he could hear, not with the ambient restaurant noise grumbling around us. "And they say true love is dead," Jenny said. "I'd call you a gold-digger if I didn't want to high five you so much. Made any progress with the investments?"

"A little. Not as much as I'd like, because Michael doesn't talk business with me. He always tells me not to worry my pretty head, that he'll take care of the finances and I should just have fun with my allowance."

Jenny curled her lip. "You're not five. I hate this asshole already."

Hating him was my job, and I had that covered. Still, I had to defend him for anyone who might be reporting back. "He's very generous. I get presents all the time."

"Money is not love," she said.

I smirked. "Yeah, well. If I could have love and no lunch or no love and a steak dinner, which do you think I'd pick?"

"You're a mess," she said, laughing.

We'd both had a rough childhood, and we'd learned to sacrifice when we had to. I felt confident that after clawing to get to this point, if I had to put up with more crazy shit to keep my promise—to Dee and to myself—I'd do whatever it took to stay the course. I just had to hope I wouldn't stumble across the line and experience who Michael Durst really was beneath the skin. Not before I was ready.

I remembered—

The bite of angry fingers on my wrist, the fury in his eyes over what seemed like nothing, me cowering on the floor, glass dust raining down. I thought of Dee and Leslie, wondered if they'd had plans, too. Fear could undermine me if I let it.

I'd come too far to hesitate now.

"Everyone's a mess," I answered, eventually. "Some of us just hide it better than others."

"I don't like that look, Marlena."

"Which is?"

"Like you're accepting some inevitable fate. We make our own destiny, okay?"

It was more like I was accepting the fact of facing off against Michael Durst. And maybe I was born to do that. "Noted. Don't worry, I can hang on. I'll text you the details."

That would take more effort, but in the safety of the restaurant, we worked out a series of numeric codes, ways I could ask Jenny for things without putting the requests into words. If he asked me about the numbers I was texting to her, it would be the same as admitting he was spying on me. And if he went that far, it would mean he was done with our relationship and that I needed to proceed to the next stage.

"Good. I feel better, even if I can't do much as your backup." Jenny touched my hand softly and then went back to her steak.

That was our last night together before she flew out. I wanted to take her to the airport, but Michael was coming back and he preferred me to be at home, waiting for him. She'd be living here soon, but I couldn't see her too often or I'd risk setting him off. I said goodbye to her in the foyer, hugging her tight and breathing in her sweetness. I wanted to kiss her, but I couldn't.

My love might get her killed.

14

I had dinner warming in the oven when my life exploded.

The first sign came from the raised voices outside the front door, and the scuffling and thud of fists against bodies. That noise died fast and then two large men stormed into the condo. I recognized one of them from the snake tattoo winding around his neck. His shiny suit was gone, replaced by all black and heavy work boots. His companion was tall and skeletal with a broad forehead and nearly nonexistent jaw, a series of numbers tattooed on the back of his neck.

They grabbed me without a word, and I fought, I did, but I couldn't break free. I managed to scream "Vin!" before the lanky one slammed a bony hand across my mouth. I bit him.

That earned me a closed-fist to the temple. While the punch didn't knock me out, it left me so dizzy that they dragged me out easily. Vin was on the floor, bleeding sluggishly from a busted head. Snake Neck threw me over one shoulder like a sack of laundry and hauled ass to the elevator. They bypassed the lobby and went to the garage sub-level, where a black-panel van was waiting, engine hot.

Snake Neck threw me in back and Death Face got the duct tape, sealing my mouth first, then taping my wrists and ankles while his cohort got into the driver's seat. The doors slammed, a perfect kidnapping in under a minute. My heart slammed in my ears as I tried to work out what was happening.

Since Snake Neck had been at the wedding, he must've been on good terms with Michael at one time. Possibly their deal went sour and now I was being taken as ... what, collateral? To ensure Snake Neck got what he wanted, whatever that was. Michael's paranoia might have roots in reality after all.

I twisted, testing my bonds, but Death Face was watching me and dropped a boot on my neck. Without a word, I understood that he wasn't playing. Suddenly it occurred to me that they hadn't hidden their faces or blindfolded me, which meant they didn't intend to leave me alive to bear witness. In that moment I was too scared to cry.

My captors were silent. The only noise came from the radio, where Justin Timberlake was promising to bring sexy back, and the song added to the surreal feeling. The steak in the oven was going to dry out, turn into charcoal briquettes. Tape over my mouth meant gulping breaths through my nose, and I felt each bump in the road, roaring beneath my ear.

It was impossible to say how long we drove, how long I lay there. Eventually they hauled me out and I had the fleeting impression of yellow lights above, too tall for streetlights, a big metal structure, doors that ground over dirty cement while opening. Inside it was all open space and darkness, a few scant bulbs burning at a distance.

"We brought her," Death Face said in Russian-accented English. "After tonight, I owe you nothing, yes?"

"We're square when this is finished. Wait outside until I call, both of you." That voice, I recognized that voice, and my head came up with a mixture of shock and trepidation.

Michael.

He stepped out of the shadows, crisp in navy pinstripes. His suit jacket was slung on the back of a chair, yet he didn't look as disheveled as he should. More like he'd just left a business meeting and was off for cocktails with his colleagues. I couldn't see his eyes, but I knew how they would look; I'd seen that expression when he threw me to the floor.

He waited until the two goons left, until I couldn't hear the scuff of their boots anymore. "You lied to me, Marlena."

I couldn't answer; my mouth was still taped.

But he didn't want a response anyway. He moved closer until he towered over me. One kick could shatter my jaw or cave in my sternum. I'd never felt so small, so helpless. I didn't dare move, just waited for more of his furious words to rain down like grenades.

"You said there had never been anyone before me. I thought you were different, but it turns out you're just another lying whore."

Michael turned, then, kicking something from a chair. I wasn't sure what until it rolled close to me, reeking of terror, vomit, and blood. The circle of harsh yellow light illuminated the barely recognizable Bobby Ray Hudgens. His chest rose and fell in shallow breaths, still alive but not conscious. I remembered vowing that he would pay after he raped me, so I couldn't figure out how I felt—a complex twist of morbid glee and mortal terror for my own survival.

"Why was this asshole bragging on shock radio that he'd banged the beautiful, allegedly untouchable Mrs. Durst?"

Bobby Ray, you dumb son of a bitch.

Michael went in on a seething tone, "I checked the facts. You starred in one of his videos. Staff from the shoot say you spent time in his trailer."

You know then, you already know.

Tired of my silence, he ripped the tape from my mouth, taking some skin with it. Blood trickled from those raw spots, and I gasped for breath while the coppery tang leaked into my mouth. I didn't meet his gaze, though he knelt so close I could smell his cologne.

"He raped me," I finally managed to say.

He swore with such ferocity that I flinched. His hands bit into my shoulders, forcing me to look at him. "You were both in the wrong. Him for what he did to you, and you for lying to me. Because you did lie, Marlena. You made me think I was the first man to touch you, *and* you denied me the opportunity to avenge you."

I sucked down a scream along with my blood and saliva. It was my truth to tell, or not, and the idea that anything Bobby Ray had done could reduce my worth, which was weighed by my husband in purity, made me want to claw both their faces off. Hate nearly drowned me in a red wave of loathing for both of them.

Fortunately, Michael moved off then or he would've seen it, and I doubt I would have left that warehouse alive. Instead, he focused his wrath on Bobby Ray's prone form. "You disgusting bastard. How dare you. How *dare* you lay a finger on what's mine. And then to brag about it? You truly are a brainless sack of shit." That last sentence, each word was punctuated with a vicious kick.

At first Bobby Ray groaned, but those sounds died away into animal whimpers. I'd be lying if I said I felt no pleasure at all, watching my husband inflict that punishment. Only I couldn't cling to that satisfaction when I knew my turn was coming.

"This pig touched you without permission. Do you think I'm going to let him live?"

I wasn't really thinking at all. I made some sound, not an answer.

"Understand, I'm doing this for you. You'll sleep better knowing this shit stain is gone." His voice softened, and the tenderness was so out of place, so unnerving, that I shuddered when he stroked my hair. "This is a public service. I understand why you didn't come forward. The police would've treated you like a criminal … but you should've told *me*. I will always be your sword and shield."

I couldn't staunch the tears and words were tumbling out like my voice was a waterfall. "I thought you wouldn't want me if you knew."

Lies. I was so good at lying, I'd forgotten how the truth tasted. More to the point, I didn't care what Michael thought about my past. It wasn't his to forgive or forget.

"I told you before, men are animals. Why did you let me find out from the radio, Marlena? There shouldn't be any secrets between a husband and wife."

That didn't sound sane or healthy; everyone had deep wells of silence that they preferred not to delve into, but there was no room for debate. Here, Michael was a king making a proclamation and I was still bound at my wrists and ankles, weeping in exhausted bursts. I could only stammer incoherent apologies while Bobby Ray wheezed nearby.

Michael kissed my forehead, like he was a priest capable of bestowing benediction. Then he rose, fetching a bottle from somewhere beyond my range of sight. He emptied most of the contents onto Bobby Ray, cheap rotgut by the smell of it, and poured the rest down the asshole's throat.

He tapped a few keys on his phone. "Ready for cleanup."

Snake Neck came in alone and left with Bobby Ray's inert body. I wouldn't see him alive again.

In an easy motion, Michael lifted me into his arms, but it wasn't to leave this place. "You've done wrong. Do you understand that? Tell me you do."

"I was wrong," I whispered.

"You've said that before. I need to believe you mean it this time— that you really want to be my good girl."

Since I'd thought I would die there, I babbled anything to save myself. Promises poured out until Michael put a finger to my lips. "That's enough. I promised I would never hurt you, but there must be punishment for trespasses, don't you agree?"

Sick and scared, I shivered as he carried me out of the warehouse to a dark room. Turning on the light didn't help; it was a torturer's dream, with rusty tools and a stained wooden table. If there had been plastic sheets on the floor, I would have pissed myself.

"You don't have to do this," I said. Begged, really.

I couldn't let things end here. Had to survive, somehow.

Gently Michael brushed the hair away from my face, and then he stepped back. "Oh, it won't be me, Marlena. You'll find that I always keep my promises. Don't worry, I'll stay with you, and I'll hold you when it's over."

When he unbuckled his belt, it was a sinister promise of punishment to come. He snapped it in his hands, once, twice. Death Face entered. Michael gave him the strap.

I screamed with all my breath and thought I might never, ever stop.

PART TWO
LIVING HELL

15

I woke in a strange bed, my entire body ablaze with agony. On my stomach, I couldn't see much of the room, only a dusty blue carpet and a hint of dark paneling. This was nowhere Michael had brought me before; it smelled musty from disuse and a little damp. Stripes of fire blazed across my back. I had welts and bruises from my shoulders down, all the way to my calves, and it hurt so much that I couldn't even roll over when the door opened.

"Madam?"

The voice belonged to Vin, not Michael, and I let out a shaky breath. Pure relief that I didn't have to face my husband yet, *and* that Vin was alive. When Snake Neck and Death Face took me from the penthouse, I hadn't been able tell how badly Vin was hurt.

"Glad you're all right," I tried to say, but my voice came out in a raw, unintelligible rasp.

"Have some water." He put the straw in my mouth because sitting up was too much effort when I could barely turn my head.

Greedily I sucked the liquid down; nothing had ever tasted so good. If I weren't so battered, I could have almost believed the warehouse was a bad dream. Except I did have these injuries, and I could never forget the sound of Bobby Ray Hudgens choking on the liquor Michael had poured down his throat.

Is he dead now?

Probably I should worry about myself. I dropped my cheek onto the pillow to indicate I'd had enough. Everything hurt, breathing too.

"See if you can swallow this medicine. It should take the edge off." Vin put the tablet on my tongue.

I had the fleeting thought that he could be giving me anything, painkiller or cyanide capsule. When he followed with the straw, I gulped water and the pill together. I wasn't even distressed at the idea of going out that way. At least it would be by Vin's hand, not my husband's.

"Would you kill me?" I asked softly. Even I didn't know how much I meant it.

The words were audible, and Vin froze. "I know you're miserable, but you shouldn't say that."

Getting better just seemed like so much effort. At this point my prospects were bleak. I would be living only to please Michael Durst, yet he wasn't a man who could be satisfied by any woman, so eventually his obsession would flip completely to a loathing so ferocious it could only be extinguished with my extinction. My plans were months away from fruition. I was still gathering the people and the power I needed to take Michael on.

I didn't see a way out.

"Why not? It's how I feel."

"Well, even if you want to be put out of your misery, I'm not doing it. That's murder, and Mr. Durst would kill me for laying a finger on you."

I let out a bitter laugh at the conjoined absurdity of those two statements. "It's fine for him to have me beaten half to death, but God forbid anyone else touch what's his."

"You understand him well," Vin said. "That might even save you."

"I doubt it."

He changed the subject. "It's time for me to put the balm on your back. Promotes healing, reduces the risk of scarring. I'll be gentle."

At least he warned me before removing the covers. "Where are we anyway?" I asked.

"It's a lake cottage Mr. Durst inherited from his uncle. The least impressive of his properties."

I filed that away and went digging for more info, something that might help. "How long have you worked for him?"

If Vin was willing to follow orders after being coldcocked by Russian thugs, I probably had no hope of swaying him. This was the longest conversation we'd ever had when we weren't jogging with Bluetooth headsets, even though he'd been shepherding me around for quite a while. Yet he *had* fought them, which meant he had some concern for me.

"Five years."

"And you're okay with the shit he makes you do? Like this?" I couldn't move to point at my ruined back, but his hand stilled on my skin and I caught a puff of breath.

A sigh. Frustration or remorse?

"I'm not all right with any of this," he said finally.

"Then do the right thing. Take me to the hospital. Call the police. You said once you'd let me leave if I wanted to."

This was more of a test. Since he'd refused to kill me, I needed to keep working on him, as Michael had once accused me of doing. Now more than ever, gaining Vin's loyalty was a matter of life and death.

"That ship has sailed, Marlena." In his agitation, Vin didn't seem to realize he'd called me by name. I noticed, though. "You saw him kill a man. You think he'll let either of us walk away? If I take you, the police can't stop what will happen next."

"Which is?" I had goose bumps all down my arms and legs because I didn't really need for him to say it. It had already happened to Dee and Leslie. I'd seen firsthand how he dealt with Bobby Ray.

"We both have soft spots. Mr. Durst knows about your friend Jenny, and the minute you walk, she's dead. And then he'll come for you."

I could stand anything but that. No matter the cost, I couldn't let Michael hurt Jenny. This was between him and me. Thank God he hadn't figured out how much she knew. If he had an inkling how she was digging into him, he wouldn't leave her be.

"You said we *both* have soft spots?"

Vin hesitated before evidently deciding he might as well answer. "My family. I have three younger sisters and a disabled father. My paycheck is all that stands between them and the street."

"Got it. You're fine with me suffering as long as your family is safe." That was a shitty thing to say when he wasn't the real villain of the piece.

"It's a living hell, but I can't get off this train. Neither can you. And that sucks, but who said life was fair?"

"Not me."

There was a silence, where he didn't speak and neither did I. The ointment he was using must have had an analgesic quality, because it was helping ... or maybe it was the pill. Either way, the pain was dropping to bearable levels.

"I'm almost done here. I'm sorry, but I have to ..."

"Touch my butt? It's fine. I guess Michael's okay with it too or he wouldn't have assigned you as my attendant."

"A real nurse would report these kinds of injuries," Vin said quietly. "And Mr. Durst doesn't trust many people with his deepest secrets."

"Like the fact that he's a monster?"

Vin laughed, then quickly throttled the sound, like it troubled him to be bonding with me. He *should* have been worried, because if he showed me a gap in his defenses, I'd squirm inside until he couldn't stand seeing what Michael did to me. Since this was a war I had to win, I'd use whatever weapons came to hand.

Sorry, Vin. I think you need to fall in love with me.

"It's funny how much he likes those 'Durst is a philanthropist' headlines for a minor donation to charity when he's doing dirty deals with the Russians and grabbing land from people who don't even understand the papers they're signing."

It seemed like Vin had wanted to vent for a while, and I was a captive audience. I encouraged him. "I guess I deserve this. I saw what he could give me, and I wanted to be a princess too much. This is what people mean when they say, 'If something seems too good to be true, it probably is.'"

Of course, I'd seen the monster in the moat long before I married him, and I'd known that the sharp-fanged beast that swam in those murky waters also liked to dress up as a prince at formal gatherings. I just hadn't counted on things going south so fast. I'd thought I had more time—fucking Bobby Ray Hudgens. Small comfort that he was likely dead. Before he went, he'd screwed me over twice.

Vin's hands had been on my ass this whole time, applying salve to the welts and bruises. They stilled, then, but I didn't think he was copping a feel. "This isn't your fault. It's not a sin to want a better life. From what I've seen, you always do your best to please Mr. Durst, even when he's acting totally fucking unhinged."

Here we go, I thought.

"Like when he accused me of seducing you with my eyes? 'You're supposed to be impervious.'" I imitated Michael's furious snarl, surprising a chuckle out of Vin. "What's that about, anyway?"

Vin sighed, finishing with the balm and draping the covers over me again. "That's personal."

"You literally just rubbed my ass. Don't I have a right to be curious?"

"Fair point." He settled on the floor beside the bed so I could see his face, an unexpected kindness factoring in my limited range of vision. "Normally I don't discuss my private life with clients, but the fact is, Mr. Durst thinks I'm gay."

I blinked. If that was true, then my plan was doomed. "Oh?"

"Before he hired me, his investigators dug into my life. I had a boyfriend at the time, and that was all Durst needed to know, apparently."

"Since you say 'at the time,' I guess that means you didn't always." I was careful, tiptoeing toward what I wanted to know.

Vin shrugged. "I'm bi. No set criteria, though I am drawn to humor and kindness. But as far as your husband is concerned, any man who's ever touched a dick other than his own is gay, forever and ever, amen."

"He tends to be black and white in his thinking." Suddenly I couldn't stop laughing.

"What's so funny?"

"Michael thinks you're the safest person he could leave me with. Because you had a boyfriend. He's such an idiot."

Vin smiled too, the most unguarded expression I'd seen from him. "Does that mean you're going to try to seduce me?"

My mouth twisted. "How? I can't even roll over. Unless you find bruises sexy, I don't see how that would work."

But he'd given me the keys to start his engine. The effort might take time, yet I understood how to win him over. He wouldn't see it coming; men never did.

"Sorry, no. I've seen every inch of you and I just feel bad. That he had this done to you and that I can't stop it from happening again." Real frustration laced his voice, and he clenched his fist on his leg.

"It's not your fault. And hey, these injuries won't disappear overnight, so at least we get a break from his bullshit. Maybe we can stretch out our stay here?"

"He'll want pictures to see how you're healing, but I'll keep you safe as long as I can," Vin promised.

16

The pain pill knocked me out, so it was the next day before I woke, my head throbbing like the worst hangover I'd ever had—almost bad enough to take my mind off the rest of my problems. I also had to pee so much that it was a miracle I didn't wet the bed.

"Vin!" I called.

He appeared in the doorway wearing different clothes than the day before—loose black sweats and a white T-shirt. Great, at least he had luggage packed. "What's wrong?"

"Bathroom," I whimpered.

He didn't waste time, just scooped me up in his arms and carried me there. The pain was considerable, but I endured. Somehow I held the stream until he set me on the toilet, but I couldn't wait until he closed the door.

The small indignity didn't bother me, but when I called for him when I was done, his ears were red. *Not used this kind of intimacy, check.*

He probably wasn't accustomed to casual nudity, either. Attitudes were different in some parts of Europe.

"Is there any way I could shower? The salve made me sticky and I smell like blood."

Vin hesitated, looking everywhere but at me. "It might be tough. You're dehydrated, and you haven't eaten in two days."

"Then help me," I begged.

His gaze flickered over the front of me. I wasn't hiding anything on the porcelain throne, and the front of me looked fine, untouched by the violence Death Face had inflicted on Michael's orders.

"Are you sure?" he asked.

"You're here to take care of me, right? This is part of the job." I stared longingly at the shower curtain, transparent plastic printed with tropical fish.

His posture told me he would give in, though he stalled a bit longer by peering in cupboards in search of clean towels. "Fine, let me get the water warmed up."

"Thanks."

The bathroom was thirty years out of date, a relic of a time when colored enamel tubs were popular. This one was a sunny lemon, with dizzying orange and yellow tile on the walls. I hadn't seen Linoleum in years, but here it was beneath my feet, a rusty hue peeling near the wallboards. As Vin turned the water on, the pipes groaned. The lake house definitely wasn't a luxurious retreat; more the place where Michael hid his secrets from the world.

Like his battered wife.

One day he'll pay, I thought.

"This is awkward, but … if I don't strip down and get in with you, we'll get water everywhere."

"I trust you," I said.

Politely I shifted my gaze so Vin could take off his clothes. Once his back was turned, I silently checked him out. He had a body that showed better bare, taut and well-muscled, more scars than normal. Each one told a story, probably; I'd work on getting him to share them. He left his briefs on, probably for the sake of propriety.

The amenities were scant here. No loofah, no sea sponges, just an old washcloth and what smelled like Castile soap. Vin stepped in first, then lifted me over the rim of the tub, his body blocking me from the shower spray. That was for the best, as even water would sting the hell out of my back.

The cloth hovered inches from my shoulder, and he wore a frustrated expression. "I don't know how to do this."

"Just wash me," I said, taking his hand and setting it on my arm.

That was a safe place to start, and he was quick as he soaped me up from fingers to collarbone. He shifted enough to get rinse water on me and then went to the other side.

I could tell he was skittish about my chest, so I put his hand there next and smiled up at him. He wasn't quite as brisk on my breasts, but he didn't linger either. He couldn't meet my eyes as he turned to rinse out the cloth.

It did feel good when he moved to my stomach, as I'd always liked having my belly rubbed, so I couldn't restrain a little sound. He pulled his hand back like I'd bitten him.

"Marlena, if you sound like that, it'll make this feel like … something else. And I'll have to stop."

"Sorry." I wasn't at all, because that proved he wasn't impervious. "Give me the washcloth. I can help."

When he handed it to me, I whimpered as I raised my leg to prop it on the tub's edge, and then completely without shame, washed between my thighs. He couldn't look away while I did it, and his intensity turned me on a little, especially since I was in complete control.

I didn't think for a minute that Vin wanted to get entangled with me; that would make his life worse in every conceivable way.

Too damn bad. I had to make him mine before we went back.

When I was finished, I handed him the cloth to rinse. "Could you do my legs and feet? I don't think I can bend that much."

"Sure," he said calmly, but his cheeks were ruddy. "Hold still."

He washed my thighs with great care, moving to my calves, my feet. Then he adjusted the showerhead to spray the suds away. Steeling myself, I spun slowly, knowing my back would be pure agony, but I wouldn't feel clean unless we did a thorough job.

"Hair next," I said.

It was long and dark, tangled and greasy from too many days without washing. Vin tipped my head against his shoulder and guided the stream of water to get my hair wet. This close, I could feel how warm and hard his body was, could feel the furious thump of his heart against my back.

Not impervious at all.

He lathered my hair, using a generic herbal shampoo that smelled like the tea old ladies drank to settle their nerves. I closed my eyes and leaned my head against him fully as the warm water sluiced over us. Then I stepped forward so he had better access to my ruined back.

"I'm ready," I whispered.

"This is going to hurt. I'm sorry." Husky voice, real concern.

That was a mild word. I bit down on the heel of my hand until I nearly drew blood. The soap stung the slices in my skin and the water felt like tiny hammers on my bruises. By the time he rinsed me off, I was shaking, and he had to lift me out of the bath and wrap me in a towel because I couldn't manage it between the shivering and crying.

Another towel went around my wet hair.

"Tell me when you can handle me touching you again and I'll take you to your room."

A few minutes later, I finally nodded. "I'm good now."

Vin carried me like I was made of spun glass, fragile and precious. As I stood dripping on the braided rag rug, he laid out a clean nightgown and undies. I'd never seen either article of clothing before; they were old-fashioned, a loose cotton shift and granny panties.

"Did we borrow these from someone's auntie?" I asked.

"I'm glad you can still joke."

He was close enough for me to touch the scab on his forehead and the deep bruise on the side of his jaw. "How are you feeling, anyway? You shouldn't have fought."

Vin pulled my hand away but I caught a flash of pleasure, too. "Are you in any position to worry about me? And I didn't *decide* to fight. They were just suddenly on me, yelling in Russian, and I reacted."

"Still, thank you," I said softly.

The consistent gentleness and gratitude were working on him, because he cleared his throat. "Anyway, you've already been through a lot, but we need to apply the salve before you get dressed."

In answer, I shuffled to the bed and carefully stretched out on my stomach. It was full daylight, sunshine streaming through the dirty window. No hiding a single blemish or bruise. The mattress depressed when he sat down beside me, another change from yesterday when he'd sat on the floor. Whether he realized it or not, that was a step closer.

"I'm so sorry," he said as he got started.

"You're just doing your job." The kinder I was to him, the less I blamed him, the more he'd fault himself.

"So were the soldiers of the Third Reich," he muttered.

"You're not a Nazi, Vin."

"I'm not a good guy, either. If I was, I'd get my family safe and then..."

"Then...?" I prompted.

"I'd go scorched earth on your asshole husband. For a thousand reasons, but not least for what he's doing to you."

Incredibly, actual tears prickled to my eyes. "If you knew what my life's been like, you'd understand that I don't expect anyone to save me. Hell, I may not even be able to save myself."

"Don't say that, Marlena."

I would've shrugged but it was too much effort. While he finished smearing balm on my back, I didn't say anything else. Afterward, he helped me into my panties and nightgown. Unless I'd misread him, he wasn't the type of man who could repeat these intimacies day after day and react like he was made of stone.

Once we left the lake house, things would be different for me, one way or another.

17

Two days of rest, along with plenty of tea and light meals, had me feeling well enough to move around on my own. The damage to my back would probably take at least another week to heal fully, so I had to make the most of this time.

As Vin had predicted, Michael was asking for photo updates. The first time Vin took the pictures, I asked, "Could you send them to me too?"

Vin tilted his head, seeming to try to figure me out. "What are you planning?"

"I don't intend to take the pics to the cops, if that's what you're worried about. I have to protect Jenny. I just ... I think this evidence may come in handy later."

"Like if you kill him one day, you'll need proof it was self-defense?" The cool question startled me.

I'd detected no judgment in his voice, but I shook my head. "Do you really see me as a murderer?"

"Nobody knows what they're capable of when someone pushes them all the way to the wall."

"I guess that's true."

He seemed to decide, then. "What's your email?"

I spelled it out, directing him to an old, free account that Michael didn't know about. I had ten thousand spam emails in that box, which made it a great place to hide evidence.

Now that I was ambulatory, I could explore the small lake cottage. It didn't take long. There were two bedrooms, one so small that it was more of a glorified closet with a twin bed wedged in it. I had the larger room, but it wasn't big either, barely fitting a full-sized bed, a night table, and a slim chest of drawers. Apart from the linoleum in the bathroom, the cottage had rough indoor-outdoor carpet on the floors, including in the tiny kitchen. There was no living room to speak of, just an open space that had a dingy plaid couch and a small Formica table that dated from the 1950s.

There were doors on either side of the living room; one set were glass and led out to a sagging deck with a questionable view of a murky, algae-choked pond, and the other opened onto the gravel driveway. There were no houses close by, and no lights, either. Michael's uncle must have built the place as a serious retreat from the world. There was no television. No telephone, either. I did find an old radio, but when I switched it on, it produced only static.

I sighed. "It's probably broken."

"Did you want to listen to some music?"

"It's pretty quiet. Gives me the creeps." More to the point, it reminded me of the shotgun shack I'd left behind, though at least we had lights and a working fridge in the lake house, courtesy of the rumbling generator outside.

Besides that machine grumble, I could only hear the insects through the open windows, crickets calling for a mate. There were angry squirrels in the trees, too, though I'd been gone from the countryside long enough to mistake them for birds at first. Funny how you forget things that were once so familiar, but I'd been a city girl for over ten years, long enough to scrape away my backwoods accent and to fool people into believing I was born in Europe.

"I'll look into it," Vin was saying. "Maybe I can fix it."

"Is that your specialty, fixing broken things?" I tried to smile, but I could tell from his expression that I wasn't entirely successful.

"I dabble," he said.

In a few moments, he had the radio cracked open and was tinkering with its electrical guts. He tightened various wires and cleaned off some parts, then put it back together. When he plugged it back in, I wasn't even surprised that a torch song drifted out of that antique.

"Melancholy," Vin said. "I'll change it."

"No, it's fine. 'Every Time We Say Goodbye' fits the mood."

"If you say so. Are you hungry?"

I wasn't, but if I lost weight, I'd be punished for failing to take care of my body, and I didn't have the strength to go through this again so soon. Until that night, the punishments had been mild, either captivity or isolation, until I rectified whatever was bothering Michael. I kept telling myself it was the price I had to pay. Cinderella couldn't have a lavish lifestyle and complete freedom, right?

It's funny what we can accept to survive. But here's the thing about monsters: they can't be satisfied, because that hunger can never be quelled. I could have fed every scrap of my identity to Michael and it wouldn't have been enough. Dee and Leslie had perceived this too, I supposed. I'd told myself that I couldn't be caught if I jumped into the net of my own free will, but a mermaid without legs still can't run.

Time to adapt or die.

"It's my turn to cook," I said then.

By Vin's expression, you'd think I had offered to levitate multiple chairs. "You're hurt. I can't let you—"

"You can't stop me," I cut in.

It felt good to move after spending days in bed. Maybe I wouldn't set any land speed records, but I could put a meal together from the packaged stuff in the cabinets. Saltine crackers, canned tomatoes, tuna, noodles … only someone who had grown up poor would be able to make a meal out of the odds and ends we had in stock. Canned soup, too, but I was dead tired of that.

I used the tomatoes to make a basic pomodoro sauce and boiled the water for the noodles. Then I crumbled the crackers into the drained tuna and shaped the mixture into patties, frying up the fish cakes in a bit of oil.

"I didn't know you could cook," Vin said, watching me with increased interest.

He didn't realize how close he was standing, and I didn't move him off. This was unspooling according to plan. It didn't take long to finish off the pasta and I plated our food.

"Zesty red noodles, fish cakes, and …" I checked the fridge. "Carrot sticks. I hope that's all right."

"Anyone who complains about homemade food they didn't have to cook is an asshole. But this looks great," he hastened to add.

The food did taste pretty good, mostly because it reminded me of the days back at the cramped apartment in Nashville. Once a week, one of us would cook something for all the girls who were at home. It was like a holiday from the water and raw vegetables that kept us thin enough to work.

After dinner, Vin did the dishes and I sat on the plaid couch, curled to the side to keep the pressure off my back. The radio kept delivering mournful music about unrequited love and people who left without a second glance. This cabin didn't deliver much entertainment but it was safe and peaceful. Those two things were almost enough to make me wish I could just stay there, hiding from the world, forever.

"Here, I made you some tea … and here's your nightly tablet."

I must have drifted off, because his voice startled me so much that I almost knocked the cup out of his hands. Though I couldn't remember what I'd been dreaming, it had been bad; I could tell that much from the cold sweat on my temples and my trembling hands as I reached for the mug.

"Marlena …" His hands flexed like he wanted to comfort me but he didn't know how.

I helped by leaning my head forward, so his big palm eventually settled on top of my head. He petted my hair in clumsy strokes that said he wasn't often called on for this sort of thing. Vin did have the look of a man who delivered beatings and rough sex more than gentleness, but I already knew the latter was what he craved most.

Once I finished the tea and took my medicine, I slid forward even more, giving him two choices: catch me or let me fall. And since I was already hurt, he was too nice to opt for the latter. I ended up cuddled to his chest, his arms looped around my hips to avoid touching my back.

With him crouched, it was an awkward position, and it couldn't last. He eased me back after a few minutes, slowly so as not to aggravate my injuries.

"I know you're hungry for comfort, but we shouldn't."

He didn't finish the sentence. Or maybe that was the end, left for me to fill in as I pleased. *Shouldn't … get close? Touch too much?* Whatever he intended, I was aiming for the opposite, but I couldn't push. Slow and steady would get this done. I hated myself a bit for this, but I needed an ally more than a clean conscience. Maybe I'd break Vin's heart, but it was even more probable that Michael would break my neck if I faced him alone.

"Sorry," I whispered. "I'm going to bed now. But I can't keep staying in the bigger room. That little bed you have is way too short for you. From now on, we'll swap."

I ignored his attempts to argue and went into the tiny room and shut the door. The generator was just outside, so it was loud as hell. Starlight streamed through the tiny window, and a gibbous moon shining on the pond laid a silver trail and almost made this place beautiful. The sheets and pillow smelled like Vin, soap and the salty, sea-swept deodorant he used. That, too, was part of the plan. If I was smelling him, then he'd spend the night breathing me in, too.

In the morning, I'd press a little closer, test my progress in scaling his walls.

18

There was nothing like the smell of frying bacon and fresh-brewed coffee to wake me up in a good mood. I stretched in bed and nearly knocked my elbow on the wall. Since I only had nightgowns, I didn't get dressed, just stepped out of my room and took two steps to the kitchen counter; that was how small the cottage was.

"We didn't have bacon or coffee last night," I said.

Vin smiled at me. Seemed like a night in a bigger bed had improved his mood. "I went into town early for some provisions."

"What town would that be?"

"I'm not supposed to tell you," he said reluctantly.

"Seriously? Why? Because Michael doesn't want me to be able to show the police where I was held while recovering from the injuries he inflicted?"

"He didn't say that, but ..."

"Probably." My disgust for the man I'd married rivaled my fear. "Doesn't he understand that they can check what properties he owns, and I can identify the place once they narrow it down? He can't have many shitty two-bedroom lake cottages."

"That's assuming the place is in his name, not under some shell company."

I sighed, my surge of defiance dying away. "Right. I forgot that he's the devil, who can't be caged by conventional means."

The early morning light lent Vin's rugged features a somber air, enhanced by the days of scruff he hadn't shaved. "I wouldn't go that far, but I think it'll take someone more powerful to take Mr. Durst down. And since he has some terrifying alliances, it may never happen at all."

"It's wrong for you to depress me this much before breakfast," I said.

"Sorry. Eat up before it gets cold. And then, hopefully, you'll be happy to hear that I brought you some actual clothes. I think your back's healed enough to tolerate a loose shirt."

"Bless you." Impulsively, I stretched up and kissed his cheek in thanks.

He didn't draw back, and the smile stayed. Yeah, a night in a bed that smelled like me made a difference.

I didn't sit down to eat until he did, and I was impressed at the spread: bacon, sliced tomatoes, fried eggs, and toast. I assembled a sandwich out of everything on the table, grinning at his reaction. "I guess this is a BET?"

"It's your breakfast, call it whatever you want." The smile went all the way to his eyes, which meant he was starting to enjoy my company.

Attraction was the next step. Too bad I couldn't ask him to shower with me again; since I was well enough to walk around and even cook, I doubted he would go for it.

Time to push another of his buttons.

"I wonder if I could ask a favor, when we leave?"

He didn't stop eating, but I caught the flash of wariness in the look he shot me. *Don't worry, it's not what you're expecting me to say.*

"Depends on what it is."

"I've been saving my allowance, and I want to send some money to my family, but I'm not sure if Michael knows about them. If he doesn't, I don't want to give him more hostages. He'll definitely find out if I send the money personally."

I hadn't wanted to waste my hard-earned cash on my mama's habit, but it would be worth it to get closer to Vin, no matter how she spent it. Maybe I was wrong about her and she'd be clean when she got the funds and use it for the youngers.

"I don't see how I can help you with that," he said.

But I could tell he wanted to.

"I'll give you my ATM card and my pin. You can take out the money and wire it to the Western Union closest to my mama's house. I'll also need you to mail her a card saying that there's money waiting."

I expected my family to be where I left them, as moving houses took money. In our neck of the woods, people stayed in the shacks they were born in until they were arrested or they died. Whole families didn't disappear without the funds to do so, though sometimes people got out on their thumbs, as I had. Good thing the truck driver who'd brought me to the bus station didn't have bad deeds in mind.

"She doesn't have a phone?" he asked.

Most people would be surprised at that, but the holler where I grew up was like the land time forgot in many ways. There might be cell service out there by now, but it was hard for me to imagine cell towers built in those hills.

I shrugged. "She didn't when I left. You can check the listings. I haven't stayed in touch, at first because I was scared I'd get sent back, and then later because I was scared for other reasons."

Vin knew why; no need for me to belabor the point. While we finished eating, he thought over my request. As I got up to clear the dishes, he said, "I'll check into your family quietly, Marlena. Once I find them, then we'll talk again about how you can help them without tipping Mr. Durst off to what you're doing."

Perfect. He was willing to conspire with me, though he knew damn well it would infuriate Michael. I turned suddenly, so Vin nearly walked into me. He staggered, flinging his arms wide to keep from dropping the dishes he had in each hand. I pretended to take the gesture as an offer of a hug and stepped into his space, leaning my head against his chest. When he didn't pull back, I wrapped my arms around his waist.

"I think maybe I can live because of you," I said simply.

"You don't mean that. It's just that I'm here and you need somebody. There's a word for it when patients think they're falling for the therapists who make them feel better."

"Transference," I supplied. I'd taken a few psychology classes along with all the art history Michael made me study. "But that's not what this is. You've been genuinely good to me and I appreciate it. Or is that forbidden, too?" Constant rejection would make anyone sad, so I didn't have to fake the tears. "It sucks that I'm not even allowed to have friends. Wait, I do have one, and she's in danger of being murdered to keep me in line. And you wonder why I asked you to kill me."

That got his attention in a big way. Vin angled in what looked like a painful twist to set the dishes in the sink and then he did hug me, sort of, hands on my hips. That drew us together in a way that didn't feel innocent at all.

"It's shit right now, but as long as you're alive, there's a chance it could get better. Promise me you won't quit?"

I rubbed my cheek against his chest. "I don't like to make promises I may not be able to keep. I don't know if I'm strong enough to see the other side of this. Maybe not in this world, anyway."

"You're killing me," he whispered. "I hate how he's hurt you."

"Sorry. You made me this nice breakfast and I made you feel shitty. That's not a good trade at all."

I tilted my head back and tried to smile at him. He answered with what had to be an impulsive kiss to my forehead. Nobody had ever done that before. Then he wiped away my tears with gentle thumbs.

"Durst would pull my head off," he said, more to himself than me.

"Well, he's not here, and we'd know if we had someone spying on us."

"True. You can hear cars coming from a mile off."

"So we might as well enjoy our freedom. We'll be living according to his whims again soon enough."

"Maybe I've got Stockholm Syndrome, because everything you said makes perfect sense."

"Wouldn't I be the one suffering from that?" I joked. "But that still doesn't track, since you're saving me. This isn't an abduction so much as an intervention."

"You give me too much credit."

"Then tell me your darkest secrets, so I can stop thinking you're a good person just because you're kind to me and you care about your family."

Vin ducked his head, unconsciously resting his chin on the top of my head. It wasn't worrying him anymore to be this close. Baby steps, all the way to where I wanted him.

"Dark secrets, huh? You already know something I haven't told my family."

"That you're not strictly heterosexual?"

"Got it in one."

"Your dad wouldn't understand?"

120

"Doubtful. He's a veteran, former Green Beret, tough as they come."

"He might surprise you ... but it's your choice. For what it's worth, I think people should love who they love."

"That's nice to hear."

We couldn't hug forever, and it would set me back if he broke contact first. As PT Barnum supposedly said, "Always leave them wanting more." I finally pulled away and got started on the dishes. Vin helped me and there were lots of opportunities to brush against him or touch his hand when passing off a clean plate.

This all felt so domestic; I just needed to nudge him toward wanting me. Not in an obvious way. He wasn't overly visual, so a straightforward seduction was out, and I wasn't experienced in making men desire me. The ones who did had twice taken without asking, and that made me skittish, so I'd been pretty close to pure when I married Michael.

I had the sense that Vin was primed. In campfire terms, I had built the triangle of wood and laid the kindling. Now I just need the proper spark to make him burn. Unfortunately, although I was sure he'd warmed to me emotionally, I was less sure how to pull him in the rest of the way.

An idea came to me, slowly, but I didn't know if I had the guts—or the acting chops—to pull it off. Bracing myself, I took a breath and decided to go for it. If this gambit failed, it would put him on his guard in addition to making me look like a complete idiot.

Be brave, I told myself. *Time to go all in.*

19

"I'm taking a shower now, unless you need the bathroom?" I said. Vin shook his head. "Go ahead."

My heart was pounding like I had a great crime planned. I washed up quickly, including my hair, and when finished, I dropped the soap and stepped on it. I didn't try to control my fall and screamed as I went down. My head hit the tub wall so hard I saw stars.

As I'd hoped, Vin burst in within seconds, and he lifted me out into his arms. His hands were everywhere on my wet body, checking me for injury. My head hurt like hell, and a knot was forming. He winced when he found it.

"Oh God, are you all right? Look at me, Marlena. Show me your eyes."

I didn't think I had a concussion, but Vin stared into my face with great attention, peering at my pupils.

"Am I dying, doc?"

"Not on my watch."

I'd accomplished my first goal, getting him to touch me while I was naked. Now I needed to escalate. Shivering, I put my face in his neck, letting him feel my quick breaths, and soon the tenor of his touch shifted. He still had his hands on me, but stroking softly, not checking for new wounds.

"Vin," I whimpered, wrapping my arms around his neck like I was looking for reassurance, and that sealed my bare wet breasts against him. My nipples were sharp from the sudden shock of going from warm bath to cold floor, and he had to feel that, too.

"You scare me to death. Half the time I'm afraid you're going to disappear."

His breath roughened against my ear, and I didn't resist when he shifted me, trying to slide me away from the erection he couldn't entirely control. He'd gotten hard in the shower too, but I'd pretended not to notice.

I wouldn't be doing that again.

Softly I rubbed my cheek against his throat, not quite nuzzling. Vin put his hands on my hips because that was the safest place to touch, but I moved so that he ended up cupping my butt. The damage was light there, so I only felt a faint sting of pain.

I feared he might let go, but when he flexed his fingers and caressed me there too, I knew I had him. A flush of pleasure suffused me then, giving me the assurance that this wouldn't be like all the other times. He was so slow and tentative that I was setting the pace.

Talking would probably make him remember all the reasons why we couldn't do this, so I scraped my fingers down his back. Not a comforting touch, an inciting one, and it earned a little growl. He nudged my head up and kissed me, rough lips, soft tongue, and he was so hard now that when I rubbed against him, he lifted his hips. *Still dressed, that won't work.* It had to be his move, though. He might regret it later if I was too aggressive.

To make sure he wanted it too much to stop, I stroked every inch of his chest and shoulders, while kissing him with everything I had. This had started as a strategy, but I really wanted him as I squirmed on his lap. We had to finish this. Had to.

Finally Vin pulled his lips away, and I almost cried, but it was only to lift me up and carry me to the room I'd given up for him. His voice was so low I almost didn't recognize it when he said, "I'm not doing you on the bathroom floor."

His clothes came off and then he pulled me on top of him. That move was a question, one I answered by sinking down on him. The control was still all mine, and I rode him until we both came, sweating and shuddering.

Between the fall and the hard, quick sex, I was dizzy. He held on to me, cuddled me to his chest, so I could hear his heart beat while I settled.

"This was a terrible idea," he said eventually.

"I wanted you."

"Me too," he admitted. "That doesn't mean we should yield to every impulse."

"Then look on it as revenge. How does it feel, knowing you went balls deep in the woman who's married to the man you hate most?" That was only a guess, of course.

Vin confirmed it with a twist of his mouth and by tightening his arms. "It makes me want to do it again. And to lick you until you can't think straight."

"I'm willing," I said. "Since this might be the only revenge I ever get, I intend to make the most of it."

In answer, Vin pulled me onto his face and kept his promise.

———

The week passed in a delicious flurry of sex and snuggling. I had Vin exactly where I wanted him, between my legs and whispering secrets beside me in bed at night. I brought him fully onto my team; we made plans and promises. We were curled up in the bigger bedroom, my head on his shoulder. He liked playing with my hair, idly rubbing the strands between his fingers.

"You never did tell me how you became a bodyguard?" I said.

"True. Do I take that to mean you're curious?"

"Insatiably." Turning onto my side, I settled into the crook of his arm so I could watch his face.

He stayed on his back, an arm behind his head, staring up at the pop-corn ceiling, a look that had been popular thirty years ago. "I don't know if I should be telling you my life story. What if you use it against me?"

"You already know how much power I have."

Vin cupped my head in one big hand. "I'm teasing, Marlena. It's not that exciting, that's all."

"I still want to know. This is probably all the time we have, and when I remember you, I want to know things about you that other people don't."

That earned me a kiss on the temple. Or maybe that was the wrong way to look at it. Vin wasn't like Michael, rewarding me for pleasing him. He just wanted to do that.

"You're sweet. But you make it sound like we'll never see each other again."

Sadly, I whispered, "Not like this."

"Well, since you're curious … I joined the Marines right out of high school, followed in my old man's footsteps. I was stationed in Okinawa for most of my tour. I didn't re-up, and I got into security work after that. Started as a guard but I pursued higher training in tech and martial arts so I could command better pay. Eventually quit the agency and started freelancing. My last job was with the CEO of a pharmaceutical company."

"How did you end up with Michael?" I asked.

"Honestly? He made me an offer I couldn't refuse. Double my current salary, three weeks of paid holiday time a year, and a full benefits package. I got greedy, didn't ask too many questions."

"I know what that's like."

"He didn't show me who he was right away. I got drawn in little by little, and by the time I realized I'd seen too much, there was no safe way to extricate."

"Because of your family." In that moment, my heart moved for Vin, but the sympathy wasn't enough to keep me from using him. I'd come too far to quit now. He'd become part of my plan. Whether he liked it or not.

Against my hair, he whispered, "Just so you don't think I'm spineless, I tried to quit once. Before he married you. You know what it's like to have him produce pictures of your baby sisters and talk about how pretty they are?"

I shuddered. "God forbid he brings me pictures of mine."

Vin cut me an intense look. "That won't end well, Marlena."

"I know. I left five youngers back home, three brothers and two sisters. I had someone who was like a big sis to me once ..."

I didn't like talking about Dee. Besides, if I told Vin too much, that information could be extracted from him. Jenny was the only person I trusted that much. Even if the worst happened, she'd die before telling Michael anything he wanted to know. And I'd do the same for her if her stepfather ever got ahold of me.

"Big family," was all Vin said.

I heard what he didn't say—that it was more leverage for Michael to use against me. Sighing, I whispered, "Wish there was some way out ... for both of us."

"It only ends if he dies," Vin said.

He wasn't wrong.

"I guess you've seen some things." It was a general prompt since I was hoping to score some dirt on Michael. You never knew what intel would come in handy. "Have you encountered Snake Neck and company before?"

"You mean the assholes who jumped me and took you?"

"Yeah."

Vin shook his head. "I've been kept out of his Russian dealings. Before, he was constantly in Croatia, but I guess alliances have shifted. He swindled four families that I can name off the top of my head. They thought they were getting a share of the resort in return for selling their land, because that was how he made it sound, but the actual paperwork—"

"Said something else entirely. What a bastard."

"There's nothing like preying on gullible elderly people."

"It's hard to catch him, isn't it? Because he does so much of his dirty business overseas."

"Between the paper companies and the partners who help him clean his dirty money, Durst looks like a legit businessman. He owns several resorts and hotels outright and has shares in actual companies. That lends credence to the big picture."

I had some half-assed idea that maybe I could gather evidence and present it. The IRS had managed to lock Al Capone up for tax fraud, and that was probably the least of Michael's offenses. That would mean getting into his computer, though, the one I'd been expressly warned never to touch. So far I'd obeyed that edict, mostly in fear of him having a key logger that would record my intrusion.

That was before he had you beaten like a dirty rug. Everything's different now. From this point on, we are at war. One I had to win.

Vin kept sending pictures and getting terse replies from Michael. On the tenth day, my bruises were so faded that we probably wouldn't be allowed to stay much longer. Sure enough, Michael sent a peremptory *come back tomorrow.* I shivered when I read it because it meant the respite was over. Time to resume the battle.

"You scared?" he asked.

I shuddered. "To death. I wish we could just stay here."

Hiding wouldn't save me, though. The only way out was through. From here on out, I had to step up my plans and dedicate myself to collecting evidence. Michael had to pay, not only for what he'd done to Dee and Leslie, but for what I'd suffered too. He thought money put him above suffering the consequences of his actions. I'd prove, emphatically, that it wasn't true.

"We could run." It was a joke, not a good one. I could tell Vin didn't mean it from the rueful twist to his mouth.

I shook my head. "And leave our loved ones to take the hit? No thanks."

"Knew you'd say that. Your heart's in the right place."

"It's really not," I said with a sly half-smile.

Vin laughed softly. "It's going to be so hard to pretend you're nothing to me after this. You know that, right?" He lifted me and set me on the kitchen counter, leaning close. "One for the road?"

"Who says revenge is best served cold?" I kissed him fiercely.

Vin fucked me on the kitchen counter the night before we left, slow and deep, and though he didn't say it aloud, I knew he was mine.

20

Before we left the cottage that morning, I scrubbed every inch of my body until my skin was nearly raw. Vin had been careful and not left any marks, so there couldn't be a single sign of what happened here. Michael was particular about cleanliness, so if there was even a whiff of Vin on me, he'd notice.

Which meant we couldn't touch again.

I came out of the bathroom half an hour later, glowing and as close to recovery as I could be. The outfit I had on was a radical departure from the white and ivory Michael previously insisted on, so I reckoned he was sending me a message.

Black on black, touch of lace. Perfect for a lying whore.

I hadn't left the cabin in two weeks and it felt strange to step out onto the gravel drive, where the nondescript rental car was waiting. Vin handed me a narrow strip of cloth.

"Sorry, but if he's got people watching us on the way back, he'll know if I don't follow his orders."

"I don't want you to get in trouble."

I got into the car, buckled up, and tied on the blindfold, ready for a long drive. If I knew Michael, he would avoid routing me through an airport, where I might have the chance to disappear. While I wouldn't run for so many reasons, *he* wasn't sure of that, and so he'd reduce the risks, limit my opportunities. Bare bones, I'd need my passport and ID to flee, and I had neither.

"You don't know how much I hate handing you back to him."

"This is my problem, and I'll solve it. But …" An idea came to me, another secret we could share. "We could work out a silent code to communicate right in front of him."

"ASL would be a little obvious," he teased.

"More like gambling signals. You adjust your tie, it means something. And if I brush back my hair as Michael's talking, it means 'what an asshole.' Might be fun and it would help keep me sane."

"You'll need an excellent poker face, Marlena. Or this could be trouble."

"He'll never notice anything from me," I promised. "Can you keep up?"

Thus challenged, Vin said, "Damn straight."

We spent the next several hours working out a simple code, matching phrases with gestures. I had no illusions about what my life would be like. If I'd thought it was restrictive before … well, I probably couldn't imagine how else Michael would narrow my existence.

The closer we got, the more my foreboding intensified. We stopped once, at a rest stop, where I took off my blindfold and used the bathroom. Mentally I noted that the car still had half a tank of gas, so the cottage had to be within reasonable proximity to New York.

"Are you worried?" he asked as we got back in the car.

I put the cloth back on without him asking. This was a generic road stop, nothing to distinguish it from a hundred others in America, so he'd kept his promise to my husband and not let anything slip about where we'd been hiding.

There was no point in lying. "Very. I know it will be bad, but I get queasy when I try to imagine the particulars."

A muscle flexed in his jaw. "Times like this, I wish that bastard would fall from something high."

I smiled slightly. "Maybe he'll take up skydiving."

"Never. He's got terrible vertigo. Once we were at a party and somebody was playing a platform game on a massive TV. Durst had to leave the room. He couldn't complete the deal in there."

Vin let me take my blindfold off for good when we crossed into New York state. My stomach got heavier with each mile, and when we came into the city, I started shivering. By the time we pulled into the parking garage, I was a fucking wreck.

"I can't hold you, Marlena, but you're making me want to. Get your shit together before I crack and ruin us both."

One breath, two, and then I climbed out of the car in my funeral attire: black slacks, loose-cut black blazer, black lace camisole beneath. Squaring my shoulders, I mustered my model walk, and that self-confidence carried me to the small elevator foyer. Vin used his card pass to activate the direct-to-penthouse lift command.

He was in full bodyguard mode again, standing behind me by a full five paces at the back of the elevator, while I stood with arms crossed at the front. It occurred to me that I was being delivered like a fucking package, since I didn't have house keys, didn't have my purse or any way to provide for myself. No phone, no bank card—I might as well be a statue that Michael had bought. He might have even changed the pin on the electronic lock to make me feel more helpless, more dependent.

Vin had the passcode, at least, since he keyed it in for me and gestured. He didn't accompany me in, though I could tell he wanted to. I shook my head slightly to relieve him of that guilt and went to meet my tormentor.

You knew it might get bad before it got better. Push onward.

Durst was waiting for me in the living room, arms locked behind him as he stared out at the panoramic cityscape like modern-day Ozymandias. *"Look on my Works, ye Mighty, and despair!"* But Michael should've read to the end of the fucking poem, about how the monument had fallen to shit, completely wrecked and forgotten.

I will be your sands of time.

Long moments passed in silence; he didn't turn or acknowledge me. The bastard made me speak first.

"I'm home," I said.

"There's a newspaper on the table." His voice was a knife, carved from a glacier. "Pick it up. Turn to page 7."

Rock and roller taken tragically, before his time. I skimmed the article, an obituary for Bobby Ray Hudgens, who had struggled with addictions his whole life and finally achieved success with his fourth band, Mad Misfits. *The singer-songwriter made the fatal error of driving under the influence, but fortunately the accident claimed no other lives.* The rest was about Bobby Ray's accomplishments and how fans were grieving all over the world.

"I did that for you. Do you feel vindicated?"

The worst part was, I couldn't muster up a flicker of sympathy for Bobby Ray. I'd married a monster, but the singer had been one too.

There was only one way to answer this question. "Yes. Thank you."

If I protested or acted ungrateful, it would go worse for me. He would find it offensive and incomprehensible if I screamed that he was the devil and that I'd rather starve on the streets than spend another night in this gilded cage. I breathed. Held it in. I thought of

Jenny and remembered that while she was willing to sacrifice any-thing, everything, for me, I couldn't let her. Her help had to come carefully, if at all.

"Now that I've had a chance to calm down, I realize I may have overreacted. It's not fair to blame you for that bastard's trespasses. But if you're keeping any other secrets, tell me now. I can't guarantee my goodwill can be relied upon a second time."

"I'm an open book," I whispered.

Michael turned and stared at me, hard, as if trying to decide whether that was true. *The liar always thinks people will deceive him.* I dropped my eyes and hoped he took it for submission instead of vis-ceral terror.

"All right then, princess."

If he was calling me that again, maybe I'd run the gamut back to his good graces. I tried a smile and wished Vin was there instead of outside the door.

Setting his hands on my shoulders, Michael turned me toward the dining room table, piled high with cards, flowers, and gifts. "People have been worried about you. You'll need to reassure them at the next event that you're completely recovered."

From the beating you ordered. Those words lodged like razor blades in my throat.

"Will and Helen Stone are very concerned, though I haven't speci-fied your illness. You can set their minds at ease?"

"Of course. But please don't let that awful man fondle me."

That was exactly what my fiend of a husband wanted to hear. "Haven't I proved that I'll keep my promises? Anyone touches you without my permission, and I'll burn them to the ground."

For a moment, maybe due to extreme fear or a trick of the light, I saw actual flames dancing in his eyes.

21

Surreal.

That was the only word to describe this situation. Michael seemed willing to act like the slate was clear between us and that we were candidates to live happily ever after. The next day, he bought me a platinum collar that he expected me to wear everywhere. It wouldn't have surprised me if there was a tracking device in it.

On day three, he gave me back my phone, but I already knew I couldn't use it for real communication. Anything I sent, he would see.

Jenny was living in the city now. From her latest email, she'd started her new job at the electric company. She'd sent so many messages, but I didn't know what to say. After all, she knew perfectly well that vanishing and going off the grid hadn't been part of my original plan. I couldn't even warn her that we were officially off-script, except with a numeric code at the end of a banal message. I chose the one for caution to keep her from doing anything rash.

I stared at my phone, begging her silently: *Please be patient. Don't provoke him. This is my fight, sweetheart.*

"Did the dress arrive?"

I juggled my phone and nearly dropped it. It took all my composure not to jump when my husband's arms slid around me from behind and he kissed the soft spot behind my ear. Smiling with a plastic pleasure that I hoped concealed my utter revulsion, I turned and lifted my mouth for a peck.

"It did. It's hanging in the bedroom. What time should I be ready?"

"Eight. The stylist and makeup artist will be here at six. Vin knows they're coming and will authorize their entry."

"Thank you for taking care of it."

"My pleasure," he said.

The truly insane part was that I thought he meant it. Staring up at him, I wondered, *how did you get this twisted?*

I kept hoping for Michael to leave on one of his extended trips, but so far, he'd stayed close to home, with teleconferences in the library and meetings in the city. He was never gone for more than a few hours, and the constant pretense was wearing on me. I didn't know how long I could feign affection.

As if I'd never been abducted, never pleaded for my life on a filthy warehouse floor, I went with the helpers at the appointed time and let them make me beautiful, according to Michael's standards. In a silent message, he dressed me in gray, telling me I hadn't redeemed myself entirely. The gown was gorgeous, mermaid cut, with sequins that might have been scales, a scalloped neck, and long lace sleeves. He liked to show me off without revealing skin.

The stylist piled my hair on top of my head, better to display the necklace Michael had given me. He watched as they worked, silently smug over owning such a rare treasure. Was that how Pygmalion looked, chiseling away at the white block of stone? I felt like Galatea in the flesh. I sat quiet while the girl made up my face, every bit as skilled as any artist who did cosmetics for my shoots. Only the best for the third Mrs. Durst.

He lost interest part way through the process and went into the living room. I let out a little breath, which the woman working on me caught. "Your husband is a little …" She trailed off, either at a loss for words or not wishing to offend a client.

"Intense?" I offered.

"Yes, exactly. My hands were shaking the whole time he was here." She didn't ask how I could live with him.

Just as well. Finally she said, "You look lovely," and turned me so I could see what she'd done. It didn't matter what I thought anyway, only whether Michael approved. If he didn't like the look she'd created, I'd be sent back like a plate of poorly prepared food.

"Thank you." I'd perfected an empty smile by then, one that cloaked my feelings entirely. Those layers of protection would save my life, time and again, safeguard me from Michael's wrath. Ironically, he loved that expression, called it regal composure, worthy of his name.

But whenever I looked like that, whenever my lips curved just so, I was always wishing one of us were dead.

I glided into the living room where Michael was waiting. He surveyed me as if I was land he might acquire and then gave an approving nod. "Perfect."

That damned word again. Impossible, unattainable. It was cruel and unusual to hang that label on me. If I met that standard once, I wouldn't always.

"I'm ready," I said.

At least a social event would provide a break from the monotony. I took his arm and he led me out of the condo, past Vin, who signaled me with a tug of his tie.

I miss you.

I responded by turning the bracelet on my wrist. *Thinking of you.*

That was our first covert exchange, as I'd been kept inside the penthouse all this time. I didn't dare ask Michael for any favors, let alone one involving Vin. It would be a while before he let me off the leash, if ever.

"I won't be needing you tonight," Michael said to Vin.

"You're not coming back after the party?" he asked.

"I have a surprise planned for Marlena. You can take the night off."

Oh God. My stomach dropped.

To his credit, Vin maintained the same flat expression he always showed Michael. "Understood, sir. May I ride down with you?"

"Feel free. I can drop you at the station, if you like." That felt like a test, somehow.

Vin didn't drive to work, so it wasn't surprising for him to accept, but it still made me nervous for him to climb into the backseat behind me. I wondered if he was thinking about everything we'd done at the cottage, if his insides were boiling.

We didn't speak on the short drive to the subway entrance, and Vin got out with a terse "Thanks" directed at Michael. That seemed to satisfy him, as he whistled in turning the car toward the highway. Though I was curious, I didn't ask exactly where we were going. On all counts, Michael preferred a Stepford wife to a real one.

"There will be a lot of important people tonight. Try to make a good impression." He didn't say "you're a reflection on me" this time.

He didn't need to.

"I'll do my best. And I'll make sure that the Stones aren't worried about me."

"I've been thinking…"

I said, "Yes?" because the pause implied that he wanted me to respond.

"New York might not be the best place for my base of operations anymore. I have several projects ongoing in California. How would you feel about moving?"

Michael didn't give a shit how I felt about anything. This had to be another test, just like the one he'd set for Vin. Since I hated the penthouse and would love for him to be three thousand miles away from Jenny, I offered a bright smile.

"That sounds exciting. I've always thought it was beautiful there."

"Are you sure you don't mind leaving everything behind?"

"My only ties that matter are to you," I said.

I'd chosen to chain myself to him, but Michael was the rock in my pocket as I tried to swim. I had to be strong enough to keep my head above water or the dark murk of his "love" would fill my lungs and leave me unable to see sunlight again.

It made me sick, how good I was getting at saying empty words because he wanted to hear them. If lying was an Olympic sport, I'd take the gold.

"Didn't your friend move here recently?" More probing.

I clenched my jaw, forced myself to relax. "She came for the job market, not me. We can keep in touch via email, just like we did while I was living in Germany."

Oh, he liked that. Nothing and nobody had better be more important than Michael Durst. He stroked the back of my head. "Once we get settled out west, maybe we should bump up the timetable on having a baby."

Oh no. Hell no.

I couldn't just agree, not this time, but fighting him would be a disaster too. "You said I had to wait two years."

Like reproduction was a privilege he had the power to bestow or withhold. But that was the right tone. According to his terms, I needed to be at the pinnacle of wifely virtue to be worthy of incubating his seed, and he had to consider the shitstorm with Bobby Ray as a fault. I did too, just not of the same shade.

"I'll think on it," he said, smiling.

Thankfully, he was quiet the rest of the way. We arrived at a brightly lit country club in the posh suburbs. A valet in a red vest and black trousers opened the door and tried to help me out. I was careful to avoid his hand and did it on my own, a move that Michael noticed, because he was a fucking obsessive maniac. I hated his smile. I hated his eyes, roving over me with complete pride of ownership.

We followed the red carpet up the steps to a grand venue. Inside, it was the stuff of dreams. I had no idea what cause we were raising money for that night, but it didn't matter. What did? Seeing the right people, impressing them, making them think we belonged in the highest echelons. Michael hadn't been born a blue blood, or he wouldn't be scratching so hard at that glass ceiling. For me, it was just another reason to hate him.

Ahead of us, there was a crowd of brightly dressed socialites fluttering like butterflies. A few were already tipsy and giggling. I read Michael's palpable scorn as we moved past them. In his eyes, there were so many ways to fail as a woman—gaining weight, losing it, drinking too much or too little. Decorum and beauty intersected on a narrow line, one that defined my existence.

I wouldn't be Michael's dress-up doll forever, but for now, like the ballerina trapped atop a child's music box, I'd dance to his tune. Ahead, I spotted the Stones, my first hurdle of the night.

Showtime.

22

I made sure my smile was brilliant as I approached. Avoiding William's outstretched hand, I took Helen's and pressed it warmly. "So good to see you again. I'm sorry we haven't managed to align our schedules yet."

"Michael tells us you were ill."

"Nothing serious," I said, before he could assign me some incurable ailment. "Just a bit of bronchitis. I was recovering in the country, and I'm feeling much better now."

"Glad to hear it, my dear." Helen had the kind of upscale New England accent that was almost impossible to replicate outside of years in the right schools, associating with people who spoke in exactly that manner.

I made small talk, conscious of the cameras flashing on the sidelines, photographers circulating among the crowd and occasionally asking the most attractive guests to pose. When the paparazzo passed, he took a second look at me and then signaled for a smile.

I'd rather bite his face off, but I settled against Michael's shoulder as if we truly were the happy, perfect couple who would be featured in tomorrow's society pages. His fingers felt like steel bands digging into my shoulder, and I wished I could break his arm off at the wrist.

"Look this way. Smile!"

"What a lovely couple," Helen said. "Don't you think so, Will? They're perfect together, aren't they?"

That word, again.

There was a minuscule pause before Will replied, "Certainly."

Michael hated this man for some reason, maybe with no rational justification, so he gripped my arm and steered me away. He didn't allow me to drink any wine, but he gave me a glass to hold.

"Pretend to sip it. The last thing I need is for you to show your true colors."

I clenched my jaw, because I'd never embarrassed him, never done anything to reveal that I wasn't the elegant diplomat's daughter he'd invented. Part of me wished I could drink until I got sloppy; that humiliation would humble Durst like nothing else. The memory of how he'd punished me reverberated in the back of my head, and I burned to even the scales.

Not now. Not yet. Be patient.

Despite my reluctance about being there, I still experienced a little of Cinderella's wonder at being included in such a dazzling array. As we circulated, I recognized a prominent playwright, a Broadway actress, several heiresses who were mostly famous for being rich though they also dabbled in music, clothing lines, and perfumes. If Michael had married one of them—

He wouldn't have control.

They might have had the background he was looking for, but they also had powerful families who would crush him for mistreating their daughters. Given his criteria, that was why he'd married someone like me, malleable and … disposable.

My stomach was so empty, and the shoes pinched my feet. None of this showed in my frozen smile. Life had taught me that it only mattered if you were beautiful in a certain shape, not if you were safe, comfortable, or happy.

Michael dug his fingers into my arm. "Stay focused. Talk to Mrs. Van Houten if you can. Since I don't know her, you'll be my introduction later. Make it look natural."

"I will."

With that instruction, he let me go, like a monkey he'd trained to pilfer trinkets from the crowd. I smiled and made eye contact as I traversed the room, measured enough so it wouldn't be obvious I was heading for the venerable dowager who came from the oldest Dutch money. I'd seen her at charity events in Europe—before Michael had proved beyond any doubt what a devil he was—but we'd never spoken.

I chatted with a few acquaintances along the way, women I'd met when I was still modeling, because a fair number of us had ended up in this circle. Eventually I hovered near Mrs. Van Houten at the edge of the room, where she was holding court in a circle of chairs. Most attendees were relegated to standing, eating off tiny plates at tall tables, but the staff clearly understood who the VIPs were. Michael must hate just being another millionaire, not so powerful that people stumbled over their feet when they saw his face.

I had no doubt that was his desired endgame, and there was no question he'd sacrifice anything or anyone to make it happen.

My timing had to be impeccable, so I waited for a break in the conversation to make it seem as if I'd noticed her brooch in passing. "That's so lovely. I saw a similar piece at a museum in the Hague."

Her attention sharpened, but my smile didn't falter. I might have been forced to study art history, but this was all true. She glanced down at the antique pinned to her gown. "Most people don't recognize Bolin's work at a glance, or they take it for a cunning reproduction."

"Impossible. I never imagined I'd be privileged enough to see one of their designs outside a glass case. You must treasure it."

"This has been passed down for generations. I don't often dare wear it, but I'm glad I did tonight. Would you care for a closer look?"

I'd clearly chosen the right tactic. Michael might be a fiend, but he'd known what he was doing when he nudged me toward art history. This knowledge base gave me all kinds of instant credit with old-money types.

Normally it would be weird to kneel next to someone you'd just met and study their chest, but she'd given me permission. I didn't reach for the brooch, and that restraint earned me points. I saw that in the faint easing of her expression. My posture was ridiculous in evening wear, but I managed to straighten without falling over after I concluded my inspection.

"That is simply beautiful," I said. "Thank you. I'm sorry I barged into your conversation, but I fear that I tend to be impulsive when I'm captivated by such a splendid historic piece."

"Not at all, my dear. But ... have we met somewhere before? You look familiar."

That was my opening, the one Michael had sent me to acquire. "I don't think so, but I know I saw you at one of Clotilde's shows years ago, and there was a fundraiser fashion walk in Antwerp ..."

There, that should be enough to jog her memory.

"Oh, yes. You were signed to Celestial for a while. I knew I'd seen you. My memory's not as sharp as it used to be when it comes to names, but I hardly ever forget a face."

Guilt flickered through me, because whatever Michael wanted with this woman, it wouldn't be in her best interests. Even the "deals" he included people in usually ended up with the least powerful party getting screwed. Most likely that wouldn't be Mrs. Van Houten, however; she had sufficient clout to crush him like a bug, and I hoped she did.

She exuded an air even more regal than Clotilde, so that I had the old-school urge to curtsy as if I were in the presence of a queen. I constrained that impulse to a simple inclination of my head. "I'm Marlena Durst. A pleasure to meet you."

Hate using his name.

"I'm Joanna Van Houten, and I must admit I'm curious. How did you go from modeling for Celestial to recognizing an original Bolin on sight?"

Smiling, I explained how I'd studied in Heidelberg, and one by one the other party guests drifted off, as it became clear I wasn't going to relinquish Mrs. Van Houten's attention now that I had it. She even invited me to join her and called for wine and a sampling of their best amuse-bouches while she solicited my thoughts on Rubens, Rembrandt, and Vermeer.

Michael joined us when we'd been talking for ten minutes. As I smelled his cologne, my stomach twisted into knots. *I don't want to do this. I have to do this.* At least until I stepped up the timetable and found a way to make him suffer.

He rested a hand on my shoulder. "I wondered where you'd gotten to, darling."

You never call me that.

"I've made a new friend," I said brightly. Then I bit my lip, adding, "Or is that too presumptuous to say, so soon?"

Mrs. Van Houten laughed. "No, indeed. I'd quite enjoy touring museums and private collections with you, if that sounds at all enticing."

I got a gentle pat on the shoulder, Michael's way of saying well done. Unlikely he'd ever speak the words.

"It would be my pleasure. Oh, and please meet my husband, Michael Durst." I didn't say what he did because I'd noticed that it seemed to be considered gauche, at a certain level, to discuss how one made money, and he was striving desperately, like a salmon upstream, for those highest echelons.

"Delighted," she said.

Just then, he pressed hard on my shoulder, and when I glanced up at him, his expression said *Go. Now.*

I rose calmly. "Would you mind keeping Mrs. Van Houten company? I need to visit the powder room."

She started to protest, but he cut in smoothly. "As long as she doesn't mind the imposition."

"Oh, not at all."

Don't be fooled, I told her silently as I walked away. *Don't let him suck you in.*

23

Five minutes alone.

That was all Michael had given me, but it felt as profound a gift as when he'd handed me a Cartier box with a diamond tennis bracelet in it. Letting out a soft sigh, I went straight to the ladies' room. There was no way to know if I was under surveillance, but it seemed wise to assume the answer was yes.

From the marble hallway, I stepped into what looked like a lounge, with opulently upholstered furniture and a makeup counter that ran the length of the wall, a huge mirror, and lighting appropriate for professional touch-ups. I'd done photo shoots in rooms that weren't as well appointed. In places like this, sometimes it was even hard for me to remember that my family's entire house had been about twice the size of this space, cut up into cramped little rooms with flypaper on the windows and cracks in the wood that let the winter wind slice through.

A couple of women were sitting in the anteroom, and I nodded in passing. Best to be polite—you never knew when a resting bitch face would backfire and turn into a petty feud you never wanted.

The bathroom itself was a wonderland with a uniformed maid offering hot towels to dry your hands. She also had a full array of toiletries, almost anything you could desire, along with feminine hygiene products and pain and upset stomach medicine. I smiled at her as I stepped into the large frosted-glass stall. These were supposed to be elegant, but I hated them. You could always see the other person's shadow, watch them moving, and I was provincial enough to be bothered.

Though I had zero desire to return to the party, if I hid for too long, I'd pay later, so I finished up and washed my hands, careful not to splash my dress.

I fully expected to find Michael still bending Joanna Van Houten's ear, but when I stepped back into the ballroom, she was once again holding court for a small circle of elite partygoers. For a lovely moment, I thought maybe Michael had abandoned me. In that case, I could call Vin to take me home and I wouldn't have to face whatever heinous surprise Michael had in mind for afterward.

A passing waiter handed me a glass of wine, and I took it on reflex, drinking half of it before my husband could stop me. It was a small rebellion, one of the few I would allow myself.

From across the room, I finally spotted Michael, and at first I couldn't believe my eyes. The girl he was chatting up couldn't have been more than nineteen, slim as a sylph, with a cascade of dark curls and melting brown eyes. You could say the man had a type, because she had that same waif look that I'd worked so well early in my career. As I watched, the girl sparkled at him and tossed her hair. He brushed a curl off her shoulder, just as he used to with me, back when he was grooming me to be the perfect wife.

Did this mean I was about to be discarded? No, there was no way he'd do that without recouping his investment. What Michael had claimed, he didn't part with casually, and he wouldn't dispose of me until he got whatever he wanted from Joanna Van Houten. His ambition gave me a little breathing room, but I couldn't count on being safe forever. When he was done with me, our relationship wouldn't end in divorce. From what I'd seen, he didn't believe in that. No, he gave his wives a much more permanent dismissal.

Just consider Dee and Leslie.

For a few seconds longer, I watched him flirt with the girl, then pasted on a bright expression. I couldn't let it seem like this was bothering me or shaking my confidence. If he took a mistress, that would give me more freedom, a break from his mind games. My expression was warm when I joined them.

"Sorry I made you wait," I said cheerfully.

Michael gave me a dark look, as if I should have lurked a bit and let him finish … whatever this was. Still, he did glance around to make sure no men were paying me overt attention. It reminded me that I was still one of his possessions, not a person with free will.

He didn't make introductions. "I'll call you later," he said.

The girl giggled and flashed me a pitying glance. It ricocheted off my *fuck you* force field as she melted away into the crowd.

"Are you ready to go?" he asked, surprising me.

"Don't you need to circulate more?"

Michael shook his head. "I've spoken to the key figures in my next deal and you helped me with Joanna Van Houten. I got her number, by the way. You need to call her. Not tomorrow, that's too soon. The day after, I think."

I bit my lip to keep from protesting. *Do this, do that, I'm not your bitch.*

Except I was, and he even had my pedigree papers.

"All right," I murmured.

He preferred that submissive tone, as if all my own thoughts had melted and drained out my ears.

"Good girl."

Horror washed over me in a slow, inexorable wave. The next time he said that, I might jump out a window, no matter what floor we were on. How long could I live like this? Sometimes I felt as if my whole body was fissuring and one good quake would break me. When I'd stepped into the funhouse, I didn't know how bad it would be. I *thought* I was prepared. I was wrong.

"This way, princess." His affection weighed on me like asbestos, poisonous and smothering.

Michael steered me through the crowd, down the red carpet, to the valet stand. The young man ran up with Michael's keys, likely recognizing an impatient asshole when he saw one. In response, he flipped the kid a fifty-dollar bill and laughed when it hit the pavement and almost blew away so the boy had to scramble for it.

The embarrassed valet opened my door, and as Michael got in the Lincoln I whispered, "I'm sorry." Our eyes met for a second and he gave me a wry half-smile.

I slid into the car. "Where are we going now?"

"Didn't I tell you? It's a surprise."

That did not reassure me.

The ride passed in silence, back into the city proper. It was late enough that traffic didn't have everything on lockdown, though it was still heavy to me since I'd grown up in an area where four cars constituted a jam-up, and later, in Europe, I'd biked everywhere.

Finally, he parked on a street where we shopped, close to the condo where it was all posh boutiques and precious upscale cafes. Women with tiny purse dogs loved this area, and they always got driven, even if they were only going three blocks.

Since I'd asked once, I wouldn't give him the satisfaction of doing it again. I merely stared, waiting for an explanation. None of the shops were even open, if he was planning to buy me something as a reward. It was possible he'd bribed someone to stay later, however, as he loved power plays like that.

"Close your eyes." That was a command, not a request.

Yet I swallowed an instinctive refusal and a twist of fear. Michael wasn't Vin; I couldn't trust him. He might lead me out into the street to die. Hell, that might even be my surprise, now that he'd found a girl to replace me.

Till death do us part, right, you bastard?

Fear-sweat pooled under my arms, beneath my breasts, as I reluctantly obeyed him. I heard the slam of his car door and then he opened mine, pulling me out with a quickness that told me he enjoyed having me helpless. The night air blew up my dress, and I stumbled when he tugged me toward him. His cologne washed over me, sickly sweet, too much almond and vanilla.

Isn't there a poison that smells like almonds? Fitting.

"This way."

No endearments, now that we were alone. He claimed this was a fresh start, but in his mind, I wasn't pure and worthy anymore. Nothing could wash away what Bobby Ray had done in that trailer, not even death.

Impossible to judge how far we walked, but I was terrified the whole time—that he'd shove me or push me in front of a car. I was trembling when we stopped, and he said, "You can look."

At first I didn't know what I was seeing; then I read the sign. *Durst Gallery.* I glanced at Michael, who was smiling with all his teeth but not his eyes.

"What's this?"

"Your reward. If we're not having a baby right away, you need to keep busy, and this will be helpful even if you don't immediately turn a profit."

I'll be cleaning your dirty money, I realized.

Galleries were great for that, as the value of art was subjective and driven by how much a collector wanted a piece. I didn't realize I'd spoken until Michael smiled and patted my head. The contact started gentle and then his fingers pressed into my skull.

"I knew you were a clever girl. You're not perfect, but you *will* be useful."

24

The next day, there was a picture of Michael and me in the society pages. We looked like a million bucks together, complete proof that pictures aren't worth a thousand words. Images can lie, just like smiles.

That afternoon, I went to the gallery to check on the work in progress. There was still a lot yet to do, and I had no experience in this area. There was no art on the walls to be purchased, for example. I did have an office set up and Michael had already furnished it to his taste, white leather and sharp edges.

Might as well do some work while I'm here.

I fired up my desktop computer, which still needed to be set up. Did that mean I could use this equipment freely? *Maybe not.* Michael might send someone to add monitoring software later. It was so tough to tell what was probable and what was paranoia. With half-hearted interest, I posted employment ads for a couple of sales agents and an experienced gallery manager. I also read a few articles on starting a business, which still left me unprepared.

I suspected Michael didn't expect me to do much more than look pretty and make connections at exhibitions. Well, that and he could use my name to hide assets from the government and to launder money. This marriage was the gift that kept on giving.

Finally, I consulted with the work crew and changed a few of Michael's orders. This should test how much actual authority I had here. The foreman didn't immediately call Michael to check, so maybe he was giving me enough rope to hang myself.

It was late afternoon by the time I stepped out of the gallery. I was messaging Vin to pick me up when a luxury car paused at the curb, window rolling down. I recognized Joanna Van Houten right away, though she was dressed more casually, in a linen pantsuit.

"I see your interest in art wasn't exaggerated." She glanced past me toward the gallery in progress.

"I'd love your advice on what emerging artists I should feature," I said. "I don't want to focus on established talent. And I could use some guidance because I can't decide what the theme of the first show should be." All of this was certainly true, but I wished I could get to know her without being bound to Michael's agenda.

The older woman brightened. "If you have time, we could get coffee and discuss some possibilities."

I made a quick decision. "I'd love that."

Deviating from Michael's plan might anger him; I'd take that chance. "Where should I meet you?"

"Just get in the car, my dear. Your driver can collect you later."

Before Michael, I wouldn't have hesitated over such a kind offer. Eventually I got in, and I texted Vin after finding out where we were headed.

The entire time we were bonding over art, quiet terror thrummed in my veins. *I don't have permission to do this. Even if it's what he wants, Michael might—*

"Marlena? Are you quite all right?"

"It's late. I ... think I'd better get home."

"You have my number. Call me soon. I enjoyed talking with you." Beneath her posh exterior, Joanna was a lonely woman; it didn't take a genius to read it. And I felt like an utter bitch for getting close to her on Michael's orders.

As it turned out, he wasn't even in the condo when I got home. I'd worried for nothing. That was par for the course. He did what he wanted and I feared setting him off.

The next week or so, I didn't see him much. Two nights, he didn't even come home. I met Joanna twice more and gave her a tour of the gallery. She helped me compile a list of artists who were worth pursuing, and I felt like she deserved a co-credit on the gallery name plaque.

When I said so, she laughed. "This is so much fun for me. I don't have the energy to tackle something like this full-time, but as a consultant? It's delightful."

I bought her lunch that day, after we left the gallery, and as we were finishing up, I lost—or won—the war with my conscience. "Joanna ..."

"Yes, dear?"

"I think my husband means to pull you into some project he has planned. Just ... proceed carefully." *Don't trust him,* I added silently.

Hopefully she'd get the message from what I said. I didn't dare say more because if she mentioned the warning to Michael—

He'll kill me.

"I understand," she said softly. "Maybe better than you know."

From the sharpening of her gaze, I thought she did. There was still a lot to do before the grand opening, so I hurried out of the restaurant so Vin could take me back to the gallery to begin interviewing job applicants.

———

A few days later, gossip sites got wind of something, reposting the picture and hints of Michael's infidelity. He came home furious, but for once it wasn't at me.

He ranted for over an hour, smashed up some dishes, but didn't hit me. I flinched with each crash, each smash. Finally he calmed down enough to say, "I will sue the shit out of them. I'll be in the library on the phone with Anton."

Right. The pale-eyed attorney I'd met in Germany. I didn't ask for an explanation. If I had to guess, I'd say he must've met up with the giggling girl. Whether he'd had sex with her or not, I didn't even care.

I had more critical issues to worry about. Such as the fact that I'd never run a business before.

When Michael first presented me with the gallery, I'd expected him to stare over my shoulder the whole time, but possibly due to wrangling his scandal, he was giving me more freedom than I'd known since marrying him. I kept meeting with Joanna, and under her tutelage, I hired a skilled manager and a couple of sales agents, and together we filled the gallery with work I admired. While this wouldn't have been my first choice for a career, I started to enjoy it.

It seemed as if I might reach an equilibrium with Michael after all. I still hated him, but it was tolerable, which is probably difficult for most people to understand. As for Michael, he seemed to remain busy with the girl he'd met at the charity event. The only downside was that I had to turn a blind eye to certain transactions that he demanded.

Now that I was working, I didn't see Vin as much. He only showed up to escort me home, ostensibly for my protection, but really it was to make sure I didn't meet anyone while Michael was traveling. He was in Switzerland at the moment.

When I'd asked him about our supposed move to California, he'd said, "That was a test ... to see if you would follow where I led. You passed, and if you do well with the gallery, we'll definitely have a baby next year."

So it seemed we weren't going after all, but that made it harder. I wanted to see Jenny so much it hurt, but it was safer if Michael believed that I'd drifted away from her, like I had with everyone else in my former life. These days, I only sent the occasional brief message with a code tacked on at the end. I still hadn't found enough evidence on Michael to make my move. I was getting bolder about searching when he wasn't home, but I suspected any real dirt would be found in his office at work, and I had no excuse to go there. I let out a frustrated sigh.

"Something wrong?" Vin asked.

For weeks, he'd checked the car every time we got in it, making sure Michael didn't leave any recording devices. I'd thought he was paranoid until the day he found one. He tweaked it so it wouldn't transmit anything while seeming to be working if Michael ran a diagnostic on it. Now we could talk freely.

"I'm worried about Jenny," I said.

"That's the friend from your modeling days?"

"Right."

"You still think he might do something to her?" Vin asked.

"Right now, he's leaving her be because he's relatively satisfied with me. The minute I disappoint him again ..." I shrugged. No sense in elaborating; Vin had seen those consequences firsthand. "I'm more afraid that she might do something reckless if she gets too worried."

Since Michael had protected himself well, finding the opportunity to strike wouldn't come easy. I needed him to attack me first; only then could I push forward with my own schemes. As long as he maintained the status quo, I had no proof of what a monster he was.

"I can mail a letter to her for you, if you want," Vin said.

Low-tech, relatively hard to track or spy on. That was a great solution. I wanted to kiss him but I restrained the impulse. "Are you sure? I don't want to get you in trouble."

"It'll be fine. Just write the letter. I'll take care of the rest."

"Don't you need her address?"

"I can get it."

He probably had his own contacts related to his service days and security work. This was a small matter.

"Thank you. I don't want Michael targeting her if I can prevent it."

"There's only so much you can do," he said.

"I know." I paused, meeting his gaze in the rearview mirror. "I miss you." It was nice to speak the words instead of using the silent gestures we'd worked out.

"Me too. It's … bad when I'm standing outside, wondering what he's doing to you. Sometimes I imagine kicking down the door, throwing him off the roof, and running away with you."

"I wouldn't want you to do that," I said quickly. "It would hurt your family too much. Think how your sisters would feel."

Vin flicked me another look in the rearview mirror. For once I was grateful for the ridiculous traffic that made traveling in the city more feasible for pedestrians. We wouldn't be able to talk this long otherwise without drawing suspicion.

"I never said I would. If people could be convicted on bad thoughts alone, there wouldn't be a free soul left in America."

"That's probably true," I admitted.

"We're here." I heard the regret in his voice as we turned into the parking garage.

Michael might not have been home, but that didn't mean Vin could come in with me, eat dinner, and watch TV. If only I'd been brave enough to fuck him in the bed I shared with Michael—but I wasn't. When—not if—we got caught, I wouldn't be penalized alone.

Kill Michael Durst, a little voice whispered. *It's the only way out.*

25

Like Vin said, for most people bad thoughts couldn't become deeds.

He let me out at the sublevel foyer door. I had my own key card for the elevator and I knew the condo's pin code, which was progress, but any of these "earned" freedoms could be revoked on a whim, which made them meaningless. I went up alone while Vin parked because that would look better to Michael on surveillance. Otherwise he'd claim that I wanted to stretch out the time with my bodyguard.

True, but I couldn't let him learn that.

Jenny sent me a text as I got in the elevator. I answered it quickly, knowing Michael might well be reading my messages. He'd probably cloned this phone to keep tabs on me. My response was mundane.

Not bad, how're you? Just so busy with the gallery! Hope the job is going well. Then I closed with the numeric code we used. That additional message was *sit tight.* But she must have been worried, especially after the way I'd disappeared. I wished I could email her a proper update, but I couldn't trust any of the hardware Michael had given me.

I was in a grim mood when I stepped off on the penthouse floor, but I couldn't put off writing the letter to Jenny. There was so much I had to say that couldn't fit neatly in a coded message. We had alternate plans to make. The letter needed to be sent quickly, before Michael ruined the opportunity. As I finished pouring my heart out and begging for her support, the phone rang.

"Yes?"

I expected it to be Michael checking up on me. Even when he was in Europe, he knew where I was every minute of every day.

"Mrs. Durst?" I didn't recognize this voice.

"Yes."

"This is Brian at reception. There's a girl here asking for you. We didn't have any instructions left about a visitor, so I'm checking to see if you're expecting someone."

Oh shit, it might be Jenny.

"Who is it, please?"

"Just a moment." I could hear some conversation taking place but couldn't make out the words being spoken. "She says to tell you that Ariella is here."

I staggered, all the blood rushing away from my head. The shock was so great, I had to brace against the wall. Of all the youngers, I'd never pictured Ariella tracking me down. She was next to smallest, only eight or so when I'd left home. That meant she was... how old, now? Dizzily I did the math and realized she was near eighteen, give or take.

"Mrs. Durst? Do you know her? Or should I see her out?"

My heart raced so hard I saw stars and I clutched the counter for support. *Breathe. Protect Ariella. Breathe.* Of all complications I could have foreseen, this one never came to mind. Somehow Barrettville felt like another world, one that didn't even contain a bridge to my current reality. I couldn't have been more wrong.

"I'll be right down," I managed to say.

Vin glanced up, astonished, when I raced out of the condo. "Marlena? What's wrong?"

I just shook my head. His involvement wouldn't make things better. I called the elevator with a shaking hand.

"Think for a minute. I *have* to go with you."

Right. Cutting him out would only raise more questions. This was already a huge firestorm, a blaze that I might not be able to put out. I got on the elevator, Vin close behind me. There was no audio in there, just cameras, so I stayed a good distance from him as I explained, "My baby sister's here."

"Oh shit," Vin said.

I could see I didn't need to clarify. Just like with Bobby Ray Hudgens, I'd pay for this. Pay and pay and pay.

Since it had been so long, I wouldn't have recognized her from the little girl I'd left behind. She stood an inch or so shorter than me with a more delicate frame. Her thin face was heart-shaped, and her dark hair had gold streaks. Thickly-lashed amber eyes, wide mouth, light brown skin, and—dear God, I could *never* let Michael see her. The horror of that prospect might slay me before I could get a single word out.

When Ariella spotted me, she took a step as if she'd throw herself into my arms, then caught sight of Vin looming behind me and hesitated. "It's me, Marlie. I finally found you. I been looking for years, but you vanished off the face of the earth."

"You're all grown up," I finally said.

This reunion, when I'd rarely let myself imagine it, always took place after I'd wrapped things up with Michael Durst. To have Ariella arrive now? This was the worst possible timing. I had no leverage to protect her, but I couldn't kick her into the street either. Tightness in my chest made me feel like passing out, but I reached for my sister anyway. Memories popped in my head, like golden corn kernels seared at high heat.

I used to hold her on my hip, walking the floor with her when I was only half grown myself. Long nights when she couldn't sleep for the hunger in her stomach, and she'd cry until the snot ran down my neck, her thin body almost more weight than I could carry. Tears started in my eyes as I pulled her into an inevitable hug. Maybe I'd left the youngers, just like Dee had, but I'd never forgotten them.

She clenched her arms around me, smelling of road dust and old sweat. I could tell she'd been traveling for days, probably not a proper bath in sight. There was nothing I could do but take her in, even as the fear of Michael's reprisal multiplied exponentially; terror-spiders hatched and laid eggs, scurrying in my head until I could hardly think.

He'd had me beaten over Bobby Ray Hudgens, and I'd lied to his face, lied outright, about not having any more secrets. I'd even said, "I'm an open book." God only knew what he'd do next.

But not to Ariella. I had to get her out. Somehow. My half-formed plans disintegrated in the face of this new urgency. *Breathe. Keep walking. Normal people have visitors.* Trying to seem calm, I picked up her bag and smiled at the concierge.

"Thanks, Brian." Best not to make the situation look odd or unusual to onlookers. Michael would hurt me more, later, if we made a scene. I stilled my instinctive shudder, envisioning his reaction to her grimy duffel and her unkempt hair. To Michael Durst, poverty must seem like a contagious illness. Whatever. I could survive whatever he dished out, as long as I got Ariella to safety first.

Not part of the plan. This is so not part of the plan.

"Let's go upstairs," I said softly, guiding her toward the elevator.

Ariella beamed at me, all wide-eyed appreciation. "Can't wait to see your place." *Aaay,* like *paint,* in the word *can't.* Compression of vowels, *your* to *yer.* I'd fought so hard to shuck that accent, sticky as pine gum.

Without a word, Vin took the bag from me as I called the penthouse elevator with my card. Ariella glanced between us.

Then she whispered, "Is this your husband? He sure looks different than in the paper, and he don't say much."

"This is Vin Rivera, our chief of security." Honestly, I didn't even know what his job title was.

A long pause while she processed that info. "Oh. Why do you need one of those?"

I waved the question away, fear gnawing at my stomach. There was no way I could explain my life to her. None at all. I couldn't afford another casualty in this cold war. Already I was losing my mind worrying about Jenny and Vin. With Ariella here, I could've collapsed on the floor and cried.

"How is everyone?" I asked.

Ariella bit her lip as the doors swished open. "It feels strange to say it out, but waiting won't make it easier. Marlie, Mama's gone."

I'd taken one step out of the lift and I spun to stare at her. "She, what?"

"Gone, as in passed away, not ran off. We didn't know how to get in touch with you."

All this time, my mother had been dead and I didn't even know. That seemed wrong, *really* wrong. I could never claim to be a good person, but this ... even if I'd sometimes hated her, Kitty Altizer had given me life.

A queasy sickness stole over me. Now I could never do anything for her—send her to rehab or tell her off once she got her head on straight. There would never be anything, anymore. I'd thought I had plenty of time, like the hours didn't move the same in Lee County or something.

"What happened? Was she sick, or ...?" I could hardly get the words out.

"Overdose. We were on our own for a couple of weeks before the state came to check on us. They split us up then, sent us to different foster homes."

"Did you finish school?"

She nodded. "I graduated, but I couldn't find work and then I saw you in the paper on the internet, couldn't believe my eyes."

If only you'd waited—

But I couldn't blame her for this. The way I'd chased after Dee, Ariella had come searching for me. There was no gain in hurting her feelings just because I was dead frightened about how bad this could be. So I tried for a welcoming smile as I put in the pin code and took her bag from Vin.

"This is it," I said.

Her eyes widened as she took in the posh entryway. Part of me wondered if she'd slip anything into her duffel; she'd always been a light-fingered little thing. Her awe struck a chord, though, as I knew exactly how she felt.

As we stepped into the condo, Vin said, "I'll be here until ten if you need me."

"Thank you."

Edmund, the night guard who took over Vin's shift, would keep an eye on us until morning, but I'd never talked to him. As my thoughts

164

whirled on how to deal with this crisis, I led the way into the penthouse.

"Wow, what a place!" Ariella's excited voice sounded even louder, echoing off the marble and glass.

She wandered around touching everything, leaving smears on the glass cabinets and tables. Michael would hate that. And I'd pay for it however I had to, so Ariella wouldn't.

"Sit down," I finally said, pointing to the white leather couch. "Make yourself comfortable."

I couldn't worry her or raise her suspicions. Maybe I could spend a night with her and then send her off with some money. It didn't matter what happened once she was safe. If he didn't kill me over this, I still had a chance, however remote, of making him pay.

Taking me at my word, Ariella pulled off her holey sneakers and flung herself on the sofa. She sighed and stretched out. "This was worth all that time on the bus. I wasn't sure you'd even want to see me since you left without a word."

"How do you know I didn't try? You haven't been at the old house for years. I actually asked Vin to look for you."

"You did?" Her face brightened like I'd said Santa was real.

Guilt pricked me because I'd only said that to make him like me more. "I was going to send money."

Leaning forward, she rummaged in her bag to produce a battered mini-notebook. "I can give you everybody's addresses. Benton tried to stop me. He said you abandoned us like stray cats and we shouldn't think about you anymore."

Benton was the closest to me in age and the smartest of all the youngers. *You should've listened to him, Ariella.* I wasn't nearly as nice as she seemed to think, and I had secrets that would make her run screaming.

165

"Are you hungry? I can warm up some food while you shower." It was impossible not to be impressed that she'd tracked me down using the internet. If she put that determination toward a safer goal, she could accomplish remarkable things.

"That sounds real good. But you're gonna do it? I thought you'd have a cook, a maid, and maybe even a butler."

"Michael doesn't like live-in help."

Ariella cocked her head, looking thoughtful. "Guess it would be strange, having people constantly around to fetch and carry. It's good to know all rich people don't lose their sense. Where's the bathroom?"

I showed her and gave her clean towels, so plush that she couldn't resist rubbing her face against them like they were toys I'd won for her at the county fair. Once she understood how all the shower attachments and knobs and dials worked, I went to the kitchen. Mechanically I got a random meal from the freezer and stuck it in the microwave. That was the extent of my housekeeping. In the morning, the maid would clean the place, top to bottom, including the removal of those fingerprints.

I was expecting Michael in two days. That would be long enough to hide Ariella, right? The explosion of temper would be catastrophic, but if she was gone by then, that was fine. I'd survived so much already. Still, I remembered the pain of the strap and the long recovery from those wounds. Shivering, I jumped when the microwave beeped, signaling me to remove the food. I plated it nicely and set it on the counter to wait.

Ariella took over half an hour, not that I blamed her. When she came out, she was wearing ragged pajamas, her hair wet and tousled. I heated her food again for a minute and passed her the plate.

"Looks delicious," she said, already shoveling like she hadn't eaten in days.

From the look of her, it might have been true. I had no idea how she'd afforded the ticket from Kentucky to New York. It must've been a long bus ride, lots of transfers and dirty stations and creepy assholes between there and here.

Poor girl had no idea I was married to one, too.

26

Though the consequences might be dire, it felt good to have Ariella there, a reminder of where I came from and why I was fighting Michael Durst. I let out a breath, resolving to enjoy this visit, however brief it might be. She caught me up on the youngers as she ate.

Benton was stationed in the Middle East, distinguishing himself in the army, while Terrell had been adopted by his foster parents; currently he was enrolled in technical school. Baby Evelina was about to graduate from high school. A surprise piano prodigy, she'd already earned a complete music scholarship.

"You didn't mention Norton," I said.

"Don't know. Last I heard, he was in bad company, headed west and following in Mama's footsteps."

"Damn." She must mean he was a junkie. If not Oxy, something worse.

"We couldn't all turn out good." Her tone was philosophical. "I was mad at you for a long time. You didn't even leave a note."

"I'm sorry." I was, too. In some ways. Maybe not the ones that mattered.

Ariella got up and hugged me. "I forgave you a while ago. You're still family, Marlie. No matter how far you ran or how long you were gone."

The sound of the door opening almost stopped my heart. I tried to twist away, but Ariella couldn't read the mood; she didn't let go. Michael stepped in, thirty-six hours early, wearing the expression that haunted me.

"What an unexpected pretty picture, my dear wife. Care to make the introductions?"

I could hardly speak. "This is my sister. Ariella."

"You're such a beauty," Michael said, taking her hand and holding it longer than he should have.

She laughed. "Ain't you sweet? I was afraid Marlie's man might mind me barging in, but I can see you're a good one."

"Marlie? How cute." He let go of Ariella and set his case down. "I wish we were better set up for guests, but you'll have to spend the night on the couch."

"Oh, no worries. Hand me a blanket and I can curl up on the floor."

"Just like a puppy," Michael said icily.

Ariella laughed like that was a real joke, not an insult, but I just kept getting colder. Right on cue, Michael wrapped an arm around my shoulders and pulled me toward him, forcefully. To Ariella it probably looked sweet. She couldn't feel the bite of his fingers, digging into the meat of my upper arm.

"Wait for me in the bedroom, Marlie? I'll shower and join you. I hope you don't mind if we retire early, Ariella? I've been flying for a full day to get back to my lovely wife."

"That's just fine. Do whatever you need to. And thank you for having me."

"My pleasure." Michael smiled at me. His eyes were glaciers, sunk in a murky sea.

"I'll get you some bedding," I told Ariella.

Each footstep returning to the master suite felt like a hundred miles. Quietly I sat down on the bed to wait, digging at my skin out of sheer nerves. If I understood Michael at all, he wouldn't act while she was there to bear witness, but as soon as she left, he would strike. I'd suffer, and she would become another tool he could use to keep me in line.

Silently he joined me ten minutes later and closed the door with a quiet click. It would've been less terrifying if he'd screamed at me, because then I'd have a witness to his behavior. But he just sat down beside me on the bed and, with casual cruelty, knotted his fist in my hair and pulled so hard that I thought my hair would yank free of my scalp in a bloody patch. I leaned with the tug so that my face was right against his.

"Another lie, Marlena? I'm not big on second chances."

"My mother was a drug addict, and she's dead. I had no reason to think I'd ever see my half-siblings again!"

"And yet here she is, curled up on my five-thousand-dollar sofa." He slid me a look that was pure, distilled evil. "Do you know, I think she's even prettier than you were at her age. That accent is hideous, of course. I wonder if she's ... teachable."

I hit the floor without him throwing me. It was incredible how well I'd learned to kneel, like begging was my natural state. He'd stripped my dignity, my pride, everything but a stubborn spark that wouldn't let me die, though I sometimes wanted to. That frisson kept me going, past what was reasonable, clinging to the faint hope that somebody like me might one day gain the upper hand.

"Don't," I whispered. "Please don't. Stay away from Ariella. I'll take full responsibility. I'll make sure she understands that we can't take her in. I'll send her to school somewhere. Just, please. Keep this between you and me. Please, Michael."

"Odd. You seem desperate to protect someone you thought you'd never see again."

"She's still my sister."

"Exactly," he snarled. "This is *something else* I should've heard from your mouth. How many others are there who can crawl up to my doorstep like cockroaches, begging for handouts? How many?"

"Four. Three brothers, one sister."

"All with different fathers?" Michael shook his head with such obvious scorn that I trembled. "Well, I suppose you became such a lying whore through your mother's example. I would never have married you if I'd known. Did you *pay* someone to tidy up your past?"

Which meant he'd run a check on me and I came up clean. The old courthouse did burn down, and Lee County record-keeping was never the best. I bet his private investigator hadn't turned up much, especially after Mama died and the youngers were split up.

"I'm sorry."

"Your apologies are worthless." His hand curled into a fist, and I could see he was dying to use it on me.

Go ahead, break your promise never to hit me.

Instead he slammed it soundlessly against the mattress. "I don't want to sleep with you, but we can't let your pretty sister worry, can we?"

I shook my head. It wouldn't bother me to sleep on the floor; I'd done it often at home, and at least this room had thick, clean carpeting to keep me warm. Should've known it wouldn't be that simple. With Michael, it never was.

"You're a filthy fucking animal. I don't even want to look at you. You'll sleep in the closet tonight."

That was better, honestly. He threw a pillow at my head and I let it hit me. Shielding my face would just make him angrier, because he was dying to inflict some pain. I took the pillow and crawled with it all the way to the walk-in. He closed the door behind me with an angry snick and I knew he would've locked it if he could.

That was a long night. I curled up beneath a couple of coats and tried to sleep.

I must have, because Durst terrified me awake by dragging me out by my hair, daring me to make a sound. Jamming my knuckles into my mouth, I held it in. Once I was in the bedroom, he let go.

"I've been thinking and I'm willing to make a deal. You know I'm a businessman, right, Marlena?"

He was using my name, not good.

"I know," I got out.

"If I let your sister go, you owe me. You said you'll take all the responsibility. Did you mean it?"

"Yes." My voice was hoarse, and I had to pee so much it hurt. I'd been holding it for hours, but I couldn't use the toilet without his permission.

Hell, he didn't even want me to breathe right now.

"Then you agree it's fair for me to punish you as I see fit."

"Yes," I lied.

My genuine answer was endless screaming.

"You've landed me in a predicament, you little bitch. I can't have your worthless relatives showing up here. Do you know what people would say, how they'd laugh at me? Stocks would plummet in at least two companies if investors found out I married a little hillbilly whore."

He paced, circling me like he wanted to kick me until I stopped breathing. "I made you, don't you understand that? You were nothing.

Yet you don't appreciate anything I gave you, anything I do, it's not enough. You *still* keep fucking stabbing me in the back."

I made myself as small as I could, tears trickling through my lashes. This was worse because he was whispering, because I was afraid he would explode like an IED and take Ariella out with him.

"Why aren't you answering me?"

"Whatever you want, you can do anything you want. I deserve it." Those words burbled out before I could stop them.

He finally paused that sharkish circling. "At last you said something worth hearing. Just remember your words later and don't say you were unwilling."

Oh God, what's he going to do?

"It's fine. I agree to that deal."

"You're a shitty negotiator," he said.

Like I had any bargaining chips at this moment.

"I'm going to work," he went on. "Teleconferences as usual. You check in at the gallery, dress that girl so she doesn't embarrass me. You have two days to get rid of her. If she's not gone by then, I step in. And trust me, you do *not* want that."

"I'll take care of it."

His lip curled. "Get out. You smell."

He was right; I did. Fear-sweat was sour and acrid, and I'd been sleeping on the closet floor like an unwanted dog. Somehow I pinned on a bright smile as I left the room. Bath and toilet first, then I'd figure out what to do with Ariella.

It might have been too late for me, but I'd do my best to save her.

The time with my sister was bittersweet. I couldn't let on about my devil's bargain, so I brought her with me to the gallery, as instructed, and took her shopping afterward. We came back to the condo with Vin laden down with parcels, and I got her a proper suitcase to replace that torn duffel bag.

On the second day, I said, "I have a surprise for you."

Ariella glanced up from her scrambled eggs, the only meal I'd ever cooked for her with my own hands. "What is it? I mean, I hope it's nothing big. You done so much already."

"Here's a credit card you can use. It'll come in handy while you're traveling."

"Traveling?" Her brows pulled together. "I'd rather stay with you for a while."

"That … it won't work out too well, long-term. And you need to see more of the world. Do you have a passport, by any chance?"

Please say yes.

To my vast relief, she nodded. "My foster mom helped me apply for one when I turned eighteen. They took me on a trip to Cancun. So I have that and a state ID." She started to dig in her bag to prove her words, but I waved that offer away.

"I'm sending you to Europe for a few months. Travel around, use the rail system, meet people, admire the art and architecture. If you like it there, I have some contacts who can help you enroll in university."

"That'll be so expensive." But her amber eyes were shining like it was her birthday and Christmas rolled into one.

Thank God.

"I can afford it, though if you feel bad, you could choose a public college, where the tuition is reasonable."

"Can I really just … go to Europe?"

Ariella's cheeks were flushed with excitement, but I understood her trepidation. I'd felt the same way when Del Morton told me I had a job waiting in Germany on Michael Durst's recommendation. Seemed so long ago now. When I chose that road, I didn't foresee all the twists and turns, though I did expect that it might get rough.

"Definitely. I'll help you pack. Your flight leaves at midnight. You'll be landing in London, and you'll want to buy a cell phone at some point. I'll write down my number in case you have any problems. I've booked a week for you at this hostel..." I showed her the reservation on my phone. "After that, you can roam wherever you want. Just ... be careful."

So much more I wanted to say, but I couldn't. I was already in too deep.

27

I woke in the hospital, an IV in my wrist. The room was dim, no light from the window, and I heard nothing but the quiet beep of the heart monitor. My head hurt; it was hard to focus.

What the hell am I doing here?

As I tried to focus, a nurse crept in. "Oh, you're awake. Your husband told us to notify him as soon as—"

"Wait," I rasped.

"Yes, Mrs. Durst?" There was something overly kind in her expression; pity, maybe?

"What happened?"

"You don't remember?"

When she parried my question with another, the pain in my head intensified. Her gaze slide away from mine. Then she said, "It's better to wait until your husband gets here."

She checked my vitals and made some notes on my chart. When she left, she kept the door open so I could hear the quiet murmur in the hall, soft footsteps passing, though I couldn't see anyone. That meant I wouldn't have any warning when Michael got here.

Tentatively I stretched my fingers and my toes, not finding any external injuries. *What the hell.* Getting agitated, I pulled back the covers, and I looked fine. There didn't seem to be any reason for me to be here. I pressed my memory harder, and my head went white with event fragments.

Flash, I was shopping with Ariella. I had the sense that I'd sent her on a trip, but I couldn't remember the details. Not yet. My memory had to come back, right?

Flash, I was on the couch with Michael. He was smiling at me as I downed a glass of blood red wine. *How long ago was that?*

I heard solid footfalls in the hall outside and instinctively gathered the blanket as a shield. My whole body eased when I spotted Vin, but I didn't know if it was safe to speak, so I waited until he finished whatever he was doing with the gadget he had in his hand.

"Clear," he said. "I didn't think Durst had a chance to plant anything, but it's best to be sure."

"What's happening?" I demanded.

Vin took one of my hands in both of his, so anxious that in that moment, I might've loved him a little. "That's what *I* want to know. The official story is that you tried to kill yourself by mixing sedatives and alcohol. Durst found you 'just in time' and brought you to the hospital, where they pumped your stomach and stabilized you."

He put something in the wine? That was all I could think of. It was coming back to me in patches; he'd praised me for getting rid of Ariella so quickly and offered to celebrate our second new beginning.

Because the tone of his toast was slightly ominous, his words had rung true. "Mark me, you won't survive a third strike. You're 0-2,

Marlena. I won't send you back to the dugout if you fail me again."
Then he'd handed me a glass of wine.

"This is a warning," I whispered. "That my life is in his hands. It also gets me on file as emotionally unstable and at risk for self-harm, which he can use later."

"If and when you 'succeed.'" Vin clenched his jaw and forced himself to let go of my hand. "Wish I could stay, but he'll be here soon."

"Just send my letter to Jenny." Quickly, I told him where I'd stashed it before Ariella arrived, breaking my life wide open.

She's in London now, right? I got her out.

"Don't know if that's possible, but I'll try." He slipped away then, hopefully avoiding cameras as he went.

Michael might not have the power to review footage in a hospital, but I couldn't rule it out. Money opened so many doors that it was terrifying.

According to the clock on my monitor, ten minutes passed before Michael arrived to play the frantic husband, rushing in to grab my hands. "I'm so glad you're all right, princess. I shouldn't have left you alone so much this year. I know how sensitive you are."

Beyond his shoulder, the nurse sighed wistfully and stepped out to grant us some privacy. Once she shut the door, he dropped my hands like I'd burned him. "You see, Marlena? I can do anything I want. I *own* you. Just try to tell your side of the story. Nobody will believe you."

"You tried to kill me." Even I found the words hard to speak.

"Trust me, if I wanted you dead, you would be. You're only alive right now because Joanna Van Houten likes you."

First, he'd had me beaten, and now this. Michael was right; I wouldn't survive strike three. Now I wondered again if second wife, Leslie, had been driven to suicide or if he'd only made it look that way. I'd believe anything of him at this point, but I couldn't help wondering, why wasn't anyone curious about his track record?

"Nothing to say?"

Mutely I shook my head. This was my lowest point, and I was losing hope in the idea that I could defeat him. Not the way the world worked. Recently I'd read a terrifying statistic that nearly fifty percent of murdered women died at the hands of their romantic partners. *I don't want to add to that number. I don't know how to get out.*

While I feared my own violent demise, Michael sat at my bedside, the exemplar of a devoted husband. All the nurses whispered about how lucky I was, and one of them mumbled about how difficult it was to stand by someone who developed a mental illness. She was quickly shushed and rushed out of the room, but Michael heard her and so did I.

"You see? *They* realize how blessed you are, Marlena. Not many men would take such loving care of a sick wife."

You made me this way, I wanted to scream. *You poisoned me, then saved me to prove a point.* Impotent rage howled in my head like a hungry wolf, but I'd seen the movies. Overt agitation would only get me sedated.

In the morning, the doctor stopped by and checked on me. My body was doing well enough, but … "I'm worried about your mental health, Mrs. Durst. You need to be evaluated before we discharge you."

Nobody had told me how long I'd been in the hospital. I had some vague idea that there was a required waiting period to make sure I wouldn't immediately leave and try to end myself again, but did it count if I'd been unconscious for part of that time?

"Okay," I said.

"Do you feel up to answering some questions?"

I shrugged. At this breaking point, I wanted to spill everything, show the pictures Vin had emailed to my private account, but that would mean betraying him. Then he'd have a target on his back, along with Jenny and Ariella.

How long do I have to do this? I couldn't bring myself to dump the boiling oil over their heads, but this was getting hard to carry on my own. Then reality crashed down on me hard, sealing my mouth shut. The evidence might not be enough to keep Michael in jail, and I could imagine how his attorney, Anton, would spin it. *Unstable wife making shit up.* If I showed the doctors those pictures, they might tell me that could be anybody's back. Since my face wasn't shown, it could be anyone.

Michael warned me with his eyes not to attempt to tell the truth, and I only smiled. Let him sweat a little. While he might be 95 percent sure he had me pinned like a butterfly to a collection board, that final 5 percent would chew at him while I was closeted with the shrink.

The doctor nodded, acknowledging my reticence. "I'll let you have breakfast before contacting Dr. Bowers."

My terrifying husband stayed with me while I had breakfast and then he kissed my forehead. "I'll be back this afternoon. Be careful while I'm gone."

That might sound sweet to an outsider, but I heard it clearly for the warning it was. I said nothing as he left, reaction setting in. Whatever pills he'd dissolved in the wine had nearly killed me and also screwed with my memory, so I couldn't quite remember what had happened with Ariella. I had the vague sense that I'd offered to let her see the world with the promise to help her get into college later, but when I pushed my brain for more specific info, a dagger jabbed into the side of my head.

Did Michael do something to Ariella?

No matter how hard I tried, I couldn't remember taking her to the airport. There was a gap between our morning conversation and me drinking that tainted wine with Michael. I wished I had my phone, but I was cocooned in here. There was a landline, but I didn't have any numbers memorized.

Maybe it would be better for everyone if I died. I might not be full-on suicidal yet, but that qualified as ideation, the fleeting wish that my life would just end without me acting to make it so. There was a word for that, but I'd forgotten it.

The door swung open, admitting a thirty-something Black woman with her hair up in a twist of braids. Judging by her notepad, she was here to decide whether I was damaged enough to keep for further treatment. She smiled at me as she pulled up a chair.

"I'm Dr. Bowers. It's very nice to meet you."

28

The session took place in Dr. Bower's office. This room was meant to be restful, cream and blue, with cushions I could hold if I got twitchy. There was no eliminating the faint tang of disinfectant, no disguising that this office was part of a hospital. Dr. Bowers did her best to make me feel comfortable, offered hot tea and took her time warming me up.

At first, the questions were easy, and I answered from the script Michael made me memorize.

It boggled me that his fiction could withstand scrutiny from a hospital, but Dr. Bowers didn't question that I had been born abroad. All so complicated, but it read better than admitting I had no idea what my father even looked like and that my mama had been an Oxy addict for most of her life, her sole distinction being to have babies by lots of different men. That wasn't the kind of shit you put in the society pages.

"That's a lot of adjustment," the doctor said when I finished my recitation. "Moving to America, constantly being scrutinized by the media. You must miss your parents." It wasn't phrased like a question, but it felt like one.

I nodded, because I was supposed to.

"What were you thinking when you decided to take those pills, Mrs. Durst?"

Nothing. I didn't know the wine had been poisoned.

"I don't remember." There was nothing for it but evasion.

Her expression sharpened. "It's possible there's been some blurring after the trauma, but you must have been sad for a while. Let's talk about that."

"There's just ... a lot of pressure. Sometimes I want to run away." Best to skirt the line between fact and fiction, right?

"Excellent, let's examine those feelings in more depth. How is your relationship with your husband?"

This was my chance to spill everything. And I wanted to. God, I did. I opened my mouth, ready to tell this kind-eyed woman everything. If she gave me her phone, here and now, I could produce some basic proof.

She read my silence wrong, as unwillingness to share. "I assure you, anything you say is confidential, Mrs. Durst. I won't even divulge the information to your husband, unless it's something he needs to know for the sake of your well-being."

"Michael is ... demanding," I said finally.

"You mean ...?" She let the sentence trail off, a good strategy, inviting me to finish what she'd started.

"A perfectionist ... and he's controlling. He picks out my clothes, decides what I should weigh, what I eat, where I go, where I work." Shit, maybe I'd said too much.

Dr. Bowers made a note. "And how does that make you feel?"

"Trapped."

"I see."

More notes.

"Do you think you'd be happier if your husband allowed you more freedom?"

"Definitely."

I'd also like it if he stopped beating and almost killing me to prove a point. The ridiculous urge to laugh tickled my throat, because this session was so futile and absurd. Not because I didn't believe in the power of therapy, but because Michael would never allow Dr. Bowers to truly help me.

"We can tackle that issue in couples counseling," she said.

"I doubt he'll want to. He's very … old school. Mental toughness, self-made, that sort of thing."

For the first time, I caught a flicker of sympathy in her professional veneer. "He will if he wants you to feel better," she said firmly.

No, he'd rather murder me.

"If you say so." I wasn't about to argue with an expert who was patient enough to listen to people's suffering and fears, day after day.

"Your husband told me that you were hit hard by the news that it will be difficult for you to have children. Would you like to talk about that?"

"I … what?" I cocked my head, utterly unable to fathom what she was talking about.

"You don't remember?" Her face showed a flicker of surprise as she made a note. "It's right here in your medical file. You had a visit back in June to the OB/GYN. According to your husband, the two of you were planning to start a family soon, but your ultrasound came back with some unexpected news. You really don't remember?"

She was seriously starting to freak me out. I hadn't been to the OB/GYN since we moved to New York, and I *was* due for a checkup.

The doctor, evidently reading my expression, passed me the file so I could see the ultrasound film in it. The words *malformed uterus* leapt out at me.

"How long have you been experiencing lost time, Mrs. Durst?"

"I haven't! I don't know whose uterus that is, but it's not mine." I dropped the folder like it was fire, and on some level, I was aware that I sounded ... unhinged.

More notes. The doctor fixed a reassuring smile on me. "Calm down, all right? I'm just trying to get a sense of where you are mentally. There are no right or wrong answers."

Breathe, I told myself. *There's an explanation. This is exactly what Michael wants. He's pushing you toward a breakdown.*

But it was like once I'd started saying crazy shit, I just couldn't stop. "They're lying, okay? It's not me."

More sympathy, wrapped around practiced patience. "Accepting certain truths can be difficult. What you're feeling is denial, repressing events that make you sad, and that results in issues that you may need help dealing with."

She's not hearing me. Somehow, I locked down my protests because really, I didn't give a damn if I could have kids or not. In fact, if that part turned out to be true, I'd dance for joy over denying Michael something he wanted from me, and *this* would be a rejection he couldn't turn aside.

"Yes," I managed to say.

Not agreeing, acknowledging.

Then it occurred to me—I *did* have lost time. Both after the beating, when I'd woken up at the lake cottage, and after this fake suicide attempt. The timing for a doctor visit didn't fit with the latter, but would Michael have dragged my battered body to some back-alley doc to make sure my baby-making works hadn't been gummed up by the abuse?

Yes, definitely. It had his hideous, soulless watermark all over it.

"You've remembered something." This doctor was perceptive; too bad her diagnostic tools couldn't prepare her for what was really going on. She specialized in helping troubled people, not ferreting out the devil himself.

"Maybe," I mumbled.

"That's good. Don't force yourself. Now let's talk about those sleeping pills. How long have you been struggling with insomnia?"

Pretty much, never. I always slept well, even better when I worked out. Dr. Bowers wouldn't believe that either.

When I didn't reply, she checked the chart. "It shows you got this prescription about six months ago."

What prescription? Apparently there was no damn limit to the documents Michael could get away with falsifying. That was it; I snapped. And the words just came pouring out. "I don't have a prescription, and I don't take sleeping pills. Never have. I didn't try to kill myself, either. Michael did that. You don't understand what he's like."

Shit, shit. I have to stop. I have to—

Then all my worry for Jenny and Vin fell away, because there was open pity in her gaze. She thought I was too far gone to see it. "How long have you thought your husband wanted to harm you, Mrs. Durst?"

In that moment, I predicted the diagnosis before it came down. *Persecution complex. Delusional. Risk of self-harm.*

Michael was winning. Again. Damn him.

"Your husband may be controlling, but he loves you deeply. He's told the hospital director to spare no expense in making you well."

Money isn't love. Money isn't love. Money isn't love.

I didn't chant it out loud because it would only make me seem more unbalanced. Instead I made some noncommittal noise and she wrote away on her pad, ticking the boxes of all the problems she'd identified. Probably she was tired of dealing with rich white women who broke down because they had too much money and couldn't have babies. At the moment, I hated myself too.

None of her private thoughts showed in her serene expression as she said, "We have a lot of work to do, but as long as you're willing, you can make substantial progress here. But you'll need to stay with us a while."

"I don't want to," I said.

I'd rather not go home with the husband who wanted me dead, either.

It seemed like she was prepared for the response. "Fortunately, your husband has your best interests at heart. He's already signed the papers."

"What? It's not supposed to work like that." Didn't this shit stop in the Victorian era, when men could commit inconvenient wives?

Dr. Bowers rose. "We've received paperwork from your parents in Croatia, granting Mr. Durst full authority as your guardian. Don't worry. We'll take care of you."

What the—

The documents I'd signed. The ones he said were nothing, just a formality, when he was finalizing my adoption by Henrik and Anya. I closed my eyes and let the tears come. If there was no way out, I'd fucking play the part.

Screeching like a madwoman, I scratched at my own arms until Dr. Bowers lost her calm demeanor and summoned the orderlies to haul my crazy ass away.

PART THREE
(UN)HAPPY ENDING

29

There were benefits to being in Sherwood.

The facility was beautiful and modern. I had my own room, and they allowed me to wear my own clothes. My days were structured but not regimented; I could decide between various programs designed to help me. I didn't have a choice about group therapy, but I mostly sat quietly and listened to other people's stories. When a bereaved mother was sobbing about her lost daughter, I couldn't bring myself to lie about feeling sad about my malformed uterus.

That was a fucking relief, at least. It meant he couldn't trick me or force me to have his kid. The best part of Sherwood? I was out of Michael's reach. Dr. Bowers would say that my conviction that my husband was spying on me was part of my delusion. At the end of the first month, they decided that I was well enough to go home, but I signed on voluntarily for three more months to continue treatment because it was so *relaxing*.

This decision also served to thwart Michael, because he couldn't use me to get whatever it was he wanted out of Joanna Van Houten, and that deal fell through. I found out about it secondhand, reading the paper about how a rival company ended up buying the property he wanted. Eventually I would suffer for blocking him, but at that moment I didn't care. At Sherwood, they watched me, but I did what I wanted pretty much, as long as I followed instructions and cooperated with the staff.

Dr. Bowers was frustrated by Michael's lack of interest in attending sessions, however. I'd predicted that, but she'd fallen for his "good husband" impersonation. Now that he was busy trying to patch the holes in his business, he had no time to torment me. And it was such a welcome break that if I could, I would've lived there forever.

Sadly, that was impossible.

Today Dr. Bowers was saying, "I understand that you're nervous about resuming your old life. It probably seems impossible that things could be the same, but I think you need to consider taking the next step."

I nodded. She was right in one regard. Things *wouldn't* be the same. He'd warned me that I needed to be useful, and now that I'd actively hindered one of his deals, I had no illusions about my safety. One strike, two strikes—I had no more chances left. At the first opportunity, Michael would get rid of me. The groundwork had already been laid. Like with Leslie, he might make it look like I'd killed myself soon after release. And if he couldn't make that ending work, maybe I'd wind up like Dee and Bobby Ray Hudgens.

How many people has Michael Durst killed?

That was the sort of question that would have Dr. Bowers checking my meds and considering that I might need a different prescription. I wasn't delusional, but my depression was real as I went through the discharge procedures a few days later.

Vin was waiting for me, not Michael, a sign of how far I'd dropped in the hierarchy. He probably didn't consider me his wife any longer, just a fly to be swatted. I hated the idea that my fate rested in his hands. I was *not* in a good place mentally and couldn't see any light at the end of the tunnel. I was quiet as Vin took my things and led me out of the facility. Each step I took away from Sherwood, fear set in, real and visceral, so I was shivering by the time I got in the car.

"What can I do?" he asked, though the answer was nothing.

At this point, Vin was just another person I had to stay silent about to protect. Michael had too many people to use against me, and I had no influence over him at all. Because he didn't love—maybe couldn't— he had no weak points, and I had no energy to keep fighting,

Then an answer burst out of me. "It's time, Vin. What we talked about at the cabin has to happen now."

Vin sighed. That had to be because I was right. Then he said, "There's always a way out. You just haven't found it yet."

"If I wait for him to make a move first, that bastard wins. I've given up years of my life waiting for him to give me something I can use. And I still don't have shit. Not enough to make him pay. He's done too good a job painting our reality in his colors. Nobody will believe me without more proof." Exhausted, I leaned forward and rested my head against the back of the passenger seat, tears trickling from my eyes.

"Are you crying?" Vin glanced in the rearview mirror, but my face was hidden. I'd drag this promise out of Vin no matter what I had to do or say. If I took those photos of my back to the cops, Vin would suffer and the police would ask, "Why didn't you leave?" Like it was ever that simple.

Waiting for Michael was the sure way to die. I had to strike first. "Vin," I whispered.

Swearing, he said finally, "Fine. I'll take care of it."

I shivered, not because I'd asked to be put out of my misery but because of what Durst might do first. "Is Michael home?"

Vin shook his head. "That's why I was delegated to collect you. He told me to drop you off and not let you go anywhere."

"That sounds about right."

Today, Vin didn't drop me off at the doors to the elevator foyer. I rode with him to park the car. In the shadows, he handed me a cell phone. "This one is clean. You can contact me, or Jenny, or anyone you want. I'll use the other one just enough to make him think you still have it."

I turned the phone over in my hands, understanding what a risk Vin was taking for me. This was a damn ticket to the world. "Can the cameras see us here?"

"The pylons block them. We won't reappear until we get out of the car."

"Then we can't stay long." Impulsively I moved to kiss his cheek, but he turned his face and met my mouth with his.

It was the first time we'd kissed since leaving the cottage. This was a terrible, risky idea, but I hadn't been touched gently in so long. Resisting him proved impossible, and we kissed like we needed to breathe each other's air to live. When I pulled back, I was panting.

Good thing I hadn't put on any lipstick before leaving Sherwood, or it would be smeared all over both our faces.

"I shouldn't have done that." His tone was pure self-loathing.

I'd never asked how Vin felt about me. Better not to know, especially now. I should have gotten out of the car then; instead, I pulled on his shoulders, dragging him into the backseat with me. Now that I'd made up my mind, I'd go out with a bang. Literally.

We didn't strip, just slid our clothing aside enough to fuck fast and hard, right in Michael's car. I wasn't quite ready, so there was a little pain, but it chased my desperation perfectly. That eagerness, coupled with the fear of getting caught, and my excitement spiked. Three minutes—and I was biting down on Vin's shoulder, through his shirt and jacket. Hurriedly, I kissed him again and then scrambled to right myself. Michael wouldn't look at the footage right away, but he would eventually. Probably not soon enough for it to matter, but I liked the uncertainty.

You tried to lock me up, to make sure nobody else could have me. Trying to be perfect hadn't gotten me anywhere, so I took an incomparable pleasure in being bad to the bone.

"Go on. I'll follow in a minute or so," Vin whispered.

This time, he didn't say "I shouldn't have done that." Fierce appreciation suffused me. Above all, I didn't want to be one of his regrets. Michael had wronged us both enough.

Quickly, I clambered out of the car and hurried toward the elevators. As promised, Vin brought my bag, composed as if he'd been checking text messages.

"He'll ask," he said. "What's the story?"

"I fell asleep on the way home. You were on your phone waiting for me to wake up."

30

Vin leaned past me to press the button.

I didn't look at him, afraid the camera would show too much warmth in my expression. I wished I could hug him and thank him for what he was about to do for me—for what he'd already done. Defying Michael could get both of us killed, and I didn't flatter myself that a quickie in the car with me was worth *that* much. I couldn't bring myself to smile, but my knees were liquid with relief to be taking action at last.

The lift doors opened and I got in after Vin, standing in front of him to avoid giving an impression of intimacy. Hard to fathom that less than ten minutes ago he'd been grunting in my ear as he came. I tingled just thinking about it.

"You look like you've come to the end of a hard road," Vin whispered. "That expression bothers me."

"We both know what needs to happen now."

He fell silent for the rapid upward whoosh, basement to penthouse. The doors opened to our private floor, and I couldn't mistake Vin's flinch as he handed me my bag. "This is so risky. Are you sure? Maybe if we gather evidence—"

No, no. You can't change your mind now. Sex doesn't change anything.

"I've dug around everywhere. Michael is tidy with his affairs. We'll never find anything sufficient to lock him up. Plus, unless it's proof of a violent crime, the police won't arrest him fast enough to keep him from coming for you and your family."

"Your death doesn't solve that either!"

I pretended to struggle with the bag as I stepped from the elevator, because it gave me an excuse to linger. "It does, actually. I'm going to make it look like Michael did it."

On the surface, it sounded demented.

Your husband wants to kill you, so you frame him for your murder.

On closer scrutiny, it was genius. Twisted genius, admittedly, but consider the alternative. Most likely, Michael had gotten away with disposing of two wives before. He might get off scot-free again if I sat back and let him finish things on his terms. There would be no investigation, no trail for anyone to follow. Whereas if I hired someone to do the job, he'd make sure Michael went down, and since the asshole wanted me dead, it was a fitting punishment.

"Trust me," I said.

Vin paced himself, walking behind me as I inched toward the condo door. Anyone watching this surveillance footage would think my bag was full of bricks or that I had the upper body strength of a toddler.

"How soon do you want this done?" he finally asked.

"The quicker the better. Remember how fast Michael struck after he found out about Bobby Ray? This is more of the same." Since Michael hadn't left enough evidence for me to make him pay, I'd create some this time.

Vin spoke through his teeth as I keyed in the pin code and the front door opened. "I'll text you when it's handled, along with any instructions."

"Thank you." Real gratitude fluttered through me. I signaled him using our secret gesture code, and then I stepped inside the penthouse, the same airless prison it had been before I left. Everything gleamed despite my long absence, but I wasn't dazzled by the expensive furnishings and high-end finishes.

First thing, I dropped my bag in the bedroom, then went straight to the shower. I took my phone with me because a clean cell was more valuable than gold. With it, once I'd scrubbed off every hint of Vin, I could contact Jenny. We could talk for as long as I wanted without fear of discovery or reprisal.

Using a loofah, I scoured my body until my skin was red, then used the detachable shower nozzle to flush out Vin's semen. I kept the spray focused for a full five minutes. At that point I should have been able to pass anything but a CSI investigation. My skin stung as I dried off, and I hoped the irritated color would ease up before Michael got home. Otherwise he'd wonder why I needed to wash so vigorously.

Smell of antiseptic? Yes. I was just happy to be out of Sherwood. That's all.

After wrapping my hair in a towel, I put on my bathrobe and was about to settle in with my prized possession, my surveillance-free phone, when the doorbell rang. Vin stood impassive, offering me a flower basket. "This arrived for you this afternoon, madam. Brian just sent it up, so I'm delivering it personally."

I nodded and thanked him, then shut the door. It must be important or he wouldn't have added that last bit. The card just listed a dollar amount and what must be an account number. Ah, this was Vin's way of telling me how to pay the contractor. I'd do that right after calling Jenny.

God, it had been so long since I'd heard her voice. She picked up on the fourth beep and I spoke before she could. "It's me. New number. Vin hooked me up."

"Oh, thank God. Are you all right?"

I smiled at the sweetness of her voice, the breathy rush. It also gave me a little pang when I considered what I had planned, but if I told her now, she'd only worry longer. One more worry-free night—that was the only gift I could offer.

"Fine. Have you talked to Vin at all?" I hoped he'd kept her posted in addition to mailing her the letter I wrote.

"I have. He explained what's been happening, to some degree, and your note filled in the rest of the gaps. I had dinner with him last week and he said you might be getting out soon. I can't believe that asshole had you committed. This isn't Victorian England!"

Okay, that surprised me. Jenny and Vin? "You two met up? I hope you were careful!"

If Michael found out, it would look an awful lot like collusion. *Breathe. If nothing's happened so far, he probably doesn't know.*

Jenny sighed. "Of course we were careful. I went all the way to New Jersey. Terrible food. Still worth it."

Something in her tone made me ask, "Did you fuck him?"

A soft laugh came in response. "Are you kidding? Of *course* I did. It was almost as good as when I'm with you."

"Glad to hear it," I said. But however entertaining the topic might be, it wasn't why I'd called. "If I wanted to open Michael's computer to outside use, how would I do that?"

Like, say, for someone to plant evidence regarding a contract killing.

"Oh, that's easy. You just enable remote access. I can walk you through it." She gave me a brief tutorial.

With Michael gone, this would be the perfect time to do it, but before I could go to his office, my phone pinged with a text. "Hold on a sec, Jenny."

I tapped out of the call with her on mute to read the message from Vin: *I sent the package as requested. Arriving tomorrow.* It didn't take a genius to crack that code, considering our discussion in the car. But if the police checked into it, Vin could claim he'd literally overnighted a package. Hell, if I knew anything about him, he probably would do that just to keep the details consistent.

Still, this was happening so fast. I needed to talk to Ariella once I wrapped up with Jenny, but I didn't have her number. While I couldn't tell my sister what was going on, I could give her access to my bank accounts so she wouldn't be left destitute abroad. I wasn't clear on what happened to credit cards after a crime, but the one I'd given her would probably be frozen.

"Did something happen?" Jenny asked when I came back on the line.

"Text from Vin." I was about to say more, but another text from Vin came in, one that left my heart racing. *He's here, just got in the elevator.*

"Sorry, I have to go." My tone gave away more than I wanted, shrill despite my best efforts. Tonight would not be pleasant.

Jenny's tone sharpened in response. "Marlena—"

"Love you. Bye."

I cut the call, deleted the messages from Vin, and raced to the bedroom.

There was no time to fix my hair, but I could get dressed at least. Clothing offered a layer of protection from whatever Michael meant to do to me. *I just have to last the night. One more night.* It shouldn't have sounded so daunting. Just in time, I presented myself in the great room, a little disheveled, but at least I wasn't lounging in a satin robe.

The front door opened, and I shuddered as Michael sang out, "Daddy's home."

31

Instinctively I hid my phone, tucking it into the pocket of my slacks. Michael Durst hadn't changed in the four months since he'd locked me away, physically anyway. His suit was sharply tailored, and his expensive haircut disguised the fact that his hairline was receding. His eyes narrowed on me, mouth tightening in a displeasure that pinched lines beside his nose. Money couldn't turn time back forever, and anger revealed the fact that his ageless veneer was simply that. His face seemed like a clay mask that would soon crack and chip away, revealing the monster within.

I probably should have greeted him, but I couldn't find the words. *I hate you* or *I wish you were dead* would earn me an immediate blow to the head, and I couldn't force myself to pretend I was happy to see him. Not after everything. There was a limit to how much—and how well—I could lie.

The silence burned, making me step back as he edged forward, arm upraised as if he'd knock me into next week. He took in my wet hair and shook his head with a curled lip.

"Nothing to say? You cost me *so* much money, you little bitch. Between that expensive nuthouse and deals falling through, what should I do with you?" His pale eyes slid up and down my body. "Even if I chopped you up for parts, I'd never recoup my losses."

"You said you'd never hurt me," I whispered.

"Things were different when I made that promise. You misrepresented yourself on more than one level."

"I never said I was an orphan."

Then he did slap me, hard enough to snap my head sideways and leave my ears ringing. "There's no point in arguing with a stupid animal. Your mother didn't even file birth certificates for half of her offspring."

I didn't try to explain how things were in the hills where we lived. People couldn't imagine anyone living like that in America unless they'd taken a vow of simplicity or had chosen to abstain from technology. Other than the Mennonites and the Amish, everyone had running water, electricity, and high-speed internet, right? Wrong.

With bile in my throat, I dropped to my knees. Not that he wouldn't hit me while I was on the floor, but I understood how he read that posture: complete submission. I might not be a worthy wife, but I was still an obedient one—as far as he knew. Bowing my head, I closed my eyes, thought about fucking Vin in the car earlier that day, and waited for Michael's fist to rain down. I didn't apologize because he'd said he was sick to death of me saying sorry, and I was done with false contrition too.

The house phone rang as he swung at me and I scrambled to answer it, desperate for any potential reprieve. "Durst residence, this is Marlena."

He stared at me with hell flickering in his eyes.

"Marlena, darling, it's been ages. Are you finally back from holiday?" Joanna Van Houten's rich, plummy accent filled my ear, and I brightened with a smile that was all relief.

Is that what he told you?

"I'm home now. I missed you, Joanna. Sorry that we … lost touch. How have you been?"

"I'd love to get together tomorrow, if you have time. Tea and a gallery visit perhaps? How does noon sound?"

I repeated her invitation, as if to confirm that I'd heard correctly, but I was really warning Michael that he couldn't touch me tonight. The beating he was itching to deliver would have to wait or he'd risk Joanna noticing what he'd done. Since she was as sharp as a ceramic knife, that would be a bad risk. I knew he was still hoping to rope her into another of his projects, though the first deal had fallen through, and I was equally determined that he wouldn't make a penny off this old lady.

"That's what I said, dear." She hesitated, lowering her voice. "Are you all right? If something's wrong and you can't speak freely, say 'Picasso.' I've been worried about you ever since you disappeared. Your husband said you turned your cell phone off to *rest*, but really, who does that these days?"

Bless you, Joanna. The evidence of foul play starts here.

"Yes, I do love Picasso," I said softly.

Her voice sharpened. "Should I send my people for you? I can get you out of there right now if you're in immediate danger."

Too late for that.

"Tomorrow at noon will be fine," I answered.

"If you're sure. Do be careful."

Gently, I replaced the cordless phone in the charger and turned to face Michael, whose clenched jaw meant he knew exactly what I'd done—and why. "You bought yourself a day," he bit out. "Enjoy that meeting with the Van Houten hag. You'll pay for disappointing me soon enough."

He's not even bothering to pretend now. Thankfully, he hadn't noticed the flowers yet. The card was in my pocket, nestled against my phone. With iron self-control, I swallowed fifty angry words, and they stung my throat like killer bees, until I could barely breathe for the fury and regret.

"Should I make you something to eat?"

Only one more day. One more.

"It's the least you can do, you hillbilly whore."

Dropping my gaze to the floor, I went into the kitchen to defrost a gourmet meal. I heard him bang into the bathroom and then I scrambled for our bedroom. The meds he'd used to fake my suicide attempt *had* to be in there somewhere. Michael was a light sleeper, and there was no way I'd be able to get out of bed in the night without him noticing. And I still needed to fiddle with his laptop and send payment to the contractor.

I opened drawer after drawer, heart beating like a hammer in my ears, until I found a small white bottle tucked behind his handkerchiefs. Diazepam, this must be it. I palmed the bottle as he stepped out of the shower and came in, half-dressed in a designer robe. His hair was wet and mussed, more obviously thinning when he was disheveled like this. He no longer looked ageless to me.

"What the hell are you doing?" he demanded.

"Do you want wine with your meal?"

"How can you possibly get dumber? I swear to God, every time you open your mouth, I want to punch you in it."

"Sorry. I'll open a bottle of white to go with the chicken in mushroom sauce."

He grunted in response, selecting a pair of pajamas. *That was too close.* Trembling, I got to the kitchen and leaned against the counter, gulping in deep breaths. If he caught me at this, I had no doubt that he'd murder me right there in the penthouse and then scrub the scene and move my body. Then he might not get caught, though I'd paved the way to suspicion through my conversation with Joanna.

It's not enough. I have to go all the way.

Working quickly, I uncorked an expensive sauvignon blanc, poured a glass, and plated his meal. *Need to be fast...* I crushed a couple of the sleeping pills and dissolved them in his wine glass. Not enough to hurt him, but he had to be *out* tonight.

Just in time, I stepped away from the counter and turned to the sink, hiding the pill bottle in my pocket, then straightened to wash my hands as Michael sauntered to the island to check what I'd provided. Since it was all cooked by a professional chef, he bitched about the way I'd arranged it and took his plate and glass to the study.

Shit, he better not pass out in there.

That kept me pacing anxiously for like half an hour, but in another ten minutes, he stumbled out with bleary eyes, still alert enough to glare at me. "Get my fucking dishes, bitch. And don't you dare set foot in the bedroom tonight. Dirty, worthless slut."

Yeah, like that's a punishment.

Inwardly, I rejoiced. *I'm so close.* Feigning servility, I trudged to the study with my shoulders slumped and got his dirty dishes, rinsed them, and set them in the dishwasher. I curled up on the white leather sofa with a magazine and waited. One hour. Two. When I checked on him and he was on his back, snoring with an open mouth, I squared my shoulders. *Go time.*

Before now, I'd only come in and out of Michael's study quickly. It was definitely his room, and it spoke to his personality, sharply modern without a shred of real elegance. The space was all shiny metal and black leather, irregular shelving, and no window treatment to soften so much stark glass.

His laptop was open; password protected, of course. That was my first obstacle. I checked around, but he didn't have the password written anywhere. *His phone,* I realized. He loved gadgets and efficient techy apps, so maybe he had a password manager. I tiptoed into the bedroom to find him on his side facing the door.

Did he wake up? Moving in his sleep might mean the Diazepam wasn't working well. Stumbling back, I crouched, trembling as I stared into the darkness.

Are his eyes open?

They weren't. I let out a shaky sigh. His snores came across as low and droning while I crawled across the floor and unplugged his cell with excruciatingly slow movements. I was sweating, though it wasn't hot in the condo, fear droplets trickling down my skin. Getting caught here would mean failure, not only for me but also for Jenny, Vin, and Ariella. They might mistake this plan for altruism or even martyrdom, but really, I just couldn't lose to Michael Durst.

He believed he was fucking unbeatable, and I'd die to prove him wrong.

Outside the bedroom, I stumbled to my feet, hurrying back to the study. I'd watched him unlock his phone, so I knew his pin; I'd just never dared touch it before. Once I got into his phone, I paged through his apps and sealed my mouth to silence an excited, triumphant sound. He had his laptop keyed to his phone, so when I activated the password app, they did a digital handshake, and then the home screen popped up.

I'm in.

Now I had access to his whole damn life. I'd worried about the money trail, and now I could make Michael foot the bill for his own downfall. Desperate laughter bubbled up inside me as I pulled up his offshore account, used his phone to authorize the transaction, and sent the money for my execution off to Switzerland.

His phone beeped with a notice about the funds transfer, but I deleted it, along with all the other notices generated by my use. Quickly I activated remote access on the laptop and watched as files popped into folders and then were hidden, because it made sense that Michael wouldn't put them in a folder marked MURDERING MAR-LENA on his desktop. It only took three minutes, but I kept a sharp eye on the door the whole time.

The condo was still dark and quiet.

I checked the laptop for any clues that would give me away, then put it into sleep mode. Now I just had to replace his phone, and my part was done. My nerves jangled with each step I took toward the bedroom. *He has to be sleeping. Two pills should have knocked him out for the whole night, right?* Still, my legs shook, and I had to drop onto my knees as I peered around the door frame.

No snoring. It was hard to make out much more than the shape of his body in the bed, still facing the open door. Breathing too fast through my nose, I edged closer on all-fours, nearly within reach of the plug now. His hand lashed out and grabbed me by the hair.

I swallowed a scream, waiting for the worst.

32

"**B**itch. Deborah. You bitch. I put you in the ground. You can't be here."

Jesus Christ. He's not awake. He's dreaming of Dee Neuman. My heart twisted when I imagined how scared she must have been. Maybe he made her feel desperate and nobody believed her, either. Bringing him down might help her rest in peace too. Both his past wives were my sisters in spirit, and I was fighting for them in these trenches.

I stilled, no longer simply trying to plug the phone in and leave. Maybe … could I …? I started recording, and breathed, "When you do terrible things, the ghosts cling to you. I'm all memory and bone now, and you will *never* be free of me."

"Deborah…" His voice came out strangled, and I wondered what hooks I'd sunk into his dreams. "Kill you again. Again. Think you're … so fucking smart."

"Admit what you did to me," I whispered. "Or I'll never let you rest."

"That fucking car ... loved it more than me. Broken, like I broke you."

The vehicle must have been long gone, sold for parts or scrap, but it sounded to me like he'd done something to it, causing the fatal accident. I hurt for Dee and for Leslie. *That's enough.*

Silently, I stopped the recording and texted it to Vin. He'd know what to do with it when the time came. With great care, I deleted that text, the recording, and then plugged in the phone, leaving it as it was before I started my mission. Next, I had to crawl along the floor to the drawer where I'd found the sleeping pills. This bottle needed to go back in before he woke. Moving this slow hurt my muscles, and I froze each time he inhaled sharply or his breathing shifted. Finally I eased the handkerchief drawer shut and inched backward. I barely breathed until I'd reached the cool marble of the hallway.

Shaky, I stumbled to the sofa and collapsed on it, swiping away the sweat beaded on my forehead. I sat there for a few moments until the shaking subsided. Michael liked the house austere, so there were no fluffy pillows or afghans, but I didn't expect much sleep anyway, it being the last night of my life and all.

This was pure self-indulgence, but I had to call Jenny back; she would be worried after the way I'd bailed before. I pulled out the cell phone Vin gave me and dialed her number. She answered on the second ring. "This is Jenny."

"Hey, it's me."

Her breath caught. "I hate you. Why are you calling me after hanging up like that? You had to know that I was imagining the worst."

There was really no defense, but maybe the truth would help. "I don't have much to say. Michael came home suddenly, and you know how that goes. But ... I wanted to hear your voice tonight."

Maybe for the last time.

"What am I supposed to say?" she finally whispered.

"Whatever you're feeling. I'll listen to anything."

"You're a terrible person. You don't think of anyone but yourself. I don't know if I can forgive you for that. You don't know ..." Jenny stopped talking then, and I heard her crying softly.

"I don't know what?"

"Anything. But I'm afraid it's too late to teach you."

"Are you giving up on me? I admit it, this is all my fault ... for thinking I could handle him and come out unscathed. I bit off more than I could chew."

"I know," Jenny whispered. "I love you, Marlena. I always have."

She cut the connection then. Probably just as well. I pulled my knees up to my chest and cried silently in the sleeves of my shirt. Though I'd showered the day before, so much stress and fear-sweat left me rank. My head hurt too much to sleep, and at first light, I went to the bathroom. Turned on the hot water and showered with meticulous care, exfoliating twice, deep conditioning my hair. Afterward, I combed out all the tangles and applied silky, expensive lotion to every inch of my skin. In my head, these were rituals for the dead, done with my own hands.

Before I left the bathroom, I tore the card that had come with the flowers into tiny bits, then flushed them away. *No proof. All roads lead to Michael Durst.*

He was still unconscious, sprawled in the bed like a drunken ogre. Dispassionately I considered killing him in his sleep, but that end was too easy. I wanted him to rot in prison, stripped of all pretension to grandeur. He would hate eating the same food as everyone else, being forced into manual labor wearing a baggy jumpsuit with a number on it.

I dressed in a simple gold sheath, no jewelry, and then I sat at the vanity to apply my makeup like I meant to go to war. Though I didn't always bother with all the steps, today I followed them one by one: primer first to fill in fine lines, then foundation and concealer. Next, I did the contouring, added blush, then my eye liner and shadow. Michael preferred lash extensions to mascara, so my eyes were done. I finished with my lips, a crushed rose matte that made me look as if I had just devoured a carton of fresh raspberries.

My face had been in magazines in Europe because Michael required that validation. Possessing a woman who was authenticated as desirable made him feel superior. He enjoyed walking with the "perfect" woman on his arm, basking in the envious glances. I understood all that, and I also knew that he was a monster. I didn't care why. There could be a thousand sad stories in his personal history; it didn't excuse anything he'd done.

Nothing could.

I poached two eggs while sautéing a few potatoes with herbs and sea salt, then I made a layered Greek yogurt parfait. Normally I didn't put this much care into his meals, but I wanted to leave traces for the police to find, proof that I had been a caring and devoted wife, taking good care of my husband, right up until he killed me. To complete the picture, I made fresh squeezed orange juice and set everything on the kitchen island. Finally, I turned on the dishwasher, though it wasn't nearly full.

Time to wash away the last of the evidence.

It was almost ten o'clock, much later than he normally slept. *I should have started drugging him ages ago.*

A few minutes later, he stumbled out of the bedroom, bleary, unshaven, and vaguely haunted. I hoped Dee was circling in his head like a shark, filling his brain with utter dread. *Do you dream of them often, Michael? Of the people you've killed?* I knew about Deborah, Leslie, and Bobby Ray Hudgens, though Bobby Ray wasn't much of a loss. How many more victims had my husband claimed?

There were no "good mornings" between us, no pretense that I was the princess any longer. That was natural. If a man believed he was the pinnacle of perfection himself, how could he accept anything less? Any woman would let him down, no matter how hard she tried, especially when his expectations kept shifting.

"I made breakfast," I said. "Help yourself."

He grunted in response. Every so often, he lashed me with pallid, angry eyes, those of a child denied a toy.

"Come right back after you meet with the crone," he ordered. "I'll be waiting, and I have eyes on you at all times, Marlena."

It won't matter. It had certainly been long enough for Vin's contact to set up. Nodding, I bussed his plate with a blank expression. "I'll do that."

Everything seemed distant and surreal as the time ticked away. I stood by like a maid while Michael slurped his breakfast, then he stomped off to his study, silently enraged by his inability to torture me as he wanted. *He won't notice anything, right?* If he could tell, somehow, that I'd used his computer, maybe through a keystroke logger, I was *so* screwed. Panic threatened but I choked it down.

Focus.

I stacked the dishes in the washer and went to style my hair. Odd to be primping under the circumstances. I settled on an elegant chignon, sophisticated without being too hard to achieve on my own.

"Make me some coffee before you leave." He stood in the doorway to the study in beige slacks and a cream sweater, sleeves rolled up to reveal hairy forearms.

"My pleasure." Every little thing he requested, I'd fulfill.

More evidence that I had been a good wife, helpful and obedient. And look how he repaid me. Public outcry should be immediate and powerful.

I delivered his requested beverage and said, "I'll be going soon."

"Remember what I said."

Come right back, eyes on you.

Finally, it was time—11:55 a.m. I collected my purse and stepped out of the penthouse, stopping when I recognized Edmund instead of Vin. The older man *never* worked days.

"Where's Vin?" I shouldn't care, shouldn't be curious, but a bad feeling bubbled up, anxiety laced with foreboding.

Edmund shrugged. "Boss gave him some time off for personal reasons. I don't ask."

Vin requested this? Or did Michael suggest it?

If Michael had sent Vin away, it probably meant he was planning to dispose of me ... and soon. If Vin had asked for leave, then maybe he didn't want to stick around for the final act. Just as well. It might get messy, as the wheels were already in motion.

"Understood." I set a brisk pace toward the lift and Edmund followed me, because that was his job.

Michael probably had other people tracking me as well. That would cease to be important very soon. My nails were plain and bare, courtesy of my time in Sherwood, and I noticed how strange they looked against the gold dress I'd chosen to die in. My hands were pale and ringless, fidgeting as we waited for the elevator. I had chosen not to wear any jewelry, nothing that might confuse the police or make them think, even for a second, that this could be a crime of opportunity.

When I stepped in, Edmund did too. He didn't speak as the lift dropped, and it felt like my elegant heels weighed a hundred pounds more with each step I took across the lobby toward the front doors. The sunlight seemed odd and wrong, too bright, and everyone's faces twisted into insincere smiles, as if they all *knew.* Somehow I beat the panic back; I bundled it beneath my heart and kept walking.

"Good afternoon, Mrs. Durst." The doorman greeted me with a smile, opening the way for me with a flourish. "Lovely weather we have today, isn't it?"

Just outside, I could see the clear blue sky, sun shining and only a scattering of nimbus clouds, fluffy as cotton balls. Judging by how the people on the sidewalk were dressed, it must be warm. I admired a woman in a white sundress and cherry red shoes. She was holding hands with a pretty girl, smiling like they had all the time in the world.

"It is, yes." *A good day to die, as they say.* "Goodbye, Mr. Pettigrew." Maybe my tone sounded strange or final, because the doorman's smile dropped as I walked past him.

I recognized Joanna's car parked in front of the building, a sleek Rolls. Her driver opened the door for her, and she got out, waving with a warm smile. I took two steps toward her—didn't see an attacker with a gun—and didn't *hear* the shot either, but my chest burst with white-hot agony and I toppled.

The last thing I heard was Joanna Van Houten screaming my name.

33

"**M**rs. Durst. Can you hear me?"

At first the voice was only an echo, but it got louder and more insistent as someone lifted my eyelid and shone a light straight in. I flinched and moved my fingers—someone was holding on to them in a desperate grip.

With effort, I lifted my eyelids, battled through my lashes for the room to swim into focus. It was too bright, but when I processed what I was seeing, I realized Michael was clasping my hand in a fair facsimile of desperate grief while Joanna sat in a chair near the window. Jenny was pacing by the door, and the person fiddling with my eyes seemed to be a doctor, judging by the white coat. He had a whole crew with him, actually, all hovering in my private room.

I'm alive.

"Wh ... what ..." I couldn't get the words out.

"You were shot, Mrs. Durst. Your survival is something of a miracle."

I made some sound, groggy and queasy from the anesthetic, and tried to beg him to elaborate with a tilt of my head. "Eh?"

"Did you know that you have dextrocardia?" he asked. I was in no state to answer, and he went on. "It's a rare condition, meaning your heart is inverted, facing right rather than left. If not for that, the shot would have killed you instantly. Thankfully, the emergency team came quickly and we stabilized you for surgery. You've lost a lot of blood, but you should be fine ... in time."

"Thank—"

Glancing at Joanna, I pulled my hand out of Michael's grasp and reached for her. She hurried to my side, staring at my husband until he got up reluctantly and yielded his spot. She took my hand.

My throat hurt, so dry. I managed to rasp, "Stay, don't let ..."

Awareness sharpened her gaze and she leveled a dark look on Michael, now standing beside the window. "I understand, my dear. I won't leave you."

With the last of my strength, I held on to Joanna Van Houten and prayed she would protect me. Jenny and Vin would want to, but it took power and resources to stand against Michael Durst, at least until the investigation proceeded to a certain point and the charges against him became irrefutable. I couldn't stay awake any longer, whatever might be happening. My eyes drifted shut.

The next time I roused, it was dark and Joanna was the only one in the room. She offered me a sip of water through a straw, and then I could ask, "What's happening?"

"You spent three hours in surgery, one day in intensive care, and yesterday you were moved to a private room. You roused briefly and since then, you've slept for almost eighteen hours. How do you feel?"

"Like I've been shot." I tried to smile but the effort exhausted me. "Where's Michael?" It wasn't like him to leave me unattended.

Maybe he doesn't have a choice.

She hesitated, seeming to weigh her words. "I don't want to shock you. It seemed to me that your relationship was … troubled, but things are …"

"I can handle the truth."

Joanna nodded. "Your husband is being interrogated, Marlena. A pair of detectives came. From what I gathered, it seems they think he had something to do with the shooting."

Tears filled my eyes. Now it was time to play this for all it was worth. I let out a shuddering breath, closing my eyes so the droplets squeezed through my lashes. *Pure pathos.* "I thought he'd succeed in killing me before anyone noticed."

"My dear, what has he *done* to you?"

"I'm ashamed to tell you. I let it happen. I didn't—"

"This isn't your fault," Joanna said firmly. "No matter what he did, you didn't deserve it. Tell me everything. I'll help you in any way I can."

I told the truth then, and it was delicious. Her eyes held a too-bright shine as she heard how he'd tormented me. When I got to the part about Bobby Ray, she took my hands and cried with me. I suspected she would have hugged me like a child if I hadn't been hooked up to wires and tubes. Instead she pressed my hand between hers.

"It wasn't only me," I said between pitiful sniffs. "I'm his *third* wife. Why didn't anyone care what happened to them? Is it because he chose poor girls and groomed them to be suitable, then threw them away when he was bored?"

"Probably." But the grim line of her mouth spoke of her determination that he wouldn't get away with it this time.

She could apply pressure for me. Make sure Michael didn't bribe the right people or pull strings to get charges dropped. How *delicious* that his insistence that I meet and become close to her would ensure his downfall.

"I have proof. A friend took a picture of the bruises when he had me ... punished."

"For being raped as a young girl." There was no feigning the revulsion in her expression. "I wish you'd told me sooner. I suspected all wasn't well when you warned me, somewhat obliquely, not to trust him, and then you disappeared ... if only I had known. You could have come to me. I would have hidden you."

"That wouldn't have saved my friends or my family. I had to stay. If I ran, I was afraid he would go after them."

Now, under police scrutiny, he couldn't afford to make such vicious moves. Michael would be frantic, trying to prove his innocence. Sheer delight bubbled through me, effervescent as champagne. He must be livid over being blamed for this. Since he'd gotten away with murder before, he wouldn't have left any evidence behind of setting up my shooting if he'd actually done so.

"I understand," she said heavily.

"That's not even all of it. You mentioned that I vanished ... he put sleeping pills in my wine and told them that I tried to kill myself. He wanted me on record as unstable and suicidal." Remembering how helpless I'd felt when I woke in the hospital, it wasn't hard to cry, fat, hot tears that scalded my cheeks.

"That way, if he killed you later and made it look like suicide, nobody would question it." Joanna clenched a fist against her linen trousers. "From what you've said, it sounds as if he did exactly that with his second wife."

I nodded. "I think so. The first wife died in a car accident, but I suspect he had something to do with that as well. I didn't have the resources to dig into the incident, but I think he built his empire on Deborah Neuman's bones."

"What do you mean?"

"Insurance payout. It wouldn't surprise me if his business has hit a rough patch and he needs an influx of capital. That might be why he tr-tried to ..." Bowing my head, I didn't finish the sentence, and she stroked my hair gently, like my older sister used to, like my mother never did.

I miss you, Dee. Everything I'm doing, it's for you.

My sister never liked the nicknames Deb or Debbie. She preferred the dignity of Deborah, though she let me call her Dee because I started calling for her before I could even talk properly. She looked after us better than anyone. I remembered how she would make us corn cakes from almost nothing and serve them with honey stolen from the neighbor's hive. She'd come back all stung up, but never empty-handed. I hadn't let myself remember any of the good times for so long, fearing it would weaken my resolve. But I only had to picture her dying terrified and alone for my determination to snap back into place.

"I'll make sure to mention that to the police," Joanna said. "It might have more credibility coming from an impartial observer. In these cases, they often discount everything the wife says."

Exactly my problem, before.

Nodding, I said, "I tried to tell the doctor at Sherwood, but she didn't believe me. Maybe she would now."

"Hard to argue with a bullet in the chest," Joanna said gently.

"Could I borrow your phone? I want to show you ..." More fuel to fire the older woman's wrath. I wanted her to see me as a bird with a broken wing, someone she needed to protect at all costs.

"Of course." She unlocked it and passed it over.

I called up my secret, free email account and dug through layers of spam to find the message Vin had sent from the cabin in the woods. Two vivid, vicious snapshots of my naked back in all its damaged glory—as I peered closer, I recognized the scar beneath my shoulder blade. Before, I'd thought they'd argue that this could be anyone, but this proved beyond a shadow of a doubt that it was me.

"Here. This is how I looked after he murdered Bobby Ray Hudgens. He hid me away at some secret property he owns until I healed enough to be seen in public again."

Joanna took the phone, but my words didn't prepare her for the reality. Her hands shook as she studied the pictures. "He's an animal."

"He didn't do it himself, but he was in the room. Watching."

She shivered, rubbing her arms down her well-tailored blazer. "That's even worse. More calculated than the drunken lout who swings his fist in rage. The police must see these photos straightaway. One of the detectives left her business card with me. I'll forward them to her with your permission."

"Please do. Hiding the truth will only help him at this point."

I yawned then, and Joanna pulled up my covers. "Get some rest. I'll stay with you tonight, and in the morning I'll hire some guards."

"Won't the police make sure I'm safe?" That was a guileless question, one I already knew the answer to.

Her gaze softened and she rested a beringed hand on my arm, gently. "They can only do so much, whereas I can afford to keep you safe for as long as it's required."

"Did they catch the shooter?" I asked.

"Not yet, dear."

With a grim expression, she settled into the comfortable chair by the window and started texting. I could hear the doors slamming on Michael Durst with each character she typed, and I went to sleep smiling.

In the morning, Detectives Hunter and Wilson arrived right as I was finishing my breakfast: delicious Jell-O and broth. The nurse assured me that I could soon progress to white toast and soup if I played my cards right. I set down my spoon and silently thanked Joanna for washing my face first thing this morning; she'd also brushed my hair, so I didn't look like a desperate mess for this interview.

Joanna touched my arm. "I'll take this opportunity to head home for a shower and a change of clothes. The guards I hired will stay with you, Marlena. Don't worry, I'll be back this evening. Detectives." She gave a regal nod on her way out.

"Good morning, Mrs. Durst," Detective Hunter said, perching beside my bed.

She was a tan woman with curly brown hair carelessly caught back in a ponytail. Her outfit was pure JCPenney and her attitude was no nonsense, from her lack of lipstick to her sensible sneakers ideal for chasing down perps.

"Marlena, please. I don't want to be called Mrs. Durst anymore."

Her eyes flickered with what might be sympathy. "We're here to take your statement if you're up to it, ma'am."

The partner, Detective Wilson, was a tall Black man with a shaved head, well-dressed in a blazer and designer eyewear. I guessed he got a lot of play with having such a handsome face and bright smile, like the one he was offering as he took the vacant seat by the window. That must mean Detective Hunter was set to ask the questions. Under the circumstances, that made sense.

"I suppose I have to be. What do you want to know?"

"Let's start with your relationship with Michael Durst." She went for the facts first, confirming our relationship, the date we married, and basics like that.

"That's all correct."

"Could you tell me about the pictures Mrs. Van Houten sent? She alleged that he has a history of abusive treatment, but I need to hear the story in your words."

Last night with Joanna, that was the practice run. This was the real deal. If the police didn't find me credible, they might not dig into

Michael hard enough to find the evidence I'd left. The fact that they were investigating him was a good start, but I needed him painted guilty as sin in the press and in the courtroom.

I spoke softly, head bowed. "I first met Michael when I was really young..."

34

At first, the detectives seemed skeptical—and even I had to admit, the story was outlandish—but I had details to spare, facts they could check. They came to the hospital four times that week to request further information on something I said. I couldn't judge how the investigation was going from my hospital bed, so I was glad when the doctor said I could be discharged if I took it easy. Full recovery would take months, he said, and I should come in for regular checks.

Joanna stood by the door with my bag, two large British guards called Clive and Nigel just outside. I hesitated. This room was secure, and I hadn't seen Michael since the first time I woke, but that didn't mean I was *safe*. Vin and Jenny might not be, either.

"I won't let anything happen to you," the older woman promised. "We'll go to my brownstone and you can stay with me while this gets resolved. No arguments. I won't hear of you going home."

"No, I don't want to do that either. It's just ... this doesn't feel like it's over. I don't feel ... free."

"I know. Trauma like this doesn't just evaporate, and it will take time for you to heal. I'll make sure you have somewhere safe to do that."

"Why?" I whispered.

She was going to so much trouble for someone she hadn't known that long, and Michael had taught me to be wary of what looked like unwarranted kindness. Joanna stepped closer and took my hand.

"Do you think I was born to old Dutch money? I was a country girl from Volendam who caught the eye of a prominent banker. When he decided he had to have me, I was only fifteen. I didn't have anyone to protect me then ... and I went through *everything* alone. Until the day he died." The grim look in her eyes told me there was a story, maybe one that resembled my own. "Do you understand now?"

"I think so."

She held my hand a moment longer, and I was conscious of the knots in her knuckles and papery delicacy of her skin. Her rings scraped my skin, a tangible reminder that her appearance was deceptive, and that she had power and influence to burn.

To my surprise, I spotted Jenny pacing in the lobby downstairs as the lift doors opened. She ran to me as soon as we stepped out of the elevator. Joanna and the guards followed at a more sedate pace, politely glancing away while we hugged, a careful sideways hold that allowed for my tender chest.

"Thank you for surviving," she whispered.

I tried to smile. "Save that for when this is *truly* over." I turned to Joanna and asked, "Is it all right for Jenny to come with us?"

She nodded.

Jenny wrapped her arm around my shoulders, letting me lean on her in the progression from the lobby to the Rolls, currently double-parked out front. We'd already completed the paperwork and the British guards acted like we were presidential candidates, clearing a path to the exit, checking outside before herding us to the car. The taller one, Clive I thought, shielded me with his body in case there was a second attempt on my life.

And honestly, that might not have been paranoia. I'd fired the first shot in this war, but that didn't mean Michael would stand still. Imagining his impotent rage put a smile on my face as I slid into the backseat. The car was more than roomy enough for the three of us; that left the guards riding up front, on the other side of the glass partition.

"We're safe in here," Joanna said, as the car pulled away from the curb. "The body is reinforced, and the glass is bulletproof."

Jenny stared. "Are you expecting to drive through a war zone, or do you have terrifying enemies...?"

Self-deprecating smile. "Everyone has enemies, my dear. Such precautions are fairly common among my set."

"Thank you for helping Marlena," Jenny said quickly. "I've known she was in trouble for a while, maybe even before she did, but I wasn't sure what to do for her."

Joanna glanced out the window, avoiding both our eyes. "It's my pleasure. I think she would agree that we've become friends, so it's the least I can do."

The least would be nothing—or feigning ignorance of my situation—but I could tell she was being modest, swiping away the credit like dust from a shelf. Since Joanna wasn't in this for accolades, I did wonder if she had some other axe to grind with Michael. I didn't fool myself that her boundless generosity stemmed completely from sisterhood and affection. Possibly she remembered how he'd wanted to use her, and she didn't seem like the sort of woman who took kindly to that.

A fifteen-minute drive brought us from the hospital to her brownstone on the Upper East Side. Clive and Nigel checked obsessively before letting us out of the car, then they rushed us inside, keeping their bodies between us and potential harm.

Inside, I saw the difference between modern style and classic old-world charm. The antiques in Joanna's home must have been priceless, rugs so exquisite I was afraid to walk on them. Even the ceramics and glassware scattered on tables and shelves looked irreplaceable.

"Have a seat. I'll ask the housekeeper to prepare a nice tea."

I settled at the edge of the sofa, conscious that I was dependent on Joanna in nearly the same way I'd been on Michael. Pissing her off probably wouldn't get me beaten, though. And until I ended things with him permanently, I would never be safe, never be able to lead a normal life. His shadow would always loom over my shoulder.

"You're pale," Jenny said.

"I just want them to lock him up already. Have you heard anything about the case?" Grabbing Jenny's hand, I glanced between her and Joanna, desperate for answers or information.

"You gave them a lot to investigate," Joanna said with a sigh. "Such things take time. I'm more afraid that animal will flee the country when it becomes clear he's about to be punished for his crimes."

"I can see him running," Jenny said.

I clenched my fists. "That can't happen, or I'll never be safe."

"They're not supposed to divulge details," Joanna said softly, "but according to my sources, he's been brought in for interrogation twice. He seems to think this will all blow over if he lawyers up and keeps denying everything."

Jenny smiled. "That's not how evidence works."

"Indeed not." Joanna tapped her nails as if considering a potential revelation, then appeared to decide. "My sources also tell me that the good detectives have applied for a warrant. I think that request will be granted shortly."

I hope so.

The housekeeper carried in a silver tray laden with delicate china cups rimmed in gilt and small plates piled with dainty sandwiches and tiny fairy cakes. "Here you are, Mrs. Van Houten. Would you like anything else?"

"No, thank you, Britta. That will be all."

Joanna poured the black tea with a grace that made it hard for me to imagine her living in the Dutch countryside, even if it had been so long ago. As if she read my mind, she smiled faintly. "You can't picture me milking a cow, can you? I assure you, I was quite adept."

"How did you know?" I asked.

"I'm good at reading people. Here, Jenny. Please, help yourself. And know that you're welcome to remain as my guest as long as you'd like."

"Thank you, but I'll just stay tonight. I have to work tomorrow."

Eating and drinking shouldn't have exhausted me that much, but by the time I ate two little sandwiches and drank half a cup, I wanted to lie down. Thankfully, Joanna read that in my face too.

"Why don't you help her to her room, Jenny? I think she's at her limit."

She showed us to a pretty bedroom at the end of the first-floor hallway. Decorated in white and blue, the space was bright but tranquil. The art on the walls were all original masterpieces; the casual extravagance felt shocking. Someone had already set my shoulder bag and purse in the Queen Anne chair near the window.

"I hope you'll be comfortable here." With a little wave, Joanna shut the door, leaving me alone with Jenny.

Jenny touched my cheek with a shaking hand, her eyes shining like two dark stars. "I may never forgive you for this."

"For what?"

"You know what."

I kissed her, both because I wanted to and because it was the best way to stop this conversation. Her lips were soft and plush, and she tasted of lemon cake and milk tea. She couldn't lean into me because of my chest, but she did cup my face in her hands, stroking my cheeks. I ran my fingers through her hair and rested my head against hers once I finally broke the kiss.

"You think sex will fix this? How could you—"

I set two fingers against her mouth, glancing around the room with cautious eyes. Right now, I might be relying on Joanna Van Houten, but that didn't mean I trusted her. She might sell me to the highest bidder given half a chance.

I wouldn't say anything within her house that would contradict the story I'd told Detectives Hunter and Wilson. Not even to Jenny. Carefully, I got my phone out of my purse and typed in the notes app:

We can't speak freely here.

Once she nodded, I erased the words and stepped gingerly over to the bed. I hadn't been feigning exhaustion, as my pain meds were starting to wear off. Jenny hurried off to get some water so I could take a pill, then she curled up in bed with me.

Her hair smelled like herbs and wildflowers, a new brand of shampoo. I put my face in the curve of her neck, breathing her in. Such soft skin, her pulse quickening because I was close. I wanted her, but my body wasn't up to it, so I settled for kissing her neck, the spot behind her ears, and a shiver ran through her.

"Are you trying to turn me on? That's unfair when you can't finish what you start."

"Just a little thing called affection. Maybe you've heard of it?"

"Vaguely, from a distance. I have a bad habit of falling for people who leave me alone and make me worry about them constantly."

"I'm sorry. I *am*."

She spooned up against me from behind with a faint sigh. "Fine," she whispered. "I understood, way back, when your revenge was only an unlikely long shot. I've been waiting for you forever, it seems like. I can wait a little longer."

"You promise?"

"No need to ask."

We slept until early morning. I woke to the sound of rain plinking against the windowpane. Jenny was still holding me, just as Vin had at the cabin. I wondered how he was doing, but I couldn't call him. There couldn't be a whisper of connection between us while the police sifted through the garbage of my life. I could call Ariella, though, just to be sure she was all right. I'd found a message from her, left months ago in my old phone's voicemail. She'd called when I was locked up in Sherwood and she'd just bought a phone in the UK.

Michael had a long reach and connections in Croatia. I'd sent my sister on a European tour and I had no idea where she was.

But that was for the best. I didn't want Ariella mixed up in this.

I shifted, flinching, as I reached for my phone. The movement tugged at my stitches. Jenny half-roused, mumbling "Are you up?" But she drifted right back off.

As I unlocked the phone to call my little sister, a message pinged in from an unfamiliar number. *This isn't over, bitch. I MADE you. I OWN you. I decide whether you live or die. And I will make you wish you were dead before we're through.*

Wait for me. I'm coming for you.

35

I bit down on my knuckle to keep from frightening Jenny. This was the clean phone Vin had acquired for me. If Michael had this number—well, it meant terrible things for Vin, and maybe for his family as well. Unlike Michael, I cared about other people, and that translated to weakness he could use.

Shivering, I slipped out of bed and got Jenny's phone. I didn't want to reveal a personal link between Vin and myself that the police could use as a motive. If they found out I'd cheated on Michael, that could change the tenor of the investigation. It would get even worse if they found out how long I'd been with Jenny. People never seemed to care if women of dubious purity got hurt; public opinion might flip on me and I'd become some Jezebel who deserved to be shot. With a bitter chill, I remembered how mass murderers had been excused because some woman refused to date them.

I knew Jenny's pin because she never changed it; always my birthday, and this phone was no exception. There was no reason why my single friend couldn't call my husband's driver, right? No shame in that game.

But no matter how many times I called, no matter how long the phone rang, Vin didn't pick up. After being shunted to voicemail twenty times, I gave up. But I couldn't sleep. It was hard to say goodbye when Jenny went to work.

I was a groggy mess over breakfast, and it took two coats of concealer to make me look human enough for the visit to the police station. Joanna was livid about the text message. When I showed it to her, a vein popped out of her head.

"I haven't heard anything about an arrest," she snapped, slamming a priceless teacup onto the matching saucer. "This should be all over the papers by now. By God, I'll leak the story myself if I must."

Clive and Nigel escorted us into the precinct; so much noise and people rushing around that I took a step back. One of them braced me and I steadied. No retreat. Joanna grabbed a uniformed officer with a hand that distinctly resembled a claw tipped with ruby red polish. "Where is Detective Hunter?"

She spoke with enough force to make the officer stammer, but we got directions to their department and she swept me along like a tidal wave. I wanted to push this as much as she did, but I also wanted to convey how frightened I was. It wouldn't do for the police to realize that I'd passed the point of fear long ago, and that I lived somewhere much more desperate these days.

The detectives were interviewing someone when we stormed into their space. Joanna slammed my phone on the desk. "What the hell are you two doing? Michael Durst already tried to murder this woman once. Why is he still free to threaten her? I swear to God, you won't be satisfied until she's actually *dead*."

Detective Wilson got to his feet with a placating smile. "It seems you're angry, ma'am. Let's calm down and have a respectful conversation, shall we?"

"Read this and see if you still feel so relaxed," she snapped.

The detective accepted the cell phone and skimmed the message. He leveled a serious gaze on me. "You think this came from your husband?"

Joanna's frown deepened. "Is anyone else trying to kill her? Do your job properly, detective!"

"I don't know who else it could be," I said. "It didn't come from Michael's usual phone, but I'm sure he's smart enough to know that's easily traced."

Detective Hunter rose, offering me a warm smile. "I'm glad to see you're out of the hospital. We'll definitely look into this, but the odds are good that whoever sent that used a disposable phone."

I hadn't paid much attention to the woman sitting in front of the desk, but when she rose, I recognized Dr. Bowers at once. She reached for my hand, then hesitated. I answered that unspoken question by meeting her halfway. I hoped whatever she had to say would motivate the detectives.

"I'm so sorry. You told me. Back then, you *told* me what he was like, but I—"

"It's not your fault. Michael is so devious, and he set the scene perfectly. I understood then why you thought I was delusional. Honestly, I was happy to be away from him for a while. You kept me safe at Sherwood."

Dr. Bowers said quietly, "Looking back, I should have realized this is why you didn't want to go home."

I didn't know if she'd come in voluntarily or if the detectives had called her. Either way, she was corroborating my account of being drugged and sent to a facility against my will. "You tried your best to help me within the parameters of your understanding. It's really not your fault that you didn't realize Michael is—"

"A monster," she finished.

Glad you said it so I don't have to.

I turned to the detectives then. "Have you checked into the Bobby Ray Hudgens case? And what about his first two wives? There's a lot to unpack, I know, but *please* don't let him buy his way out of this."

The cops exchanged an uncomfortable look, so I guessed Michael must be applying pressure from above somehow. Then Detective Wilson said politely, "We can't talk about ongoing investigations, ma'am. We do take this matter seriously and we'll pursue all leads until we have sufficient—"

Just then, another officer rushed up. "Wilson, the warrant you've been waiting on just came in. Should we head over to the Durst place?"

Yes.

"He's probably already scrubbing the evidence," Joanna said bitterly.

It took all my self-control to keep from smiling. No doubt Michael absolutely would be destroying his hard drive if he had any inkling what was on there. With the chaos of the last week, he might not have noticed the wire transfer either. Now that the police had clearance, they could dig away and find all the clues.

For me, the crime was attempted murder. Even better if I could hang deaths on him as well. Life in prison without parole? That was a fitting punishment.

The officers exploded into motion, leaving us with Dr. Bowers. She stared after them with angry eyes. "I hope they nail his ass to the wall," she said.

"Me too." That was maybe the biggest understatement of my life.

I wished I could go watch it all unfold, but that would seem suspicious and I doubted they'd let me into the condo anyway, even if I claimed I needed to collect my belongings. Joanna set a gentle hand on my shoulder.

"We've done what we can for today. I'll make a few calls this afternoon, see if I can apply some pressure for a quick and satisfactory conclusion."

"I can't thank you enough for everything you've done. Lately it feels like you've become my fairy godmother."

"Don't accuse me of that, my dear. Her gifts were limited ... and they dwindled to nothing when the clock struck midnight."

As we headed for the exit, a disheveled man in his forties with dark hair and light brown skin stepped into our path. "I couldn't help but hear about your case, Mrs. Durst. I'm a crime reporter, and this seems like a story I shouldn't miss. Do you have time to answer a few questions?"

Pressure from the media would help. Without waiting for Joanna's input, I said, "I'd like to see your press credentials first."

He showed me his badge, which I guessed gave him license to loiter at police stations waiting for something interesting to pop. "Will you get a cup of coffee with me and answer some questions?" he asked. "There's a café nearby."

Joanna caught my eye and nodded emphatically. Since she'd mentioned leaking the story herself, I gathered that she wanted coverage sooner rather than later. This was the least I could do, considering everything she'd done for me, and this served my aims as well.

"Certainly," I said.

The reporter led the way, and I followed him out of the precinct. Joanna's stately elegance led people to clear a path for her, to where Clive and Nigel were waiting by the front doors.

"Are you sure you have time to shepherd me around like this?" I asked.

She smiled. "Definitely, my dear."

"I feel bad. You must have other things to do."

Her smile gained layers, and her eyes narrowed in the afternoon sunlight. "Right now, this is at the top of my agenda."

I wondered why that would be the case, but I didn't argue. Joanna must know her own schedule best, so I just nodded. The reporter had quickly outpaced us, since Joanna did move like an elderly person and was wearing heels. He'd taken the opportunity to grab a table and already had a cup of coffee cooling in front of him. At Joanna's whispered instruction, Clive went to fetch us both some tea, while Nigel assumed the guard position at a table nearby.

As we joined him, the journalist slid a business card across the table. "I'm Manny Rodriguez. Freelancer. If you look me up, you can verify where my work has been featured."

Joanna signaled to Nigel, who silently did the due diligence, and then he offered a nod as if to say "he's legit."

"Nice to meet you, Mr. Rodriguez. What did you want to know?"

Clive delivered our tea, enforcing a pause, then sat down with Nigel.

Rodriguez asked, "Is it true your husband is being investigated as a suspect? I already know that you were shot last week."

"It is, true, yes. The detectives left with a search warrant a little while ago."

He made a note. "Why do you think your husband wants to harm you?"

I'd already told the police everything. Well, almost everything.

"It's a long story, and quite painful. If you'll bear with me, I'll tell you what I know."

It took almost half an hour to go over it with Manny Rodriguez, and he had half an hour's worth of extra questions, many of them like what the detectives had asked. But his eyes were glowing by the time

I got finished. I suspected he thought this would be a career-making story if he could verify half of what I'd told him.

"He *really* found fake adoptive parents to improve your social pedigree?" His skepticism was obvious.

"There's a paper trail if you follow it. I'm an American, but I wasn't born in Croatia. My father isn't a diplomat. In fact, I've never even met him."

"If this stuff is true, that's some next-level egomania," Rodriguez said.

"Trust me, I'm aware. I've lived with him. And barely survived it."

His look softened slightly. "For what it's worth, I'm sorry. It sounds like you've been through some shit. Can I call you if I have any further questions?"

In answer, I took a picture of the business card he'd given me, then wrote my number on the back, the clean cell phone Vin had gotten me. A pang went through me, fresh fear that arrowed straight to my heart.

It must have shown in my expression, because Joanna asked, "What's the matter?" just as Rodriguez said, "Are you all right, Mrs. Durst?"

"No. I'm scared to death for people who've tried to help me." I picked up my phone, weighing my options.

Then I decided that calling Vin in front of witnesses played better than a surreptitious midnight summons. The phone rang six times, then dumped me in voicemail. "Would you try?" I asked Joanna.

"Of course. What's the number?"

I showed her the screen, my leg jumping the whole time. Imagining Vin tied up and beaten like Bobby Ray Hudgens brought me to tears. If he could have, he would have called me or Jenny back by now. She would have told me if she'd heard from him. Deep in my heart, I knew—I'd known since last night—that the only way Michael could have my new number was because he'd taken Vin and turned his place upside down to find it.

"What's happening here?" Rodriguez wanted to know.

"Vin Rivera was my driver and bodyguard. He worked for Michael. Over time, he started to feel guilty over the way Michael treated me."

The reporter made a note. "He's the one who looked after you, post-beating?"

"Yes, but now I can't get in touch with him. I haven't heard from him in over a week, or before I was shot even. The night guard was on duty when I left the condo that day, and he said Vin had taken some time off, but now—"

"Now you're worried that your husband has him," the reporter finished.

36

"I'm afraid he's been hurt for helping me," I said. "What should I do?"

Rodriguez was clicking away on his phone, but he glanced up, looking between Joanna and me. "You want my advice? Tell the cops. They need to search for him, but if it's already been over a week..." He didn't finish the sentence, but I knew.

Vin might already be dead.

I remembered his hands on me at the cabin, how hard I'd worked to seduce him. It didn't seem right that he was paying for that while I'd survived a shot to the chest. I stood, not waiting for Joanna.

"If you have more questions, call me. You can speak with Dr. Bowers at Sherwood as well. We need to go back to the police station. I'm worried about Vin."

"Now I am as well," Joanna said.

I needed to check on my sister. Having Ariella and Vin out of contact had me so scared, I could hardly think. Ariella didn't pick up, so I

238

left a voice message, and I also sent an urgent text pleading with her to ring back as soon as she got it. Though I'd just seen Jenny, I called her to check in.

She, at least, answered her phone, sounding cheerful. "What's up? Are you okay?"

I smiled. "Don't worry about me. I'm concerned about *you*."

"I'm not the one married to a murderous narcissist." Trust Jenny to joke, even at a time like this.

"Still, have you noticed anything strange? Anyone following you?"

"So far, so good. But I'll be careful."

That let me breathe a little easier, but I wouldn't rest peacefully until I heard about Vin and Ariella. The threatening text from Michael meant I had to risk mentioning Vin to the cops, even if it jeopardized my plan. The detectives still weren't back, so I made my report to a different officer. He listened to my concerns about Vin, and he seemed to take them seriously.

"I'll inform Detective Wilson that Vin Rivera may be in danger. You said he bought you a cell phone? And he wanted to help you get away from your husband?"

"There was a limit to what he could do for me. Michael threatened him, showed him pictures of his younger sisters."

The officer clenched his jaw. "The more I hear about this asshole, the happier I'll be when we lock him up. Seems like some people think money means they can do whatever the hell they want."

"I think that's the case," I said softly. "Michael *does* seem to believe he's above facing consequences, no matter what."

"We'll see," the cop muttered.

"You've already done too much today." Joanna set her hand beneath my elbow. "You'll make yourself ill, Marlena. The doctor said you need to rest."

Vin...

Losing strength in my legs, I let her help me out to the car. I'd done my best to make Vin care about me at the cottage, and now—I sighed, resting my cheek on the window as we drove back to Joanna's brownstone. My chest hurt and my heart ached. I barely made it to my room before passing out.

I woke well after dark, and the place was quiet. Joanna wasn't one to turn on music or television for background noise, so when I opened the door and stepped out of my room, I heard her voice at once. It was too late for her to be talking to one of the maids, so I crept closer quietly, not wanting to disturb her if she had a late guest.

"That's right. The article will likely be published tomorrow, and Durst stocks will drop. When they bottom out, start buying."

Well, that explained everything. I hadn't believed for a moment that Joanna Van Houten was sheltering me out of pure kindness. When she turned to find me in the doorway, she didn't display even a flicker of guilt. Instead she gave me a warm smile.

"You don't mind, do you, my dear? It's only business."

"Do I mind that you're using my personal pain for profit? Not at all. I did wonder what your hidden motive was, so it's a relief that this is the catch, and that it's not worse. I don't care what happens to Michael's company."

"I'll manage it well," she assured me.

On some level, it tickled me that she would be scooping up his life's work. After all, he'd wanted me to soften her up for some scheme of his. Maybe this could be considered poetic justice.

"I meant it when I said I'm not interested."

Joanna took that at face value. "If you say so. The housekeeper left a plate for you in the microwave. You should eat and take your medicine."

She was right; I wouldn't recover without taking care of myself, but I didn't have much appetite. I picked at the grilled chicken, mushroom risotto, and green salad, then finished with bottled spring water and my pain meds. It was past midnight, and I remembered my modeling days when I'd rather be beaten with a stick than eat this late.

I went back to my room after that. Tried calling Ariella again. Still no answer. Anxiety and dread pooled in my stomach, so my dinner felt like a huge knot. Vin didn't pick up either, not that I expected him to. Curling up in bed, I thought about texting Jenny, but she was probably asleep.

At first, I took the pain in my stomach as a physical manifestation of fear, but when the cramp hit so hard that I rolled out of bed, I got the message. If it hurt this much, even with the pain meds I'd taken, there must be something terribly wrong. Moaning, I crawled toward the door, and it took all my strength to turn the handle.

The brownstone was so big and dark, and I had no idea where Joanna's room was. A low light suggested someone might be in the parlor, but I couldn't make it that far. My mouth tasted of metal and my breath smelled oddly of garlic. I tried to stand and tipped over a table, smashing a vase that likely cost more than my net worth. It was getting hard to breathe, and I purged the contents of my stomach in a wet splatter. The sound of someone running toward me was the last thing I heard.

———

For the second time, I woke in the hospital with Joanna beside me. Her face was drawn, makeup nonexistent, and she looked *old* in a way that she hadn't before. "I'm so sorry, my dear. I failed you."

"What …" My throat hurt so much.

"You were poisoned. On *my* watch. Britta had already disposed of your leftovers, but the results of your blood test were conclusive."

Her house was like a fortress. I wanted to ask *how* that had happened, but Michael had gotten his point across. If he could get to me inside Joanna's compound, then I wasn't safe anywhere. And I never would be.

Even if I put him in prison, he could send people after me. After the ones I loved.

Where the hell are Vin and Ariella? Tears trickled down my cheeks, and I knotted my fists in the white hospital sheet.

My confidence was gone. I'd lost Vin. Maybe Ariella, too. I wished I could convince Jenny to get on a plane. I cried until I passed out.

I woke in slightly better spirits, but it didn't cheer me when Joanna said, "I've made a list of everyone who had kitchen access that day. I'll find out who betrayed me."

Even if she did, it wouldn't change the fact that someone had taken money to hurt me. If it happened once, it could happen again. I didn't feel safe even in the hospital, because I didn't know who had been touching my food.

I was weak when they discharged me, and I didn't want to go back to Joanna's place, but I had nowhere else to go. Staying with Jenny would paint a target on her. Somewhere, Michael Durst must be laughing. I could almost hear him gloating. *You thought you had the upper hand, bitch? Best you can do is mutually assured destruction.*

That night, I didn't sleep much, and in the morning, I hardly had the energy to drag myself out of bed. Showering was out of the question, so I washed up and used dry shampoo on my hair.

To my surprise, there were clothes waiting for me in the closet. I selected a blue patterned skirt and matching blouse, adding a white blazer. The fit was a bit loose, and the skirt hit above my knees, but overall I looked all right. When I came out of my room, the house-keeper was hovering, like she didn't know if she should knock.

"Mrs. Van Houten is waiting for you in the breakfast room."

"Thank you, Britta."

I found a continental feast laid out, fruit and pastries, coffee and tea. Joanna had the paper in hand and a tablet turned on beside her. She seemed to be checking stock prices.

"Morning, dear. Ah, that ensemble suits you. I've bought some things that don't work for me over the years. Britta gathered those bits and pieces and put them in your wardrobe. All the underwear is new, sent over from Neiman's this morning." She paused, then added, "I've tasted everything on this table. An hour later and I'm still fine. You can eat, I promise."

I let out a deep, weary sigh. "You shouldn't risk yourself for me like that. I feel like I've thanked you so much that the words have all lost meaning."

"Nonsense. I enjoyed your company before, and I'll appreciate all the money I make from your husband's downfall. Our relationship is win-win, my dear." She slid the tablet toward me. "Mr. Rodriguez is a fast worker. He's already got your story online. See?"

I skimmed the article, which he'd written with no embellishment. This was in a credible news journal, which meant the papers would probably snatch the story and run with it soon, featuring different angles. "They'll probably be calling for interviews."

She agreed with a sedate nod and a sip of tea. "The company's already taken a beating in the market. I'll make my move shortly."

I couldn't sit around watching my flesh knit together, wallowing in fear of Michael's next maneuver. "Speaking of beatings, could I borrow a guard? I want to start divorce proceeding and file for a restraining order."

"Of course. Do you prefer Clive or Nigel?"

"Clive, I guess?" In all honesty, I had a hard time remembering their names and faces. They were both tall and white with short brown hair, black suits, white shirts, and sunglasses, and neither of them ever said much.

"I could call my lawyer," she said. "I'm not sure if you're aware, but an attorney can handle both those issues. You don't need to go to the courthouse personally."

"Really?" In fact, I *didn't* know that.

"I'll have Mr. Fielding come directly after breakfast. There's no need for you to put a target on your back, barring absolute exigency."

It was true that I didn't love the idea of going out with Michael still running amok. I let Joanna persuade me. "Then I'll accept your offer with gratitude."

"Mr. Fielding? This is Joanna Van Houten. Please make time for me this morning. I'm at home."

What must it be like to take it for granted that people would clear their schedule and take care of your problems at once? With such privilege, it was a wonder Joanna Van Houten wasn't exactly like Michael Durst.

Maybe she is, a little voice whispered.

After eating a light meal from the food Joanna had deemed safe, I called Ariella and Vin for the twentieth time. I left messages for both of them, sent more texts while fear chewed up my insides. *Where are you? Are you all right?* I would never forgive myself if something happened to my sister. *I should have warned her before I sent her to Europe. Should have told her about Michael.* As for Vin, I'd dragged him into my problems against his will—

"Don't panic," Joanna said.

"There has to be something I can do. She started her trip at Heathrow in the UK. Can we check somehow—"

"If she's traveling in Europe, there's no way to be sure where she's gone. There would only be a record if she returned to the US. They don't stamp the passport as you're leaving the country."

"Right, I knew that. Only on entrance." I let out a breath, rubbing my knuckles against my aching temples.

I knew worry might make me physically ill. Not a good scenario when recovering from a near-fatal gunshot wound. At this rate, Michael could succeed in killing me indirectly. I shook my head in silent protest.

"I can probably find out if she's come back to the States. Let me make a call."

Joanna retreated to her office, and shortly thereafter her lawyer, Mr. Fielding, arrived. She must have briefed him, because he had all the paperwork ready for my signatures. Like her guards, he was a man of few words, middle-aged, white, and balding. He looked downright innocuous, but if he worked for Joanna he must be a shark.

"Do you have any questions, Mrs.—"

"Marlena. Just Marlena. And I'm wondering how long all of this will take?"

"The order of protection is urgent, so I'll do my best to rush it through. Since there's an investigation ongoing, I think it should be soon. The divorce is more complicated, and it will take longer, especially if Mr. Durst contests."

I tried to smile. "Then you don't know how long it will take for me to be free."

"Unfortunately, ma'am, I can't say, especially under these circumstances."

"I understand."

"I also need to caution you. Even after the protective order is granted, that doesn't mean you will be physically protected from your estranged husband. The police may opt to assign someone to protective duty, but the restraining order doesn't guarantee that."

"I'll keep that in mind." The lawyer didn't need to warn me. I already knew there was no safety for me as long as the monster I'd married was alive.

Mr. Fielding nodded. "I'll file the motions today and I will appear in court on your behalf as needed. It will be safer to minimize your public exposure as much as possible."

"Thank you for your time."

Against Mr. Fielding's protests, I walked him to the door and as he stepped out, my phone rang. I didn't recognize the number, but I answered on the first ring anyway. "Ariella? Are you safe?"

There was a short pause. "Sorry to disappoint you. This is Detective Hunter."

"Oh. Yes." She'd given me her card, but I hadn't added her to my contacts. Discouragement swept me at the knees, so I leaned against the closed door and took a deep breath. "What can I do for you?"

"Can you come down to the station? We've picked up a couple of suspects related to the case and we need you to identify them."

37

It was hard for me to leave the brownstone, though I wasn't safe there either. Even whenever Joanna managed to root out who'd taken the bribe to poison me, it wouldn't keep it from happening again. Michael had too long a reach.

Clive cleared this throat behind me as I hesitated in the doorway. "Something wrong, madam?"

Everything. This is how people develop agoraphobia.

"It doesn't matter," I said. "Let's go."

We went to the precinct without Joanna. She had work to do, presumably related to taking over Michael's company. The guard didn't make conversation as he drove, and he parked near the station in silence and shielded me with his body, head on swivel. His boss had instructed him to "guard me with his life" and it appeared he took that command seriously. The extreme protective stance didn't let up until we were inside, surrounded by a bevy of cops. Clive escorted me to

Detective Hunter and then excused himself to wait near the front doors.

"Thank you for coming so quickly. This way, please."

She led me to an interior room in the police station, on the other side of a two-way mirror. Six suspects were lined up, all tall, thin, and pale, but Death Face was unmistakable. I'd never forget how scared I was when they took me.

Before she could speak, I said, "I'm supposed to identify the man Michael paid to hurt me, right? It's him, number five."

"Are you positive?" she asked.

I nodded. "Absolutely."

"That's Sergei Petrovich. He has ties to the Bratva. Are you aware that your husband did business with these people?"

"Mr. Petrovich was at our wedding in Ibiza along with the other man, the one with the snake tattoo on his neck. I didn't know what line of work they're in. Michael never talked business with me. However, I did have some suspicions when he put the new art gallery in my name. I thought he was probably going to use it for money laundering."

The detective leveled a look on me that said she wasn't entirely persuaded by my role as an innocent victim. "How can you not be sure when you ran the place?"

"My name was on the contract, and I decorated the place with Joanna Van Houten's help. I prepared for the grand opening, but Michael had me hire a manager to handle the daily business. I haven't been there in months. You're aware that I haven't been out of Sherwood for that long?"

"That's true," Detective Hunter acknowledged. "I'll put that on the list of things for us to investigate." She tapped the intercom and spoke to someone outside. "Bring in the next group."

I had no idea how they'd found so many men with tattoos on their necks, but they came tromping in. Like Death Face, the original Snake

Tattoo was unmistakable. "It's number four. He's the one who took Bobby Ray Hudgens away."

"Constantine Kozlov. It will be difficult to get a confession from Kozlov or Petrovich. These men take their vows of silence and brotherhood seriously."

"Will you be arresting Michael soon?"

"I'm sorry I can't give you a concrete answer," she said.

The detectives had come to see me in the hospital and asked a lot of questions about the poisoning incident, but they could only follow so many leads, so fast.

I sighed. "Right now I'm living on Joanna Van Houten's good graces, but I need to resume my life soon. I want to remove my things from the condo, but I'm scared to go back there. My passport is there, along with everything I own."

She gave me a sympathetic look. "I understand your situation. I suppose it won't hurt to tell you that we searched the premises yesterday and our IT team has found enough evidence to implicate your husband. A warrant for his arrest has been issued, and officers have been dispatched to pick him up."

Yes. Finally.

I worked hard to keep my face clear of anything but relief. The triumph I swallowed whole as I sagged against the wall beside the door. "Thank you. Have you heard anything about Vin Rivera?"

"Mr. Rivera's family confirms that they haven't heard from him in over a week. We sent officers to his apartment, and when he didn't answer, the super let us in. The place was a mess. It's not my job to speculate, but he does seem to be missing."

Too easily I could imagine Michael's people bursting in on Vin. The resulting fight would have resulted in the wreckage the detective mentioned. "Did it look like the aftermath of a fight, or more like Vin packed in a hurry?"

"As I said, I deal in facts."

But judging by her expression, she was holding something back. They must have found some blood on the scene or something like that or she wouldn't look so grim. I nodded and followed her out, back into the main room.

"Is there anything else I can do to help?" I asked.

Before she could answer, Detective Wilson and another plain-clothes cop hauled a struggling suspect into the room. Because the man was so wildly disheveled, it took me a moment to recognize Michael Durst. No jacket; wrinkled blue shirt and crumpled gray slacks; unshaven so his jaw was spotted with salt-and-pepper stubble; and hair that was downright greasy. His bloodshot eyes made it seem like he hadn't slept in weeks. Between the crisis at his company and being investigated for various crimes, his life had been tough lately.

When he spotted me, he lunged, and it took both officers to retrain him. "Bitch! I don't know how you did this, but you won't get away with it. I made you! I own you!"

Wilson and Hunter exchanged a look. *Yeah, that's exactly what the text said. Make a note.* Trembling, I scrambled behind the nearest desk and stared at my nemesis with wide eyes, one hand on my chest to remind everyone that he tried to have me killed.

Then Detective Wilson put a hand on Durst's back, shoving him toward the interrogation room. "That's enough. Do you still not understand the situation?"

Michael was still shouting at me when they dragged him away. Detective Hunter hovered nearby. "Are you all right? That must have been—"

"I'll survive," I cut in. "I'm wondering if you could do me a favor? But I understand if it isn't possible."

"What is it?" Wisely, Detective Hunter didn't make any promises.

"I won't have a chance to speak to Michael during the trial. And I can't talk to him safely if he bonds out after he's charged. I won't visit him in prison, so this might be my only chance to ask him *why*. It should be safe for me to have a word if you leave the door open and wait right outside. Is that possible?"

Detective Hunter seemed torn, but she finally said, "I can give you two minutes."

"Thank you. That should be enough. He probably won't do more than rant at me anyway, but I have to try."

"This way, please."

I followed her into a corridor and she chose the second door on the left, Interrogation Room 2. Michael sat inside waiting for the questions to begin. "Two minutes," Detective Hunter cautioned.

"I'll be quick. Thank you."

Michael's head snapped up when he saw me but he didn't leave his chair, largely because he must have seen Detective Hunter in the hall. As I took the seat across from him, I was conscious of the mirror taking up most of the wall behind me; I had to be careful here.

"Where's Ariella? And what did you do to Vin?"

"I have nothing to say to you, bitch. When Anton gets me out of here, I'll make you wish you were dead." He smirked, an expression that stole my breath. In this setting he wouldn't tell me anything, but my fear doubled.

"You're not sorry?" I said loudly. "Don't you feel *any* remorse? No sympathy for Bobby Ray's family?"

"What the fuck are you talking about?" His pale eyes gleamed with manic hate, and the sheer intensity of it reminded me what a monster he was.

Detective Hunter signaled from the doorway—one minute left. No need for that much time. As I stood, I summoned pure bravado. Michael Durst wouldn't tell me shit. He could hurt me through those

I cared about, but I had weapons too, ones he'd never see coming since I'd been sharpening them in secret, hardly letting myself think of my past because breaking character meant risking my own life.

I leaned close enough to murmur a few words, so soft that it couldn't be audible to anyone observing in the next room. "Do you think it's a coincidence that you met me, Michael Durst? I waited at that burger place every night for *two* weeks until I spotted Del Morton. I knew you owned part of his company. And I've been planning to destroy you for much longer than you know. You built your empire on my sister's bones, and I would happily die if it means taking you with me."

He sucked in a sharp breath, sudden clarity cracking the wild rage that crackled through him. Before he could speak, I added so softly, "Deborah Neuman. You murdered her in Croatia. Did you think you'd never pay the price? How does it feel when nobody believes you? Get deeply familiar with that feeling, Michael. That's your fate from now on."

"Bitch!" With an incoherent snarl, he leapt for me.

He got his arms around my neck and I choked out a scream. Detectives rushed into the room, incapacitating him with a brutal arm twist. Detective Wilson forced him to the floor, where he thrashed wildly, still screaming. "Marlena, you fucking whore, I'll kill you if it's the last thing I do. You will not get away. Do you hear me? *Do you?*"

Detective Hunter guided me out of the room, and I leaned on her. The sudden choking would leave marks, I knew, and the hot trickle in my chest felt like some of my stitches had burst. I shivered uncontrollably, not just from shock and pain but also euphoria. I'd kept that secret for *so* long. Michael Durst thought he was untouchable, a god unshakable with armor made of money, but *I'd* brought him down.

Not without collateral damage. That makes you as bad as him.

"Are you all right?" the detective asked. "Did he hurt you?"

"A little. I'll stop by the hospital to get checked out." And to get the attack on record. Now the police had *seen* him get violent with me. He'd threatened me in front of witnesses.

Thank you, Michael.

"Good idea. Did you get the closure you needed?"

I sighed softly. "He's beyond reason. Thank you for the opportunity, but I can't get any sense out of him. He just hates me so much. It's not about insurance payouts any longer. I've … I don't know. Become an emblem of failure or something?"

"He certainly seems fixated on harming you," she agreed. "Be careful. Even with him in custody, I'm afraid he might—"

"Yes, he has unsavory connections. If he tells his lawyer to make a call … well, I'll be cautious, especially since he's made two attempts already."

She didn't argue with my assumption that he was behind the lacing of my food. "That's probably best. I can also request police protection. That would be prudent under the circumstances."

Refusing that offer would seem strange, like I had something to hide. I nodded at once. "Please do. I'd feel safer."

"I'll start the paperwork. Do you need a patrolman to give you a ride?"

"No, there's a driver waiting for me. Thank you for everything."

Detective Hunter took that as affirmation that we were done, and with a quick "We'll keep you posted," she hurried off to question Michael. I had no doubt he'd deny everything, but with all the evidence piled up against him, they didn't need a confession to push ahead with criminal charges. Plenty of people went to prison to await trial while insisting that they didn't do it.

Clive was waiting for me near the front doors. He stared at the red marks on my throat that would soon darken to bruises. "What happened?"

"I tried to talk to my estranged husband. Don't worry about it. We need to stop by the hospital on the way back, though. I think my stitches might need..." I trailed off as the blood seeped through my blouse.

"Right away. I'll let Mrs. Van Houten know."

He took my arm and helped me to the car, all efficient protection. "The closest hospital, or the one where you were treated before?"

"The latter, I think. They have all my records."

And I can't wait to get it documented that Michael tried to hurt me again.

38

At the hospital, Joanna Van Houten's name opened all the doors.

I bypassed the emergency room and ended up in a posh VIP area, the likes of which I didn't know existed before I joined these elite ranks. Clive stayed close to me until the doctor took over. I had two stitches replaced and my bandages changed. They took photos when I told them my husband had inflicted the damage.

As we left the hospital, I asked, "Can we stop by my condo?"

The guard hesitated. For a moment I thought he'd make me ask Joanna for permission, which would've made me feel like I was her prisoner, just as I'd been Michael's. In both cases I'd gone into the lion's den by choice, though.

Clive eventually said, "It would be polite to inform madam what has transpired."

I took the hint and called Joanna, who answered on the third ring. "Marlena, dear, did something happen?"

Quickly I summarized the morning's events and concluded, "Right now, I'm sure it's safe to go to the condo. I'd like to retrieve my personal effects while I'm sure Michael is in custody."

"Understandable. By all means take care of that while you can. But do keep Clive on watch. You never know what could happen."

That warning was entirely unnecessary, but I thanked her for it. "We'll be careful."

Clive shifted in the driver's seat and met my gaze over his shoulder, silently asking for confirmation. I said, "Yes, she's fine with it. Let's hurry."

I couldn't break character, not even for one second. I was a victim, terrorized beyond all reason. I shouldn't be smiling as we drove to the condo; I killed the satisfaction and stared out the window in silence.

Clive took us into the parking garage. "This is our spot," I said. "Let's go up."

To my surprise, Michael hadn't changed the door code. I had half-expected to need to ask security to let me in, but I input the old PIN and the door clicked open. The condo was a fucking wreck, dirty dishes on the smeared glass table. It even smelled of stale food, something Michael never permitted when I lived there. Gingerly I stepped over splintered glass from the smashed wedding portrait. He'd broken the picture and scratched my face off, probably with the blood-smeared shard on the floor.

I really got to you, Michael.

"Be careful," Clive said.

Nodding, I picked a path to the bedroom and packed my things. In movies, the heroine only collects what she'd originally owned once her mission is accomplished, but ... fuck that. I'd *earned* everything he'd bought me, putting up with his shit. Designer dresses and all the jewelry, an entire suitcase full of handbags and shoes—it took us two trips to port everything to the car. I made sure not to touch any of

Michael's stuff lest he accuse me from his prison cell of theft. Then I stopped by the bathroom. There was nothing else I needed to take, only something I had to leave.

"I need to go into Michael's office to get my passport," I said to Clive when I was done. "Could you come with me?"

"Why?"

"Because he might say I took something that doesn't belong to me."

"Understood. You want a witness, then."

"I do, if you don't mind."

"It's not a problem."

I led the way, and Clive watched as I opened the strongbox, withdrawing *only* my passport.

"If there's any doubt later, I'll verify what you took from here," he said.

"Thank you. I really can't rule anything out with that man. He's—"

"A devil," the bodyguard supplied.

I glanced at him in surprise, but Clive's expression was blank. It would help if an irreproachable British bodyguard took the stand on my behalf. I couldn't feel joy or relief yet, not with Vin missing and Ariella unresponsive. Passport in hand, I left the condo as I found it, a disgusting mess. I was done tidying up after Michael Durst.

In the car, I called Ariella. Again.

Still no answer. My insides twisted with dread, laced with stinging filaments of self-doubt. If I'd come this far, only to use people who cared about me, and get them hurt fighting my battles... well, Dee wouldn't want that. She wouldn't appreciate a bloody revenge that came at Vin and Ariella's expense.

Just because Michael was locked up didn't mean he was powerless in the real world. At some point they'd have to let him confer with his lawyer, Anton, and I knew all too well how merciless that bastard was. I remembered him saying, "Looks like you've chosen well this time" when I signed the prenup without complaint. From that I could guess that he *knew* about Michael's crimes and didn't care as long as he got paid.

Ariella ... where are you? I have to do something.

Then it hit me. I'd given Ariella a credit card before she left, so I should be able to track the last time she used it ... and where. Hurriedly, I logged in on my phone and skimmed the list. Since I was living off Joanna, I hadn't used my card in a long time; all the purchases were international, sporadic hits as my sister traveled.

"Let's see ..."

Aha. Last used at Brioche Dorée. I clicked on the charge for more information. *In-person transaction, Paris, France, Charles de Gaulle airport.* I also found the date, some numeric codes, and a link to click if I wanted to dispute the charge.

Two days ago, she was at the airport in Paris. The card hasn't been used since.

Don't panic, I told myself, but that was easier said than done. None of my plans factored in Ariella. I bit down on my thumb to quell the rising tide of fear and desperation.

No. No, no, no.

"We're almost there," Clive assured me. Probably saw I was a having a panic attack, but he couldn't know why.

Once we arrived at the brownstone, I ignored his attempt to help me out of the car. I raced for the front doors. Joanna half-rose from her chair at my noisy entrance, both brows up. She was as perfectly groomed as ever, evincing only moderate surprise at my haste.

"Breathe, dear. Whatever it is won't be improved by hyperventilation."

I stumbled to her and dropped to my knees, putting a shaking hand on the arm of her chair. "You said you'd make some calls, see if they have a record of Ariella entering the US. Did you find anything out?"

"I'm still waiting for a return call. Let me check."

I stayed where I was for her murmured conversation, and when she disconnected, I could barely breathe. "Did they tell you?"

She sighed softly. "It seems that Ariella returned yesterday. Records show that her passport was scanned in New Jersey at the Newark Airport."

I squeezed my eyes shut, trying not to cry. "There's no good reason why she won't return my calls. Michael must have lured her back somehow and when she arrived—"

"Calm down. It won't help her if you fall apart."

"But he probably has Vin and Ariella! Vin only tried to help me and Ariella doesn't know anything! She found me in the paper and—"

A sharp slap knocked my head sideways. "Pull yourself together. You knew Michael Durst was dangerous. You understood that there would be consequences for crossing him. Yes or no?"

I swallowed hard, tasting blood on my tongue from where the corner of my inner lip had split against my teeth. Joanna was coolly elegant, delivering violence with the same aplomb as she served tea. And I was at her mercy.

Fear shimmered through me. Like Michael, she might consider me expendable now that I'd caused the crisis she was using to take over his company. She might dispose of me, and the people I needed to save would be left to Michael's rage and vengeance.

"Yes," I whispered.

"Are you calmer now?"

"I am."

She indicated the chair opposite her with a graceful gesture. "Then sit down and let's discuss this rationally."

Taking one deep breath, two, I did feel better. More clearheaded. Reason reasserted itself. Joanna had no reason to harm me. She was getting what she wanted out of our association, and I didn't believe she was a sociopath, just deeply pragmatic.

"Sorry. I'm just really scared for Ariella."

"With good reason. You know what Durst may do to her."

I thought aloud, step by step. "Let's presume he took her right after she landed. I can't wait for the police to check the leads methodically. I need private help and I'm willing to put all my money toward finding her."

Joanna nodded. "I understand. Mr. Fielding can contract personnel on your behalf. If money is no object—and we're not seeking a legal conviction for her abduction—well, many more avenues open up."

"Find her, whatever it takes. Michael owns a lot of property, some of which aren't even in his name. There are paper companies…" Though I thought hard, I couldn't recall precisely what Vin had said about ownership of the cottage where I was sent. Just something about it not being in Michael's name.

"Mr. Fielding is thorough, and he will hire skilled investigators. I know it's not easy to wait, but it won't help your sister if you collapse and end up in the hospital again."

I acknowledged that with an inclination of my head. "Don't forget that we're searching for Vin too."

"I'll see to it," Joanna said. "And I'll have Mr. Fielding update you personally once the search is underway."

She set aside the newspaper she'd been reading and picked up her cell phone. This day she wore a heavy gold bangle and an ornate ruby ring that matched her blood-red manicure. "Mr. Fielding? I have an urgent job for you. I'll email you the particulars." Once she hung up, she added, "I'll go to my office now and send the instructions. I'll copy you on the email so you know what I've asked him to do."

"Thank you. And as you said, I need to build up my strength, so I can be there for Ariella when we find her. Do you want anything from the kitchen?"

"Not right now. Thank you."

Britta wasn't in the kitchen, and I hoped she wasn't territorial, but I had to eat. I didn't trust anything that I hadn't seen someone else eat first, so I went for packaged food. It would be harder to tamper with a random can, so I had soup that I made with my own hands, a protein bar, and water from the tap.

I'm probably paranoid. Michael wouldn't try the same trick twice. He wants to torment me, make me wonder how and when the next attack will come.

Joanna's kitchen was so over the top—with gleaming granite counters, stainless steel everything, pristine copper pots dangling for display, and fresh herbs in hanging baskets. The fridge was meticulously stocked with food labeled and stored in glass containers, bottled spring water lined up like soldiers, and condiments wiped so clean that the bottles shone.

She even had double baking ovens and a huge walk-in freezer. Large enough to store a body, in fact.

"Can I get you something, miss?" Britta stood behind me, hovering in her black and white uniform. She set a pile of crisply folded dish towels on the island.

I shook my head as the microwave beeped. "No, I'm fine." On impulse, I asked softly, "What's Mrs. Van Houten like to work for, anyway?"

She took a step back, eyes wide. "She's lovely, miss. Just wonderful. She's done so much for my family, too. Paid for my mother's surgery and gave me money when I was struggling to put together my son's tuition. The woman's practically an angel."

Right. Of course. What did I think she would say?

For all she knew, this was a test. As I passed her, carrying my meal toward the breakfast nook, she glanced around and whispered, "Just ... don't cross her, miss. That's all I'm saying."

39

At 2:37 a.m., the house phone rang. Since worry was keeping me up anyway, I came out of my room in time to catch the tail end of the conversation. "You may have found him? Good work. Confirm and get back to me."

I tapped hurriedly on her bedroom door, although it was partly ajar already. "Are you talking about Vin?"

"Marlena, dear. You should be resting."

"If you're talking about him, I'd like to help. Please."

Joanna sighed faintly. She was propped up in bed in a satin and lace bed jacket, all elegance even at this hour. Even her hair hadn't stirred from its careful upsweep. That spoke of powerful hair spray or superhuman self-control, or possibly both.

Finally she replied, "There's only one place left to check, and my people tell me the location has been locked down, quite recently too.

Even maintenance personnel have been prohibited, which seems ... unusual."

"Where is it? I need to go myself."

That was the least I could do for Vin, who'd sacrificed so much trying to help me. At least the police were keeping watch on his family now, in case Michael tried to go scorched earth in retaliation.

"There's no dissuading you, I suppose. Just a moment, I'll call Clive."

In less than five minutes, the guard appeared in jacket and slacks, fully alert and ready for action. Did her staff ever sleep? I felt like utter shit, exhaustion and pain from my waning meds warring for supremacy. My fear of food wasn't helping me regain my strength, either.

"I have the address," Clive told Joanna, as if I was a fixture he was meant to deliver. "Shall we go now?"

"Please. And be careful."

Outside, a pair of policemen sat in a patrol car. When they saw us exit the building, one of them stepped out. "Where are you headed?"

"We may have found Vin Rivera."

"That's your missing acquaintance, right? You should leave that to us."

Clive ignored him, escorting me into the car with brisk efficiency. The cop bit out a curse and jogged back to his vehicle. It seemed they'd decided to follow us, just in case I got myself in trouble on their watch.

At this hour, the streets were much emptier than usual, just a few late-night cabs and people on second shift making their way home after a midnight meal. Clive drove as he did everything—with silent skill—and though I didn't have the address, I recognized the warehouse when we turned down the broken gravel drive.

This is where they hurt me ... and killed Bobby Ray.

The gate was chained and locked, which meant Joanna's other team hadn't arrived. Though they'd called her to let her know this was a likely location, they might have had farther to travel. Clive hopped out and pulled a bolt cutter from a toolbox in the trunk. Briefly I wondered if there were limits to the work he'd performed for Joanna as he cut the padlock and unwrapped the chains, then opened the gate so we could drive through. As he got out again, he didn't tell me to wait in the car. Just as well; I meant to stick with him every step of the way. While it might be dangerous inside the warehouse, it was also scary to be left alone in a deserted place.

The patrol car caught up with us a minute later and parked beside us. Clive moved toward the warehouse doors with the bolt cutters and one cop protested. "You can't—"

"Whatever," the other said. "I hear something inside, don't you?"

Ah, so they were prepared to help us out? There must be some rule about being allowed to do this if there was reasonable suspicion that somebody's life was in danger.

"Do you think we need backup?" I heard the first cop ask the other one.

I didn't catch her reply as Clive cut another padlock on the warehouse door and rolled it up. Since Michael owned the property, this probably counted as breaking and entering, but I had no doubt Joanna could take care of it. As we stepped into the dark, Clive sweeping his Maglite around, I did hear … something. A low, animal sound, not even strong enough to be called a whimper.

"This way," I whispered.

The police pushed forward, then, clearing the area ahead of us. Since they had weapons, that seemed like the smart move, and Clive let them take point. A sharp gasp came from the female officer, and her partner breathed, "Jesus Christ."

I rushed up and my knees buckled when I saw what—who—they'd found. Vin's face was hardly recognizable, so bloody and swollen that his mouth looked like chewed meat. "Is he …?"

The pool of blood beneath him made my head swim, and Clive set his hand beneath my elbow, steadying me. Vin's body was bent at an unnatural angle, bound at wrist and ankle. There was no telling how long he had been lying there.

"They locked the place up and left him to die slowly," the female cop said.

The partner knelt, checking Vin's pulse. "Holy shit, he's still alive. Call for medical."

"It will take forever for an ambulance to get here," I snapped. Maybe it wasn't the right move, but waiting seemed wrong too. "Clive, can you lift him?"

"You shouldn't move an injured person," the male cop said.

I knew that, but I wanted so desperately to help him. In the end, I could only apply pressure, getting Vin's blood all over me as they called for an ambulance. Every minute that we waited, that ticked away with Vin's blood trickling through my fingers, I feared might be his last—that he'd bleed out on this filthy cement floor.

"Breathe," I begged, tears slipping down my cheeks.

But Vin didn't rouse. Not even when the ambulance zoomed up, siren and lights going. I stumbled back to let the EMTs work and then went with him in the ambulance, against Clive's protests. I shook off the guard's hands.

"Let me *go*. I have to stay with him."

If this was some master plan of Michael's to lure me out, then his goons could attack the ambulance. I wouldn't be leaving Vin's side until I knew whether he'd make it.

"Fine, I'll follow you." From his tone, Clive still didn't like it, but they wouldn't let both of us travel with the patient.

I held Vin's hand in the back of the ambulance, but he didn't seem aware of me or anything the EMTs did. Once we arrived at the hospital, they rushed him into the ER on the gurney, leaving me to follow in a daze and fill out forms as best I could. With a pang, I realized how little I knew about Vin. I couldn't supply his social security number and I didn't know how to contact his family, either. Unsurprisingly, he didn't have a phone or ID on him, so I signed off as the guarantor for his treatment costs.

The doctors were running, as the ER was jammed with other patients. I waited for a while, then grabbed a passing nurse. "The man I came in with … how's he doing?"

"Please wait, ma'am. We're doing our best."

Clive had been hovering, hard-pressed to guard me in such a crowd, and then he stepped to the side, talking quietly on his cell. I guessed he was updating Joanna on the situation. Tiredly, I sank down in a plastic chair, staring at the speckled white tile floor. Family members waiting for other patients wore similar expressions.

Around five a.m., the cops who'd been assigned to my protective detail came in. "We came to check on Mr. Rivera. Any word yet?"

I shook my head. "They won't tell me anything since I'm not family. Can the detectives get in touch with his dad?"

"We'll take care of that, ma'am. He hasn't regained consciousness?"

"I don't think so."

Just then, the doctor who'd taken Vin emerged from the treatment area. "Mr. Rivera is stable now. We're admitting him, and—"

"I'll pay for a private room," I cut in. "If there's one available."

"Check with admin on that." The doctor didn't seem to be amused at being interrupted, so I murmured an apology. "How is he?"

"Weak. He lost a lot of blood, but he should rally with proper care. If he'd gotten here any later …" Though she trailed off, I could finish that sentence.

"Thank you, doctor."

I handled the request for a private room, then waited for them to advise me where Vin was going. It was half past six in the morning by the time the hospital staff settled him. From the way he was bandaged, he'd been beaten much worse than I was, and there was evidence of knife-work too.

Clive stepped into the doorway. "The police have notified Mr. Rivera's family, madam. They should be here soon."

"Are you suggesting I leave before they arrive?" I knew that might be best. They'd have questions about who I was, my relationship with Vin. Possibly they might blame me for his injuries, and hell, they'd be right. And I didn't know if I had the strength to handle their anger and grief on top of my own.

"That's up to you," he said in a neutral tone.

"Give me five minutes."

"I'm at your disposal."

He moved off, out of my sight line, but I figured he was standing outside the door in his secret service pose. For a few seconds I stood beside Vin's bed, staring down at his battered face. Then I took his hand.

"Get better, okay? Thank you for everything. I'll take it from here."

His lashes fluttered and his fingers flexed against mine, but he didn't rouse. His pain meds were dripped steadily, a reminder that mine were overdue. I limped out of the room and beckoned to Clive.

"Let's go. I've done all I can here."

"Understood, madam."

The patrol officers were standing by; surely they'd be relieved soon, though. It had been a long-ass night.

As we left the hospital, Detectives Hunter and Wilson met us in the parking lot. Hunter spoke, but her icy tone didn't match her usual friendly demeanor. "Are you trying to do my job, Mrs. Durst?"

Since I was dead sure I'd asked them not to call me that, it had to be intentional. "Excuse me?"

"Imagine my surprise when my colleagues informed me that you did a midnight runner to check out a lead on a warehouse. It didn't occur to you to call us?"

Is this a territorial thing? Or are they mad because I was looking for Vin through private channels as well?

"Honestly? No. I just wanted to help Vin, as fast as possible. If I did something wrong—"

"We had officers with us," Clive cut in. "There was probable cause for us to believe that Mr. Rivera's life was in danger. If you have additional complaints, please contact Lewis Fielding, Joanna Van Houten's attorney."

That shut everything down, and for a few beats, neither detective spoke. Then Wilson said, "No, we're good. Just so you know, we're doing everything we can, ma'am. We're looking into his first two wives also, but it's been so long that it'll be tough to make anything stick. There will likely be lesser charges as well."

Racketeering, money laundering, possibly tax evasion. If the heavy charges stuck, Michael would rot in prison for a long time. Anything could happen inside, especially to a man who believed he was inherently superior to most other humans. That attitude might even get him killed.

"Thank you," I said sincerely. "I can breathe a little easier now. But ... I still haven't found my sister. Have you heard anything?"

Detective Hunter gave a tight smile. "Don't you have people for that? You shouldn't wait around for us."

Yeah, she was pissed.

Rather than get into an argument with the cop who should be helping me, I apologized again and let Clive lead me to the car. My head was ringing by that point, and I could barely stay awake for the drive back to the brownstone. The sun was rising over the buildings, a pallid burn in the early morning sky.

Without much hope, I dialed Ariella's number. One ring. Two. Three.

"Yes?" a deep male voice answered, with a touch of an accent that I placed as Eastern European.

My heart kicked into overdrive. "This is Ariella's number. Who is this?"

40

"I think you already know." Amusement laced the unknown voice, as if he relished toying with me on my husband's behalf.

"Michael's in custody," I snapped.

"Then you know who I work for, at least. If you want to see her alive again, you'll lose the police. Lose your bodyguard. You'll say nothing to Joanna Van Houten and by midnight, you'll arrive at the address I'm about to text you."

Clive stole a glance at me, eyes watchful. I regulated my expression. "Okay," I said quietly. "I understand."

"Good. Don't bring your cell phone or anything that could be used to track your location. I will search you and if you disobey, Ariella will suffer for it. Come alone. Are my instructions clear?"

"Completely."

"Then our business is concluded."

I couldn't reveal how shaken I was because Clive was still watching. Finally, he asked, "Is something wrong?"

"It's just been a long night."

"I'm sure your friend will pull through." He was being downright chatty, a sure sign that I looked like I might come apart at the seams.

Get it together.

My phone vibrated, a text from a number I didn't recognize. There was no message apart from the address. I pulled it up on the map ... *somewhere in Newark? That's where Ariella's passport was scanned.*

My photo app buzzed and I clicked it on instinct. I had just enough time to register the picture of Ariella, bound at wrist and ankles, with a newspaper unfolded across her chest. *Today's date. They have her. It doesn't matter that Michael is locked up. I can't—*

Panic broke over me in a drowning wave, threatening to steal my breath, and black sparks popped in my field of vision.

Enough. You can't help her this way.

I took a screenshot before the picture dissolved; that was the app's gimmick, but only a dipshit would assume that the service was foolproof. Right now I couldn't do anything with the photo, not without endangering Ariella, but it was more evidence for me to leave behind.

Somehow I held myself together until we got to the brownstone. Joanna was up, already dressed and sipping Earl Grey in the breakfast room. Britta greeted me at the door, then scurried to the kitchen for another place setting. Under the circumstances I didn't feel like eating, but I needed fuel for the nightmare ahead.

"Bad news?" Joanna asked as I joined her at the table.

"We found Vin. He's alive, currently at the hospital under guard."

"That's a relief, then. But why do you look so despondent, my dear?"

"I'm just tired." The lie rolled out automatically. Good thing I'd gotten plenty of practice at it while living with Michael.

"Have a bite to eat and get some rest. I imagine you'll want to go back to the hospital later?"

"It might be safer if I leave him to the police—and his family—for now."

Joanna pursed her lips, thoughtful. "You could be right. Wise of you to keep out of the public eye as much as possible. I hear that journalists are searching for you even now."

"Shit," I blurted. "Sorry."

Her eyes twinkled. "No need to apologize. I've been known to curse myself, if the situation demanded it."

Mechanically I smiled and declined the food Britta brought. I was still afraid to eat anything I hadn't seen being prepared, so I had another protein bar and some fruit from the plate Joanna was using. Everything tasted of ashes anyway and I washed down the flavor of failure with a glass of tap water that I fetched myself.

It seemed impossible that I could sleep with such a terrible task ahead of me, but I took three pain pills and set the alarm on my phone for 9:45 that night, just in case.

Exhaustion coupled with the pharmaceutical help knocked me out for twelve hours, and I woke up just in time for dinner. Joanna had noticed my peculiarity by now, so she acted as my taster again. I had no idea what I ate, only that I did, while quietly watching the clock.

To get to the meeting point on time, I needed to leave by ten, and I had to take the bus to guarantee nobody followed me. Getting past Clive and the police on protective detail outside ... that was the challenge. I couldn't handle it alone.

I need a distraction around 9:50 tonight, I texted to Jenny. *Can you turn off the power for a while?*

You think I'm a master hacker? she sent back.

Jen.

Fine. I can probably get you a brief brownout. Two minutes max. Will that work?

It will have to. Thank you. I added a heart to the message.

What are you up to?

Ignoring the question, I went back to my room, where I'd left all my belongings in a pile. I dug out a pair of black yoga pants, a black sweater, and plain black sneakers. No black hat, but my hair was dark anyway, so I tied it back.

The time ticked down slowly while I paced and listened to the household settle. At 9:44, I turned off my alarm and left my cell on my bedside table. No phone, nothing that could be used to track me. Leaving my phone felt like abandoning my lifeline, as if I wouldn't be coming back from this trip.

As I opened my bedroom door, the lights went out. Not just at Joanna's, but our whole side of the street.

Damn, Jenny.

That triggered the backup batteries on various electronics and the house alarm kicked on, a raucous screech that would alert the household. It would also make it harder to find me in the chaos.

I slipped out the front as the officers got out of their car, cautious, with hands on their sidearms. Crouching, I crab-walked to the short iron fence that framed the front of the brownstone and remained that way until the officers passed, knocking on the door behind me with growing agitation.

They probably think Michael's making a move. A blackout was the perfect opportunity, so they were looking for assailants, not a single woman scurrying around the corner of the building. Once I was out of sight, I climbed over the fence, whimpering as the movement pulled my stitches.

I was in no condition for this much activity, but I'd abandoned Ariella once. I wouldn't do that to her again, even if it cost me everything. My heart had broken when Dee left me behind. When I read the note she'd left, about leaving and not coming back, I wanted to die.

Later, when I found out what happened to her, I wanted Michael Durst to die.

As I reached the next block, the lights came on behind me. I'd memorized my route, the meeting point burned into my brain. I bought a transit card at a convenience store and got on at the nearest stop, rode over to the central hub, and transferred to an intercity bus headed for Newark.

Since I didn't have my phone, I was wearing a watch Michael had given me, too shiny and ridiculously expensive. I'd be lucky if someone didn't mug me for it, so I was constantly tugging my sleeve down over it as I tracked the time, silently obsessing over whether we'd hit traffic or construction.

In Newark, I transferred yet again, heading for the stop nearest to my destination. I still had to walk eight blocks, and my chest hurt like hell. No pain meds; my head had to be clear for what was about to happen.

I passed pawn shops and liquor stores, quick marts and a few run-down bars. The address turned out to be a closed business. According to the sign, it had been a used car lot, but the building was dark, windows covered with metal framework. Everything in the neighborhood was barred and shuttered. I hadn't seen any people for a couple of blocks.

11:47 p.m. I made it.

I didn't like loitering in this place, but I had no choice. My whole body prickled as I paced the broken pavement, the lines barely visible in the defunct parking lot. At midnight on the dot, a dark car pulled into the lot, kept rolling until it reached the alley. No streetlights down there, no CCTV, and no witnesses either. A nondescript man in a gray suit got out. There was nothing remarkable about him, but that was even more frightening.

"You came," he said, with a smile that chilled me to the bone.

Not the smile, exactly. His eyes. They were dead and flat, like a fish on ice at the supermarket. I tried to note details about his appearance in case I survived, but he was just relentlessly average—thinning hair, the color of his eyes too hard to see in the dark, narrow face, medium build.

"You didn't give me much choice."

"Untrue. You could've saved yourself, left your sister in my care. Michael told me you were a heartless bitch. It seems that's not entirely true."

"Michael hates women," I said.

"You know your husband well. As promised, I'll search you now. Nothing personal."

I didn't have a bag with me, just the transit card tucked into my bra, but he groped me from head to toe, searching for contraband. He found the card and tossed it. That was bad enough, but then he slipped on a pair of latex gloves. When he bent me over and went for a brutal, impersonal cavity search, I bit my lip until it bled.

He didn't give me a chance to speak. Once he was satisfied that I had followed instructions, he taped my mouth, wrapped industrial-grade tape around my wrists and ankles, and dumped me in the trunk. I made a sound through the tape as the metal slammed down. The space was too small, so I curled up in the fetal position, and various tools bit into my back. From the shape and the way they poked and pinched, I tried to distract myself by guessing what they were—hammer, crowbar, tire iron—all implements that could also be used as weapons.

I let out a shaky breath through my nose. The trunk reeked of chemicals: gas, definitely, and possibly windshield wiper fluid or antifreeze. Breathing this way left me lightheaded, though maybe that was from sucking in exhaust fumes blowing up from the tailpipe. My body tipped back and forth, according to the stop-and-go movement that told me we were still in town. Then suddenly the car accelerated.

We must be on the highway.

The car put miles and miles between me and anyone who cared what became of me. I'd known this was a trap going in, so I tried not to let fear blossom in my head like a bloodstain, but dread stayed with me like a destructive little gremlin, tapping away at my self-control. None of my plans had figured for Ariella. I'd come to save her, but I had no backup, no cell phone, no way to call for help. They hadn't even shown me proof of life before shoving me in the trunk.

This time, I might not make it out alive.

41

Hours of hell—my muscles burned from being stuck in the same position, and I needed to piss so much that it hurt. I had no sense of time in the darkness and still felt lightheaded. Hunger, inhalation of chemicals—it could be either one. The car slowed, and the way I shifted in the trunk made me think we'd finally gotten off the highway. We continued to drive, a bumpier road than before, slower too.

Sharp smells occasionally sliced through my haze: acrid skunk; stink of fertilizer; something rotten, maybe road kill. We were definitely in the country. I put my face closer to the trunk hood, desperate to breathe in something else, anything at all, and I caught a whiff of stagnant water. That reminded me of the cabin I'd been taken to before. I remembered the murky pond with the algae growing unchecked atop it; the perfect place to sink a body. Or two.

Sickness roiled in my stomach, but I couldn't throw up or I'd choke on my own vomit. The car made several turns and slowed even more, eventually leaving the pavement entirely for a gravel road. I could hear the rocks pinging against the undercarriage and crunching beneath the tires. Soon we stopped entirely and the engine cut off. I heard the car door open and slam shut, then finally saw starlight.

After so long in the dark, it hurt my eyes, but I couldn't shield them. The goon hauled me out bodily and I got a quick glimpse of Michael's cabin. Average Man slung me over his shoulder like a sack of cement, so I only saw a blur of rocks, trees, and car until he dropped me on the porch. My legs were shaky and stiff from being crammed in the trunk and I almost fell. He didn't steady me, so I hit my face on the doorframe.

The door opened as if we'd knocked, revealing a man in dark slacks and a white shirt. He was terribly handsome, but it was a plastic prettiness that made me wonder what his real face used to look like. Nobody had cheekbones that symmetrical or a jaw that could slice up a ham.

"You're late," he said to Average Man.

"I drive the speed limit. There's no gain in attracting attention. We have plenty of time before Mr. Durst joins us."

My captor dragged me inside, pushing me toward the smaller of the two bedrooms. Before, there'd barely been space for a single bed and a chest of drawers. Now the room was ominously devoid of furnishings, with the carpet torn out and clear plastic sheeting on the walls and floor.

"Welcome to the murder room," Average Man said.

He shoved me, hard enough that I hit the wall and went down on my side. I didn't try to get up for fear he'd do worse. He had given me no chance to ask questions, no sense of what his orders were other than the certainty that we were being held for Michael Durst. I didn't think a henchman would have the authority to kill us, certainly not before my husband got there, but he might bloody us before the main event.

"Ah, you can't respond, but you must be wondering…" With a mocking flourish, he moved to the closet and pulled something—no, someone—out. Ariella tumbled over, her hair spilling around her like a mermaid who was dying and would soon turn to foam. My heart froze, and—

She moved, shoving up on her elbows as best she could. Her wrists were bound in front of her and her ankles were taped as well, heavy-duty material strong enough to patch an air conditioner hose. A dark strip of the stuff covered her mouth as well. Her face was dirty and pale, her eyes sunken.

The goon said, "Stay quiet. Enjoy the reunion… while you can." Then he slammed out of the room and I heard the door lock. The radio kicked on in the other room, the same melancholy station I had listened to with Vin. I could tell that the minions were talking, but I couldn't make out the words. That was probably the reason for the background music.

I couldn't wait any longer, and with a groan of humiliation I crawled into the closet to pee. If they treated me like an animal, I'd fucking act like one. My sister didn't say anything, but from the smell of it, she'd gone in there too while she was locked up.

When I came out, Ariella half fell toward me and I managed to loop my arms around her. She didn't look good. No telling how long it had been since she'd eaten or had water. With a little maneuvering I managed to peel the tape off her mouth at least, and she did the same for me. Screaming wouldn't do us any good out here, though. I knew that much from the time I'd spent with Vin. It would only get our captors in here, pissed and ready to punish.

"I'm sorry," I whispered.

Ariella's voice was so rough and raspy, thick with thirst and disuse. "What's happenin', Marlena? Who are these assholes?"

It nearly killed me to admit, "They work for my husband."

"Shit. That answers my next question too."

"How did you end up here?"

"I got a call from Michael. He said you were awful sick and that I should get on the next plane out. He booked the tickets and everything, arranged my pickup in Newark. But instead of bringing me to you—"

"The driver brought you here."

"He drugged me first. Otherwise I would have been screaming long before ending up duct-taped in a murder room." She slammed a fist against the plastic-covered floor. "Why didn't you warn me? I would've been careful if I'd known..." She trailed off, probably unable to find words to describe our current situation.

"I just wanted to get you away as fast as possible, but you're right. I fucked up." There was no point in apologizing; some wrongs couldn't be righted with a few words.

Only action could fix this.

"You sure did," she muttered.

"I don't know how long we have before Michael gets here."

She let out a moan. "I'm *so* hungry. But the thirst is worse."

"Wish I could do more than apologize."

Ariella fluttered a sad little smile. "Just like the old days, huh, Marlie? When we didn't have anything to eat or drink at home and we made do by catching rainwater in a barrel or walking to the old artesian well."

I remembered. No electricity, no indoor plumbing. I'd followed Dee away from that life, walked where she had until I ended up here. Had she known why she was dying at the end?

Dark thoughts would only erode my ability to think on my feet. I'd survived so much. I had to keep going and get my sister out of this. She didn't factor into the plans I'd laid. Now I was working off-script, frantic and fearful.

"You were in the closet, right? Is there anything in there? Anything at all?"

"I don't think so. We can check."

The plastic crackled, so I inched across it as quietly as I could, hoping our movement wouldn't draw attention from Average Man or Plastic Guy. The only window had bars on it, hammered in place on the outside, so our only exit would be past Michael's two minions.

Finally, I got close enough to peer inside. This time I looked around but saw only dust, old wallpaper, and peeling paint. I wasn't surprised, but disappointment still flooded me.

"I'll figure something out," I promised.

From Ariella's expression, she didn't plan to hold her breath. With a little whimper, she leaned against me and closed her eyes. She slept for a bit, small, pitiful sounds escaping her even as she dozed.

Hours passed. I might have slept too. Darkness dropped gradually, creeping over the trees. From the rumble of the generator, the lights were on in the rest of the house, but we sat in the gloom, waiting.

Waiting for Michael.

Waiting to die.

For me, at least, it wouldn't be quick.

Someone's phone rang on the other side of the door, a shrill summons. I crept closer to try and make out the conversation. Thankfully the walls were built of thin paneling and not well insulated.

Since they'd turned off the radio at some point, Average Man's voice carried clearly. "How soon will you be here?" A pause. "They're docile for now but I don't know long that will last." Another silence, longer this time. "Yes, I still have what I used to sedate the girl. Understood. I'll take care of it."

Whatever he offered us to eat or drink, we had to refuse it. If my guess was correct, he planned to drug us, and when we woke up, Michael would be here. I'd wake up naked and strapped to a folding table in the murder room.

Like hell.

I still had on the stupid shiny watch Michael gave me. According to that, it took fifteen minutes for them to fix our drugged food. The door opened and the light flipped on, a bare bulb embedded in the ceiling. The sudden brightness hurt my eyes, but it also let me notice little details, like all the dead flies on the plastic by the window and how much Average Man smelled of camphor and menthol.

"You two have been so quiet that I've decided to reward you," he said. "Something to eat, ladies?" He set the tray on the floor and whistled like we were dogs. "Come and get it, be good girls."

"It's okay that we took our gags off?" I asked warily.

"You need them off to eat anyway." His false geniality scared me even more than if he'd been threatening us or slicing me with a knife, because I knew how bad it would get once Michael Durst arrived.

Ariella caught my gaze and tipped her head toward the food. I nodded. We couldn't eat it but we shouldn't antagonize our guard, either. She crawled toward him, eyes down, the picture of submission, but she was so weak or dizzy that she almost pitched face-first into the food. He lunged to keep her from messing up our dinner. He hadn't cared when I'd smacked my face, but this food? Another story.

"Clumsy moron," he muttered, shoving her back. Then he slammed the door behind him as she pulled the metal tray toward the center of the room.

"Tell me you got something," I said.

Ariella had always been fast with her hands, even as a little kid. Stumbling into him, taking the punishment? That was all to get him close enough for her to work.

She produced a collapsible baton. "It was the first thing I could grab. I don't know how long it will be before he notices."

Carefully I extended it to its full length and peered at the weapon, trying to imagine what we could do with it. It wasn't sharp enough to cut through the tape … well, we had to figure out what to do with our dinner first.

"Don't drink the water," I snapped as she picked up the glass.

With the light on, I could see it was cloudy. They'd also given us a cream soup to be drunk from tin mugs, so that could be drugged too. The sandwiches were more of a question mark because I didn't see how pills or powder could completely permeate bread, meat, lettuce, tomato, and cheese.

"Is any of it safe?" Ariella whispered.

"Let's have the meat and lettuce. If we don't feel anything from it, we can eat the cheese and vegetables too."

Since the window was barred from the outside, they hadn't bothered to secure it on the inside. I wriggled the sash up enough to pop the screen out, then dumped the contents of our mugs and plastic glasses. The roar of the generator sounded even louder close up, and suddenly I knew exactly what to do with the baton. I beckoned to Ariella in tight, frantic motions.

Angling my shoulders, I slid my arms through, baton in hand. As I'd hoped, it was just long enough to reach the generator. I bashed the connective wires with all my strength, striking again and again until they popped out of the machine.

The lights went out.

42

I listened to the assholes cursing, stumbling in the dark.

That gave me time to close the window, collapse the baton, and hide the baton in the back of my pants. It wouldn't hold up to scrutiny, but I hoped Average Man was too pissed to realize his beating stick had gone missing.

I crawled over to Ariella. "My nails might be sharp enough to unpeel the edge of your bindings. Let's give it a shot."

But before I could put my plan into action, the door slammed open. "You fucking bitches broke the generator." This was Plastic Guy, practically spitting in his rage. I prayed they hadn't noticed the soup splattered down the side of the house.

He stormed in and kicked me, then aimed for Ariella. My stitches popped as I tumbled over, pain spiking in my chest, but he only booted Ariella once before I got my body between them. I covered her as best I could, taking one kick to the thigh, another in the ribs.

When that didn't satisfy him, he swung an arm and slammed a fist into the side of my head. It snapped back and I bit my tongue, blood in my throat.

I blacked out briefly as he hit me more, roused only when the other man finally dragged Plastic Guy out of the room. "For fuck's sake, you'll get us both killed if she dies before Durst gets here! Think for a second."

"Thanks to them, we're squatting in the dark. I don't like this, Yar—"

"Shut *up*," Average Man hissed. "No real names. Do I have to remind you what's at stake? We'll find some candles, light a lamp. It will be fine."

He dragged his comrade out, the latter cussing ferociously in a language I didn't speak. They slammed the door, leaving me in a heap on the floor, one huge, throbbing bruise from head to toe. For a few seconds I could hardly think, let alone breathe, and I was still bleeding sluggishly from the chest.

"Marlie." Ariella crept toward me and lifted me so I could rest against her shoulder. "You shouldn't have done that. It would've been better to split the whooping."

Blearily I shook my head. "Old habits die hard. Used to do the same thing when—"

"I remember," she cut in. "Mama's men never laid a hand on me if you could help it."

"Dee did the same for me when she was around. I believe in paying it forward." I was too dizzy to think. Food and I hadn't been close friends since Michael had me poisoned, and I was so thirsty that my mouth and throat hurt.

I tried my plan with our bindings, but I couldn't find the right angle and all I did was scrape away my fingernails until they broke off into the quick and bled. Finally I gave up with a shaky sigh. "I'm sorry. I can't do it. We need something sharp."

"You're bleeding," she whispered.

Waving away her concern, I considered what to try next. They'd left us with the tin mugs, plastic cups, and metal tray, along with the hidden baton. "Let's see if we can break the plastic cup. If we get a sharp piece, we might be able to saw through the layers of tape. Not quickly, but …" It wasn't like we had a better idea.

Ariella took her cup, put it beneath her ass, and bounced on it. Not what I would've done, but when I heard the quiet crack, I gave her two thumbs-up. Banging it on the wall would've drawn the guards for sure.

I reached down and picked up a broken piece, a nice jagged fracture. "This might work, if they leave us alone long enough."

The cutting didn't require as much precision as peeling, and we took turns, spelling each other when our arms started to hurt. Finally the bonds popped, ragged threads fraying from the tape as we pulled free. I raised my arms and rolled my shoulders as Ariella moaned in relief.

"That feels so much better. What now?"

"We'll need to replace these soon. Just wrap them so it looks like we're still tied up."

She nodded. "So they don't realize we got free."

"Once they open the door, run if you can. Don't look back. Run until you find the nearest house and beg to use their phone."

I heard the reluctance in her soft, backcountry voice. "Promise me this ain't some big sacrifice? 'Cause you feel bad about leaving us, so you're determined to die a hero."

With a half smile, I shook my head. "That's not my style. Trust me and go."

After we stretched, we replaced the tape, but it wasn't solid anymore. When we applied pressure, it would pop off. The surprise factor wasn't much of an advantage against three armed men, but it was all we had.

Countless tense hours passed; we cuddled up together and dozed. I roused to the sound of a purring engine and tires rolling over gravel. *Michael's here.*

Our lives hung on the next few minutes.

Because Plastic Guy was probably still pissed, Average Man came for us. The smell of kerosene intensified, drifting in from the front room. Everything was flickering shadows, so that his too-careful coif looked immense, the ghost of Elvis come to drag us to his Nether-Graceland. I didn't move, and Ariella whispered a plea for mercy.

He grabbed me by the scruff of my neck and hauled me to the front room, then went back for Ariella. I stayed where he threw me, feigning a near stupor. *They think we're drugged and trussed for Michael's pleasure. He'll start here and finish up in the other room.* I wondered if he'd ever murdered anyone with such brutal intimacy before.

I made him escalate. I could take a sick sort of pride in that.

Average Man pushed Ariella to the floor, where we lay before Michael Durst. His clothes were dirty and sweat-stained, hair greasy and disheveled, and his eyes glittered with a febrile light that had to have come from something he'd snorted. He paced before us, movements abrupt and jittery, and I could smell the rage even in the sourness of his sweat.

This man was homicide incarnate.

"Go," he snapped. "Get out." He flung a white envelope at Plastic Guy, who managed to catch it. "We're done. You don't get to stay for the final act."

As the henchman left, Michael aimed a kick at my chest. I tipped sideways, trying to make it look more accidental than a coordinated dodge. He couldn't discover how alert I was before I heard the men's car drive away. Once they went, my odds against him would improve significantly.

"You had so much to say at the precinct," he spat. "But you're so fucking quiet now. I did everything for you!"

I tuned out his ranting and took the first kick in the back. *Bruises are good. Bruises are evidence of violence.* Thanks to the brutes he'd hired, I had plenty.

When I couldn't hear the car engine anymore, I rolled over in time to avoid a vicious stomp. Quickly, I signaled Ariella, who broke her bonds and scrambled toward the door. He snatched at her hair, dragging her back, and she screamed, high and agonized. Her hair came out in a bloody hank but she didn't hesitate, thank God. I popped the tape and dove, wrapping both arms around his ankles.

He slammed into the floor as she flung the door open, running as I'd begged her to do. *Get help,* I silently urged her.

"She left you to die," he taunted. "How does it feel? You need to. They all did. Dirty, worthless bitches."

My chest blazed with a pain fierce enough to steal my breath. No time to worry about it. He aimed a kick at my head, and I barely avoided the full force. It probably would've cracked my skull. I let go of him and rolled away, fumbling for the baton I'd hidden. Michael was jacked up on whatever he'd snorted, all rage as he ran at me.

I had no grace, only desperation, as I dove over the flimsy, pasteboard coffee table. I kicked it at him, and Michael flinched reflexively. That gave me the space I needed to pull the baton out of my pants. I snapped it to full length and waited for him to rush me.

"You think I'm afraid of that little stick?" He was too angry, too enraged, to consider it even slightly. He was Michael Durst. Invincible. Untouchable. It was impossible that a girl from Kentucky could break him step by step. But here we were.

And I was hurting like hell, no question. But if I died, I was taking him with me. I had no intention of wrestling with him over the baton.

As he grabbed for my arm, I stumbled to one side, then smashed the kerosene lantern onto the floor, directly in his path.

Small room, burning carpet. While he screamed and tried to put out the fire that was licking up his pants leg, I slammed the baton against his head as hard as I could. When he dropped, I did it again for good measure.

I went around the house, tipping candles and breaking lamps until the fire grew brighter, burning, burning—

He'll never get up.

Some people just need killing.

My husband thinks I'm one of them, and maybe he's right. His first wife didn't make it out alive. Neither did his second.

I'm the exception.

The flames are everywhere. It's getting hard to breathe.

We'll see who dies today.

Smoke filled my lungs, but I stumbled forward, feeling for the door, a window, anything. *I can't see. I can't breathe.*

Michael crawled toward me. Hand on my ankle. "You'll die with me. We'll burn together."

I hit him again. Again. Until his fingers uncurled, limp on the floor. Blood dripped from a cut on my head. My blood on his hands.

How fitting.

Then I dropped to my knees, crawling toward the front window. I was nearly there when a lamp smashed into me from behind, glass shards in my neck and shoulders. Darkness flickered in my head—*he almost got you*—but no, fuck that. *Ariella's waiting. So are Jenny and Vin.*

Gritting my teeth, I held on and rolled into the pain. He was bloody-faced, a beast from my nightmares. With the roaring inferno behind him, Michael didn't look remotely human anymore. My fingers fluttered on the floor and I came up with a glass shard that cut my hands. No hesitation. As he swung at me again, I sliced one leg, then the other, as deep and hard as I could. His shriek as he fell sounded like a dying pig—and I'd often heard them they were slaughtered, back in the day. When he hit the floor next to me, I stabbed deep into his thigh meat, then pulled the shard out. His blood spattered over me, and he didn't move as I hauled myself to my feet, using the windowsill for leverage.

With bloody, trembling hands, I smashed the window and dove through it because I feared I would pass out before I could unlatch it. *I'm bleeding.* God knew from how many wounds, but once I hit the ground outside, the pain reminded me I was alive.

Shivering, I pulled myself to my feet and watched the house burn. *He's dead. Finally.* If he tried to get out, I'd push him back into the fire. Michael Durst would burn in the hell he'd made.

The cabin was completely engulfed in flames when the squad car pulled up, an eternity later. Ariella stumbled out even before the policeman, and she hugged me, feeling me up and down. Her hands came away stained with blood.

Mine.

"What happened here?" one officer said. These were local cops who'd responded to the 911 call.

"Nobody could have survived that," his partner said, staring at the fiery inferno.

Luckily, the police had believed Ariella's story about my wicked husband and his terrible henchmen. They wrapped us in blankets and took our statements, corroborated by phone calls to Detectives Wilson and Hunter in New York.

Soon I was in the back of an ambulance with EMTs treating my various injuries. Ariella sat next to me, intermittently crying and cussing me out.

"That was your plan? You're insane."

"Probably. But I'm still here, as promised, and so are you."

"Thank you, Marlie."

I didn't ask what for; I knew. Closing my eyes, I let myself drift and woke to more hospital treatment, somewhere in Pennsylvania. *I bet I'll see the detectives soon.*

Sure enough, they arrived by late morning, wearing apologetic smiles. Detective Wilson said, "I'm so sorry. The prosecutor pushed for no bail, but the judge didn't see it that way."

"I'm alive," I answered.

It felt like a boast rather than a statement, a verbal way of spitting on Michael's grave.

"The coroner has identified Durst's charred remains from dental records. No open casket for him," Detective Hunter joked.

I smiled. *He'll hate that.* "I intend to have his ashes scattered. And not in a good place."

She nodded. "After what you've been through, I don't blame you. I can guess what happened, but I need to take your statement. For the record?"

See that, Michael? The winner decides what is fact and what is fiction.

I told them. How he abducted my sister as bait and I went to meet his minions to save her. How he tried to murder both of us in that terrible cabin and how in the subsequent struggle, Ariella got away. He beat me. Again. In his wild rage, he knocked over a kerosene lamp. I pushed him and ran. He nearly kept me from escaping when he broke a glass lamp on my head.

I almost died in the fire, after all. Glass slices on my front and back, bruises all over my back. Split lip, knot on my head where his hired goon had punched me. Damaged palms from self-defense.

"I hate cases like this," Detective Wilson muttered. "I'm sorry he nearly got to finish what he started."

"I'll heal," I said softly. Then I asked, "Did you ever find out anything about the person he hired to shoot me?"

Detective Hunter sighed. "Apparently he's some impossible-to-catch hit man, goes by the name of Ghost. There are at least five cases where he pops up, but nobody's even gotten him on camera."

"He's never let a target live before either," Wilson added.

I pleated the white sheet with my fingers, regarding them with the wide eyes that photographers—and Michael Durst—used to love. "Dextrocardia. Dumb luck."

I did this for revenge. I did it for money. Who says you can't have your cake and eat it too?

Outside, it was noisy as hell. The reporters had found me. *I can only imagine what the papers say. Something like SOCIALITE HOSPITALIZED AFTER HUSBAND FAILS TO KILL HER FOR THE SECOND TIME.*

Idly, I wondered if Joanna had completed the takeover. She must be pleased with how things had turned out. I should send her a flower basket, I mused, perhaps a nice selection of cheese and wine. There was no card for this occasion.

"You look tired," Wilson said. "We'll be in touch, but this looks like a pretty clear-cut case of self-defense."

"I'll make sure they leave a couple of officers on the door for a day or two at least," Hunter added. "You need time and space to recover."

The pain is worth it. Even the scars will fade. This triumph never will. Fuck Michael Durst and his prenup. I wonder how much I can squeeze from his estate.

I offered my hand to Detective Hunter, who took it with a warm smile. She must have gotten over me investigating Vin's disappearance without her. "Thank you so much for everything," I said. "I couldn't have made it without your help."

"Our pleasure."

The cops left and I switched on the news, discovering that I was the top story in this little town. A pretty brunette with a page-boy cut gave the play-by-play of my story, the abridged version.

I wonder if I can sell movie rights? Smiling, I leaned back against the pillows.

I'd stalked Michael Durst for months before I met Del Morton. I learned Durst's preferences and became that girl, one in need of Svengali's touch. Then I plotted his downfall, and now …

Michael Durst was a smoldering mass of ash and bone.

Now that it was finally over, I contemplated one final, burning question: was it still murder if someone *really* needed killing?

swan song

one year later

I pack a single bag. The rest of my belongings, I drop off at donation
boxes. My lease expires in twelve days, and I leave a cutoff order with
the utility companies for that date as well; Anton will handle the final
bills. He works for me now, like the clever Swiss mercenary he is. Late
that evening, I board a flight to Berlin.

First class is glorious with a seat that reclines into a bed, hot towels
before meals, and several glasses of wine to let me sleep. I hurry
through immigration, collect my suitcase at the carousel, and rush
past the NOTHING TO DECLARE sign at customs.

I can't wait to see them. For the last year, I've been so damned
circumspect, celibate as a saint. The papers are finally bored with me,
and the Lifetime movie has aired. Now I get on with "getting away
with it."

Outside, the cab driver speaks excellent English, but I thank him in German as I get out at the train station; ultramodern steel and glass. Up an escalator, I find the board directing me to the right track. I've traveled before, sometimes with Michael's hand on my neck. I'm acutely aware of the wind on my nape as I melt into the crowds waiting in line for snacks and coffee.

This is why I chose rail travel. Nobody has asked for ID since I cleared immigration, and there will be no border check when I pass from Germany to the Czech Republic. The EU is a wonderful place to get lost in.

The platform is bustling with a scrum of passengers shoving to get into the first-class car. There can't possibly be sufficient seats for so many people. I swing left, passing through the dining car, then through a storage car where I weave through a maze of bicycles. Just in time, the train is moving, making my progress hazardous.

I have a window seat in a six-person compartment, but first I have to find it. *Easier said than done.* The train is crowded. A Chinese tourist can't locate her assigned seat, and an American woman practically challenges her to a fistfight as the beleaguered conductor tries to keep the peace. I slip past, gratified to be so anonymous.

Nobody recognizes me as the infamous Marlena Durst.

Here, finally. I pull open the glass doors. Four of the six seats are occupied already, and two of those people are pretending to sleep, likely so I won't make conversation. Quietly I lift my bag onto the overhead rack and settle by the window, facing backward. Four hours and seventeen minutes to Prague. I hope to sleep, although I suspect that it's unlikely. At nine a.m. tomorrow, I have an appointment in Wenceslas Square, near the trolley that's been converted into a café.

It feels as if I've waited a lifetime for this reunion.

Somewhere past five p.m., I reach the last stop, Prague city center. The train station is more modern than I expect, so many shops that it's practically a mall; I even spot a Sephora on the way out, promoting K-pop cosmetics. It's a quick walk to my hotel, and I pass a basement pub called the Ferdinanda advertising *the best goulash, with dumplings or bread*, handwritten on a chalk board. The route to the hotel takes me past Wenceslas Square, past the trolley café.

The Fenix is tucked away past the plaza, up a side street, just beyond a giant sex shop and across from a gentleman's club. But the place is clean and modern, surprisingly quiet despite the neighbors. Nobody would expect to find a socialite here.

A slim clerk with a bleached ponytail checks me in, warning me that breakfast is not included. "One night only, yes?"

"Yes."

The key I'm given is strange, an enormous plastic piece with a knob at the bottom. When I touch it to the button that's been attached to the door, it unlocks, and I step into a small, clean room, satisfactory for such a short stay. No lavish celebrations yet. Leaving my suitcase, I retrace my steps, back across the square, which is too big to be called so.

I breathe in the air, brisk in my lungs but also … sweet. There's none of the acrid smell I've come to associate with other cities. Across the square, I notice a restaurant called Como, which specializes in fancy food and expensive wine, the sort of place Michael would've insisted upon. But he's dead, and I can eat whatever the hell I want. I decide on the rustic charm of the Ferdinanda and head back toward the train station.

I spot the specials board before the restaurant sign and duck inside, going down a few steps to what looks like an English pub, all burnished wood and busy, aproned staff. There's one free table, so I claim it. A harried waitress offers a menu, but I'm set on the goulash, with steamed dumplings and a dark beer.

Two dark shadows fall across the table, and I glance up. The two people I want to see most, and expected to see tomorrow, have arrived together, dressed in matching pinstriped suits. I can't decide whether to laugh or kiss them. Standing, I take Jenny's mouth first, soft and deep and full of longing. She pulls off the hat that gave her an androgynous look and her beautiful hair spills free. I stroke the glossy strands, earning a wicked grin from her. Vin has a few new scars, and I trace them with careful fingertips before coming up on tiptoe to press a lingering kiss to his lips.

"You've lost weight," Jenny says.

I quirk a brow, repressing the smile that would illuminate her like a spotlight. "Have you been watching me?"

"Like a guardian angel. We've had eyes on you ever since you left the train station."

"Sit down," I invite them.

The waitress takes their order, more goulash and beer. And I watch them across the table with the hunger I haven't let myself feel for twelve months. From the looks I get in return, it's going to be a delicious night, and I'll be wrecked in the morning.

"Can't believe we did it," Vin says. "Sorry about shooting you, love."

I grin at him. "All part of the plan."

"Easy for you to say." Jenny reaches for my hand, pulls my fingers to her mouth and bites them. "You got to beat Michael Durst. I had to let the two of you get hurt."

"It had to be convincing," I say. But she *knows* that. She just wants to complain, and I'm delighted to listen to it, since it's been so long.

"How much did you get for the condo?" Vin asks, taking a pull of his beer.

"Almost four million. Anton got me most of Michael's assets, everything that wasn't tied up in the business. We're looking at a grand total of thirty-eight million with all properties liquidated."

"Joanna cleaned up too," Jenny notes.

I laugh softly. "She holds a grudge like you wouldn't believe. Michael crossed her ten years ago, bought some land she wanted. I swear she was waiting for someone like me to come along."

I'll never forget how beautiful it was when he burned.

"Too bad we couldn't play Durst's game. Imagine how much we could've gotten in life insurance payouts." Jenny's tone is wistful.

I shake my head. "Too risky. Life insurance is motive, and we were *so* cautious."

"Too cautious," Vin grumbles. "You insisted I *had* to be abducted, but you're not the one who lay for hours bleeding on the cold cement."

Frowning at him, I say, "It worked, didn't it? The police never even asked you for an alibi for when I was shot. And that was the point."

He sighs. "Fine, fine. But I expect you to make all that pain up to me."

"Oh, I will," I purr.

Our food arrives, and the goulash is as good as the sign promised, deep and rich. I take a few bites greedily, envisioning where we'll go from here. We're still discussing our options, but I want a place in Cyprus, lemon trees, grapes grown wild on the wall, maybe a grove of olives, with ancient steps leading down to the sea.

"What did they say about Ghost?" Vin asks.

I laugh. "Still uncatchable, apparently. You and Jenny did a stellar job laying his tracks, confusing the cops. I felt *slightly* sorry watching them chase their tails."

The greatest trick the devil has ever pulled is convincing people he doesn't exist. And neither does Ghost, the legendary hit man Michael Durst hired to kill me.

"Does anyone suspect?" Jenny asks.

"I don't think so, though I did hear Detective Wilson say it's strange Michael left so much evidence. Maybe you overdid it when you dropped the files on Durst's laptop."

I stroke Jenny's hand when she bristles. She does not take criticism of her computer science skills lightly. "Don't start with me," she says.

"Anyway, it's not enough to make them reopen the case. The coke I planted when I moved my things out of the condo helped. Last I heard, they're speculating that he had a drug-induced breakdown when his empire began to crumble."

"Perfect." Jenny touches my thigh beneath the table, and my entire body trembles.

"You handled the mess with Ariella exceptionally well." Vin smiles. Raising his glass, he offers a toast and I click my mug against his. "How is she, by the way?"

Younger sisters are Vin's soft spot, and he would've done anything to take out the man who threatened his. Even shoot a woman he loves.

"She's doing well, currently in therapy and studying in Berlin. I intend to visit her on this trip, just so you know." From Ariella, my thoughts flow to the sister I lost, and I add, "I also plan to pay my respects to Dee in Croatia."

Jenny and Vin both acknowledge this as they eat a bit more of the superior goulash. I have three different Swiss bank accounts. Me, Marlena Altizer from Barrettville, Kentucky. That satisfaction is as good as sex.

"We'll go with you," Jenny says.

"Anywhere," Vin adds.

I'm still remembering that glorious fire and how Michael died. "Honestly, the cabin scenario worked out so well. I like this finale more than my original plan."

Jenny thinks it over, then nods. "There were risks associated with having him shanked in prison. We'd always have to worry about the person we paid to finish him off."

"And it was satisfying to wrap the work up with my own two hands," I say.

A large hand cups the nape of my neck and Vin pulls me in for a kiss. "It turns me on when you're vicious."

We finish dinner and step out into the Prague twilight. Vin wraps one arm around me, the other around Jenny. I bite his ear. She nibbles his throat, and then Jenny and I fall into each other, kissing like the world will end if we stop. People don't even look twice because this is Prague.

Vin hugs us both, then nudges us toward the cobblestone walk. "Come, my darlings. I have a posh suite at the Four Seasons. Shall we?"

"Sex first," Jenny agrees. "Planning later."

As I swing into the crowd with my beloved partners in crime, a song by Leonard Cohen—"The Future"—echoes from the speakers of a nearby café, a fitting soundtrack for getting away with murder.

Acknowledgments

First off, thanks to Lucienne Diver for believing in this book, and to the team at Midnight Ink for making *The Third Mrs. Durst* a reality.

Thanks to Rachel Caine for always listening. I could not ask for a better writing partner. Next, thank you to the Puppy Break squad. You know how much you've helped me this last year. As ever, thanks to my friends and colleagues, including but not limited to: Kate Elliott, Kate Kessler, Melissa Blue, Dee Carney, Shawntelle Madison, Yasmine Galenorn, and Lilith Saintcrow. Special mention goes to Annie Bellet and Victoria Helen Stone for reading the book early and encouraging me with their response.

I send much love to my family for bearing with me when I was writing and rewriting this book. This was such a challenging story to tell, and I hope my revenge fantasy worked for you, dear readers. I thank you for taking this adventure with me and I hope you'll come back for other stories. I truly appreciate your support.